The Looking Glass House

VANESSA TAIT

CORVUS

First published in hardback in Great Britain in 2015 by
Corvus, an imprint of Atlantic Books Ltd.

This paperback edition published in Great Britain
in 2016 by Corvus

1 3 5 7 9 10 8 6 4 2

A CIP catalogue record for this book is available
from the British Library.

Paperback ISBN: 978 1 78239 656 7
E-book ISBN: 978 1 78239 655 0

Printed in Great Britain

Corvus
An imprint of Atlantic Books Ltd
Ormond House
26–27 Boswell Street
London WC1N 3JZ

www.atlantic-books.co.uk

For my mother,
whose middle name is also Alice.

CHAPTER I

$\mathscr{T}$HE EXPECTATION OF A PARTY, MORE PERFECT THAN the thing itself; the music room was alive with it. All day the bell had been ringing and boys from the vintner's coming in with boxes of wine and canary and stacking them noisily on the sideboard. All day the housemaid had been on her knees at the fireplace until the orbs of the firedogs reflected the whole room in queasy miniature: the table cluttered with silver boxes, Mrs Liddell's embroidered scene of Cupid, and the Dean's chair sagging with scholarship and commandeered from his study for the evening.

On the sideboard sat a large bowl of fruit punch, the rafts of cut oranges and lemons half submerged. Next to it a cold collation: a tart of ox's tongues, which rippled out like a choppy pink sea; a minaret of stuffed larks in cases and three trembling turrets of prawns in aspic.

From above: footsteps. Across the ceiling and down the stairs they came. As the door opened, the candles juddered in their sconces and the ivy on the wallpaper swayed on its stems. A woman entered, pushing three girls in front of her, she dressed in black, they in white and each carrying a basket of posies.

'We are in a jungle, look how the wallpaper moves!' said Alice.

'What, in England?' the governess said. 'And anyway, your mother's party is as far away from a jungle as I could imagine. Do not touch anything.' Mary carried on the instructions she had begun upstairs. 'Do not touch, do not rub your dresses. Hands by your sides. Do not fiddle! Especially with your hair. Only speak when you are spoken to. Look pleasant. Be polite.'

The three girls shuffled into place in front of her, three heads in descending order of size. Ina, who was thirteen, was the prettiest; her straight hair had been curled and held back with violet ribbons. Alice, who was ten, had a blunt fringe and a white pencil-line parting drawn down the middle of her head; no ribbons at all – too plain in Mary's opinion. Edith, the youngest at nine years old, had red curly hair that reached to her shoulders. Mary reached down and tucked a lock of it behind Edith's ears; she was shy, she must not hide behind it.

Mary had brushed her own hair until the blood had drained away from her wrists and her hair spread out down her back in a shining mass. Then she had gathered it up into a thick tail and wound it into a coil. Her mouth in the looking glass was full of pins. She had pinned it up into a bun, then more pins round the edge so that no strands would fall loose. Larger pins in the middle to keep it secure. Clips everywhere else for control and tightness. And for her cheeks a pinch, hard enough to bring tears to her eyes.

The fire snapped and spat and pushed out a smell of cloves and smoke. The collar of Mary's new dress was already rubbing. She bent her neck the opposite way to try to relieve the pressure, but the collar was too tight.

The door flung open again with an exhalation and the children's mother entered in a blaze of crimson: rubies scattered in her hair, diamonds piled round her neck, the points of light from the room reflected in them all.

'My darlings, my dear ones, you all look divine!' Mrs Liddell pressed her gloves to her bosom. 'How proud I am. Now you will all be quite *quite* good, won't you, for me, for your mama. Oh, Miss Prickett, please don't stand by the cold collation, it is not a good backdrop for the children. Too much pink. Stand by the chest.'

Mary blushed. 'Yes, ma'am.' The children's bones, under the stiff material of their dresses, felt frail, like those of birds.

'The first guests are approaching, I heard their carriage,' said Dean Liddell, coming in, brushing off his sleeve. 'I had banked on a few more moments' peace.' He took up position just behind his wife, the long fingers that extended from the sleeves of his dinner jacket rubbing against each other irritably.

The doorbell rang. Mary breathed in inside her corset, her ribs grating against the whalebone struts. Now it would begin, she thought. Her life.

'Mr and Mrs Farquhar,' rang out the butler's voice.

Her life up until this moment had not been what Mary had expected, or had been led to believe to expect from her books. But now that she had been taken on as the governess to *the most important family in Oxford* (she always italicized these words to herself), it must begin to take on a weight and a motion. A velocity in fact. And this party was the first sign of it.

The diamonds that hung beneath Mrs Farquhar's ears were heavy enough to draw lines in her ear lobes. Mr Farquhar was as tight in his jacket as a fat beetle in its shell.

Mary would meet a different sort of person now, maybe even tonight. She might (she had thought of it all through the preceding night as she fell asleep in her unfamiliar bed) find herself exchanging some brief but deeply felt words. She might even leave an impression, now that she was here. She who had spun through life like a burr looking to hook its edges in.

It happened in literature; it could happen in life.

And, of course: the Queen. Someone from a fairy tale. She was the reason for all of this.

Tonight, Mary – plain, poor, obscure and little – was to breathe the very same air as the Queen and her consort, come to visit the Prince of Wales, who was matriculating at Christ Church.

In the music room looking glass Mary saw that, in spite of her efforts, her face proffered out of her collar like a dish of pork and potatoes. Her mouth was too big, looming above her high black ruffle. She pursed her lips to try and compress them into a rosebud. But she looked horrible, aggrieved, and she let them go slack. Mary was always being asked what the matter was, and had concluded that the problem lay in the shape of her lips when in repose.

The doorbell rang again and again. Nobody wanted to be

early, nobody wanted to be late, so as a result they all arrived together. Soon the music room was crammed with people. They stood or sat, with flushed cheeks and brightly coloured dresses: carmine, turquoise and vermilion silks. Cigar smoke floated above them all in an acrid sea. Mary and the children found themselves pressed back more and more on the tea chest.

'Dear me, have you moved from this spot yet? I thought not! *Circulate*, please, Miss Prickett. I want my children *seen*,' said Mrs Liddell.

Mary blushed again. She pushed the children forward a step. But there was no one to circulate *towards*. Out of all of them she recognized only old Lady Tetbury, who still wore her spaniel curls though the fashion for them had long died out, and the Vice Chancellor, Mr Arundell, with his beard that projected from his chin as a solid thing. Neither of them was approachable, either for her or the children.

Mary turned and steered them all towards the middle of the crowd. She might find someone in there, in the hubbub, the hoots of laughter, the glint and the glare. Because governesses married, all the time. Just because she had been taken on in this capacity did not mean she could not find a position in another. In fact she thought it more likely that she would find a husband now that she was a governess to the Liddells than when she was sitting at home. She was twenty-eight years old now; she had done all the sitting at home she could manage.

Circulate, Mrs Liddell had said, as if they were all air and could easily pass through this mass of human bodies, with their chattering mouths and their smell of violets and sweat. Mary gripped the children by the shoulders and pushed them in front of her, heading for the middle of the room.

Ina twisted her head back. 'Where are we going?'

Mary gestured to the centre of the room. 'We must find someone.'

'Who?'

'Someone to talk to. Someone to receive your posies.'

Mary's throat was dry. A servant appeared from somewhere with a tray of Madeira. A small glass of sherry would soothe it. She gulped it down and replaced the glass on the tray with a clatter that was lost in the noise of the room.

She squeezed her way through the crowd, pushing the children ahead. A handsome woman turned her face towards her; thin red veins criss-crossed the sides of her nostrils.

'How nice to see you. Are you well?'

Mary blushed. 'Yes, thank you.'

'I saw your father the other day. He tells me your mother is sick. I was sorry to hear it.'

Her mother was not sick. Even if she were, her father, a steward at Trinity College, would never be friends with this woman, with her emeralds clustered round her neck. A burst of heat erupted over Mary's face.

'Oh,' said the lady. She had noticed the children around Mary's skirts; now she took in the plain black dress and the collar that bristled at Mary's chin, and her hair, not ringleted, not jewelled.

All the pleasantness drained from her face. 'Excuse me, I mistook you.'

The V of the woman's back that was revealed by her dress contained two large flat moles. There was another tray to her left, on the table. Mary grabbed a glass from it. Above her head the glass drops of the chandeliers were polished to a dagger's point. A halo of pain throbbed above her eyebrows. She ought not to have pulled her hair so tight.

There was always adversity in the opening chapter. It would not make sense otherwise.

Mary put on her smile again. She must find somebody standing on their own who looked interesting, at least to have some destination. She could perhaps catch their eye and smile, then come to rest quite naturally nearby.

But the children were already talking to somebody, a man, although he was not the destination she had had in mind. This man was slight and lopsided and his skin was as smooth as a child's. His hair was long and lacquered; Mary could smell the sweetness of it. It ran smoothly over his head until it reached his ears, where it bubbled out like water over rocks.

'I have no recollection of saying such a thing!' Alice was saying to him.

'Well, if it was not *you* then it must have been the cat who said it. Although I have not yet heard a cat talk, it does not mean that they reliably *cannot*, I suppose.' He turned and put out his hand to Mary. 'You must be the new governess; Miss Prickett, is it?'

His fingers were dry and smooth, but they had a surprising grip. Mary was about to say yes, and add something else that she had not yet thought of, but just then the noise in the room dropped away, as if off a cliff, and everyone turned towards the door.

Two men backed into the room dressed in crimson robes with the white fur of three or four small animals lining the collars; and two others in three-quarter-length silver coats, also with their backs to the party and bowing deeply. Next someone who could be a footman, in a jacket ribbed with gold and festooned with a complicated system of buttons, drawn up to his full height. 'Her Majesty the Queen, Prince Albert and the Prince of Wales!' he cried, and in they swept, surrounded by ladies-in-waiting, the Queen smiling pleasantly.

Mary had stopped breathing. She could not make them out properly amongst the jostling; she fully expected them to be magnificent. But Alice's friend bent down and said to her:

'I must say I didn't expect the Queen to be so short. She may even,' he framed the word with a certain relish, 'be called *dumpy*.'

Mary stared. No one could ever have suspected that this odd man had just made such a remark; he was smiling pleasantly just like everyone else, even standing on his toes for a better view. The Queen and the Prince of Wales were moving slowly through the room.

Alice said, quite loudly: 'She does not look how a Queen ought to look at all. And I have been so looking forward to meeting her.'

'Be quiet!' said Mary.

The man whispered: 'But one must never judge by appearances. The Queen is the most powerful person in the world, despite what she looks like. Did you know she could have any one of those courtiers' heads off whenever she pleases?'

'Whenever she pleases, Mr Dodgson?' said Alice.

'If she doesn't like the look of them at breakfast, their heads will be off by dinner.'

Mr Dodgson was the name of him then. Mary would not forget it.

'Oh good,' said Alice.

Mary shifted again. She had collected stamps when she was a child, had pasted Queen Victoria's ageless profile into her book every week. She did not want to hear this man talking, this man whose eyelashes were only just darker than his lids, whose left eyelid drooped, whose lips were too pale and too smooth and uneven, with one corner hitched higher than the other. And he was thin, excessively so, and his shoulders had something irregular about them too, so that the whole impression of him was uncomfortably asymmetrical.

Where was the royal party? She strained to see over the rows of heads. They had stopped to admire the *tableau vivant*. A child was feigning sleep on a daybed, a string of pearls round her neck, her hair spread carefully over a cushion. The Prince, played by a child of about eight, was in the act of surprising the young Princess with a kiss, down on one knee, a cape thrown over his shoulder.

'We did so enjoy "Sleeping Beauty" when we were young,' said the Queen. Her voice was thin and sharp and cut through the cigar smoke.

The royal party moved off to sit on the three golden chairs

that had been placed at the top of the room for them, and gradually the party resumed its chatter. But Mr Dodgson remained still with his hands folded in front of him as if to protect himself. 'I must try to gain access to the Prince. I think the Equerry will be willing to introduce me.' He stood for a few moments, neatly contained in the riot of the room.

Mary looked at him in surprise. Perhaps he worked at the college, in some junior position, and was desperately trying to improve himself.

She moved to go, to find someone more suitable, but as she stepped forward she found herself pressed in by a group of men discussing the theories of Mr Darwin, the Dean among them.

'My part in the Science Museum has finished now that it is built,' said one with a riot of hair that curled out from his temples and reached in one unbroken mass all the way to below his chin. In the middle of it his lips were a pair of small red cherries. 'I can have nothing to do with what goes on in it. I abhor that Mr Huxley. Quite like a monkey himself. I am lucky enough to be able to perceive God in Nature – a rare gift and one that I am grateful for. Every part of a cliff or cave, or a falcon for that matter, thrills me. Mr Darwin sees in nature a seething Godless struggle.'

The Dean studied his glass. 'His idea of Nature, it seems to me, is that she selects only for that of the being which she tends, whereas Man selects only for his own good. In that respect at least Nature may be allied to a benevolent higher power, for although her means of selection can be ruthless, the end towards which she works is nothing short of a better planet.'

'My dear Henry, an elegant theory,' said the man, who, Mary realized, was probably Mr Ruskin. 'It sees the good in everything – as you do. But natural selection is clearly an absurdity.' He smiled and separated his hands with a broad gesture. 'What would the human race resemble if blushing young maidens had held a predilection for blue noses when selecting their mates? Your party would look very different. You are lucky, though; under Darwin's terms you are successful. Four children, attractive ones.' He grabbed on to Alice's hand with one of his own, his port jostling darkly in the other. 'Is there a more perfect expression of vitality and beauty in all the world?'

That Mary could be related to an ape, even distantly, was repellent. Living in the jungle, doing exactly as they pleased. No morals; fornicating and hooting and killing. Careering about naked and free, no work, no need for work, feasting on fruits of the forest. Mary closed her eyes. She felt hot, dizzy even. She had seen a chimpanzee at London Zoo once, a few years ago. It had been, as the pictures showed, all over hair, except for its black face and broad nose and lips that seemed to be another appendage. It had been eating a banana in a desultory way, squatting on a branch, haunches spread apart. With no change of expression, it had slowly defecated, reaching round with its other hand to catch it. Then it had sauntered off (Mary thought she had caught glee on the creature's face at the humans' gasps and shrieks) still holding the sausage-like form in its hand, to store it somewhere she supposed; it looked as if it had an aim in mind.

No, Man – Mary opened her eyes – civilization at its peak, could not have come from *that*.

Mr Ruskin had caught Alice awkwardly round the knuckles; the tips of her fingers were turning red in his fist.

'Perhaps you would like a posy?' Alice said, putting her basket between them.

'A posy!' said Mr Ruskin. He laughed. 'Yes. Yes, I will, I will fly in the face of convention – who could not accept such an offering from such a child?' He reached into Alice's basket and plucked a bunch of lavender out, then swooped down and pressed his lips to the top of Alice's head.

'And here is another man with no progeny,' said Mr Ruskin, looking up again. 'And happier for it, I dare say. Good evening, Mr Dodgson.'

'I have all I need in the progeny of others,' said Mr Dodgson, drawing himself up, making himself taller and thinner, if that were possible.

'And what do you think of Mr Darwin's theories?' said Mr Ruskin. 'Are we to be ape men?' He grinned and leaned towards Mr Dodgson, to the other man's visible distaste. Mary could see a speckle of Mr Ruskin's white saliva glistening on the shoulder of Mr Dodgson's coat, where it bubbled disconsolately for a moment before melting away.

'Perhaps you have seen my photograph,' said Mr Dodgson. 'The skeletons of humans and apes. They are very similar.'

Mr Ruskin spread his fingers and said: 'Ah, so you are—'

Mr Dodgson cut him off with a prim turn of his mouth: 'And yet, of course, completely dee-dee-dee-different.'

Mr Ruskin grunted and turned away. As he did so, his elbow knocked against Mary and tipped her towards Mr Dodgson.

Mary tried to step back but lost her balance, enough for the wine in her glass to splash out and down on to the back of Alice's white dress, where it quickly bloomed into a red stain.

But nobody had noticed. Not Mr Dodgson, not Alice, not Mrs Liddell.

Mary's head was heavy and hot. Her feet throbbed in time to the pulse behind her ears.

'Good evening, Mrs Liddell,' said Mr Dodgson. 'What a party you have given. It will go down in the history books.'

Mrs Liddell laughed, showing her small white teeth. 'I doubt that. History books are for the doings of men. But thank you, Mr Dodgson, all the same. Dearest Edith, go to Mrs Cornelius and her daughters, say hello. I have told them you will be coming.'

The skin behind Edith's freckles turned red. 'Must I?'

'Yes, dear, you must. Alice, please thank Mr Ruskin for your drawing lesson – he does it only out of the goodness of his heart and I think you have seen him this evening without thanking him. Ina, no one has yet presented Her Majesty with a posy. Her lady-in-waiting has indicated that the Queen may accept it.'

Mary stood waiting for her own instructions. 'And I will circulate,' she said.

Mrs Liddell turned to her in surprise.

'With the children,' Mary added, her cheeks hot.

'The children have destinations, as I have just said. But when they return, you may take them upstairs to bed.'

❦

The party was still exhaling gusts of laughter as Mary lay upstairs in her bedroom. Her head was spinning. She put a hand on her forehead – burning, as she thought. It was all the excitement, most likely, or perhaps she had a fever.

Thoughts hit the inside edges of Mary's skull with a heavy brightness. *The Queen*, but even as she saw her again in all her power, the word *dumpy* sprinted across the upper part of her forehead. She closed her eyes and faces immediately came bursting through the darkness. The Queen's soft jowls, so shockingly familiar; Mrs Liddell's mass of dark hair; Mr Dodgson's uneven smile, Alice's eyes beneath her fringe. All began to jiggle up and down and then follow each other in a figure of eight.

Ah well, plenty more chances.

As Mary began to review it in her head, she told herself that the party had in fact gone very well. She had not made a fool of herself. She had not lost control of the children. And most importantly, she had been there.

'A terrible crush in here,' said Mr Dodgson, as the whole room seemed to shrink.

The mouths, the moustaches, the pinked cheeks.

The tea chest pressed in against her calves, the ceiling down on her head.

My life has begun, my life has begun, my life.

The party spooled away in circles, away and away until Mary stopped remembering the various elements of it and only felt the rhythm of the unravelling. And then she slept, and had some memory, in the morning, of snoring.

CHAPTER 2

Mary sat at the front of the classroom, a sparse room perched at the top of the Deanery with four desks in it. She was staring out of the window at the elm tree, its bare branches knobbed with buds. An early fly was already trapped on the windowsill, on its back and frantically buzzing.

Mary, said Mrs Liddell, when she was engaged as governess, had only to continue where the last governess had left off: more reading, neater writing, general knowledge, and manners. The eldest, Harry, was away at boarding school. The girls left behind would have tutors for French, music, mathematics and art.

Mary's experience of education had so far consisted only of her own schooling: a school for girls run by another governess not much older than her, in one bare room at the top of a house. Her teacher had had a voice that never varied its register, and she'd relied entirely on books. Indeed, Mary found it hard to recall her face; it was always pointed downwards, or sometimes obscured altogether. Although if she perceived impudence or laziness, she suffered an abrupt change of character, springing out from behind her desk and leaping on the girl in question. In the winter it had been so cold that the ink froze in its pots; they had had to wear gloves to write, and it was difficult to stop the pens from slipping to the floor. And if Mary bent too many nibs she would have to go without for several weeks – which was meant to be a punishment but was not. In summer the room grew oppressively hot and airless and the droning voice of the governess made it difficult to stay awake. Once Mary had actually fallen asleep, for no more than a second, but had awoken to the irate face of her teacher, and her mouth, opened extraordinarily wide – it had been that that Mary focused on; she had never seen her open it wider than the width of a pencil before – screaming at her to wake up. She was a useless, lazy girl to whom nothing good would ever happen. She had been beaten on the back of the thighs with a cane, so hard that she had had to stand for a week.

It was silent in Mary's classroom, except for the children's nibs scratching across paper, and the fly. Each spin a desperate buzz, each buzz a desperate spin. The sound of it began to drill into Mary's forehead.

'Ina, have you finished writing out "Harriet and the Matches"?'

'Yes, Miss Prickett.'

'Stand up then, please.'

Ina stood up, smoothed down her pinafore and cleared her throat:

'But Harriet would not take advice:
She lit a match, it was so nice!
It crackled so, it burned so clear –
Exactly like the picture here.
She jumped for joy and ran about
And was too pleased to put it out.

'So she was burnt, with all her clothes,
And arms, and hands, and eyes, and nose;
Till she had nothing more to lose
Except her little scarlet shoes;
And nothing else but these was found
Among her ashes on the ground.'

'The moral?' said Mary.

'Do not light matches.'

'And?'

'Always listen to your elders.'

'Good. Thank you, Ina.'

Mary got up and went to the window. The fly seemed to sense her coming and with a desperate effort righted itself and began to blunder up and down against the pane, its back glossy with black fur, its head with its great red helmets for eyes.

Outside, daffodils stood out on the grass, mouthy and bright. A man walked through her gaze, across the bright expanse of lawn, his clothes and hat so dark Mary could not initially see his features. His back was very straight and he moved quickly, but there was something uneven about his legs; perhaps one was longer than the other. She recognized him as Mr Dodgson, the man from the party. She had the impression that his body and legs were not properly attached. He was carrying a large object with similarly long disjointed legs; she could not see what it was but the strangeness of them both caught at her.

'May I be finished now?' said Alice.

'Have you done all that I asked?'

'Yes. I have done it all before anyway.' Alice stuck out her bottom lip and blew the air upwards, deranging her fringe.

In the three weeks Mary had been at the Deanery, she had noticed that the child was full of sighs. And more than that, her sighs seemed theatrical – illustrations of sighs, meant to draw attention to the fact that she was sighing.

Her hair was bright and shiny and as waterproof as a bird's. When she was reprimanded, she shook the words off. Only the tip of one toe touched the floor; the other foot curled round her leg.

'Alice, it is not ladylike to blow out so much air. In future, if you have the desire to sigh, please hold your breath.'

'But I'll suffocate!'

'It is not possible to suffocate yourself, as you know. Just hold your breath until the desire to sigh has faded.'

'But if I hold my breath I will only want to sigh more, shan't I, when I release it?'

'Well then, when you release it, hold it again. Or breathe regularly; you must know how to do that. All this sighing is off-putting for Edith and Ina. Let me see your book.'

Alice's lips were very red, her lashes long and thick. Ink splotches littered the page.

'You have blotted your copybook! Your writing must be neater.' Mary grasped Alice's hand in her own and forced the pen along over her own pencil marks. 'You must keep an even pace. I have told you this. And it must go exactly as high as below. D'you see? A child half your age could do it. Write out ten more.'

'Yes, Miss Prickett.'

Not a crease, not a mole or thread vein or mottle intruded into the porelesss curve of Alice's cheek, but Mary saw that its natural rosiness had deepened into a darker red of anger or shame, she could not tell which.

She was, for a moment, glad. And then she was ashamed of her gladness and tried to make it up to the girl by putting her hand awkwardly on Alice's head, but Alice shrank away.

Mary turned to look out of the window once more. Mr Dodgson was there again, carrying what looked like glasses, or tubes made of glass, awkwardly, his fingers inserted into the mouths of them so that they resembled giant glass hands.

She looked at the clock. Still half an hour to go, then perhaps they could all go to the garden for some fresh air.

She turned back towards the window. The fly was perpetrating a frantic V up and down the pane. Mary reached over to Alice's desk and grasped her schoolbook, rolled it up, and brought it down with a sharp smack, twice, on the window pane. A heavy body dropped to the sill, leaving a smear on the glass.

Mary returned the book to the child and went back to her desk. The weight of her new skirts, the swish of them as she walked, still felt strange. She touched the tip of her finger to the raw patch on her neck where her collar had rubbed at the party.

Edith was gazing up at the phrenology chart Mary had put up on the schoolroom wall. It was more for Mary's benefit than the children's, though it was worthwhile to introduce them to scientific principles, if the last governess had not. Mary liked the rational world suggested by the chart; that this or that character trait could be illustrated by the concurrent area of the brain bulging up and pushing out the skull.

Order in chaos. Answers in an unfathomable world.

It was a map, she always thought, of all the different sides of human nature. She imagined the various sins simmering beneath the skull, and as each one came to the boil – laziness, or avarice say – the relevant part of the skull would pop out like an excrescence.

Dean Liddell had a very large forehead, an illustration of his brain expanding in general, due to all his scholarship. Mrs Liddell, Mary noticed, had enlargements in the area assigned to mirth, but also destructiveness. There did not seem to be any related to insolence, but children's heads were growing all the time, and were harder to read.

'What shall I do now, Miss Prickett?' asked Edith.

'Have you finished your spellings?'

'Yes, Miss Prickett.' Edith had red wavy hair and a small nose dotted with freckles. She often pulled down her hair to cover her eyes, so that she was unknowable.

'I will read to you all then.' Mary reached over and pulled a heavy black volume towards her. She had found that *Magnall's Historical and Miscellaneous Questions for the Use of Young People* was very useful during her lessons with the children. When she had emptied herself of knowledge, the closely crammed pages had it in abundance.

'"Chapter Seven. Canaan, or the Holy Land. This once populous country, the peculiar object of Divine Providence, was first called the 'land of Canaan', from Canaan, the grandson of Noah." Please study the map.'

The children looked at her.

'The map of Canaan! Come forward.'

Mary turned the book towards the small heads of the children. She had never herself been to a foreign land. It was strange to think that God had sent Jesus to so barren a place. England would have been so much more welcoming.

When the children's heads were bent over the book, Mary allowed herself to look out of the window again. Mr Dodgson's body was bent over into the shape of a C. On the inside of the curve there was a large brown box.

'"The posterity of Canaan was numerous. His eldest son, Sidon, founded the city of Sidon and was father to the Sidonians and Phoenicians. Canaan had ten other sons who were the fathers of as many tribes dwelling in Palestine and Syria; namely the Hittites, the Jebusites, the Amorites, the Girgashites, the Hivites, the Arkites, the Sinites, the Arvadites, the Zemarites, and the Hamathites."'

She read on and on, cramming what remained of the lesson

with a torrent of words and facts, until the whole schoolroom was full up with them. She stumbled a little over the unfamiliar names, but after the first few minutes she began pronouncing them as she liked; no one would know to correct her.

◆

It was not warm, but the spring sunshine was sharp. Mary had left her bonnet off and she had to squint. She knew it was unbecoming, especially in a face as thin as hers, but she was helpless against it.

The children ran on ahead, their legs stirring their new white dresses into foam.

'Girls!' she shouted into the wind, louder than she meant to. But it seemed they did not hear her and ran on. Perhaps the wind had snatched her voice away.

She strode round the hedge, her mouth hooked halfway open on the first *guh*, her eyes narrowed, and even though she had been expecting to see him, it was a shock to almost run into Mr Dodgson, her cheek moments away from his jacket.

He let out a startled *hummnnnng!* Her fingertips grazed the rough wool of his jacket. They both reared back their heads and stepped outwards. An aroma of chemicals emitted from his jacket.

'I'm sorry to sta-sta-startle you,' he said. 'I thought Mrs Liddell—'

'No, oh! I am so sorry, my own clumsiness. I was – I was chasing the girls.'

'Mrs Liddell has given me – us – permission to use the garden to-to try-try – to try for a photograph of the children. I beg your pardon! I thought perhaps she wa-wa-wa . . .' Mr Dodgson swallowed. 'She WOULD have told you.'

Mary stepped back another pace. 'She would have told me?' She had lost track of the conversation.

'She would have tah-tah . . .'

She must not stare at his mouth, but she couldn't stop herself. It was open, it ought to be singing by the look of it, but no sounds were coming out. Above it his eyes stared at her help-lessly. He had not suffered from this disease, if that was what it was, at the party. Perhaps it came on sporadically, like a coughing fit.

'She would have told you I was here!'

'Oh.' Mary dragged her mind to Mrs Liddell. 'No, she did not!'

'Oh, Mr Do-Do-Do-Dodgson,' said Alice, coming round the corner. 'Have you come to photograph me?'

'Yes, dear Alice. Look, I am all ready.' He indicated a table with a striped cloth over it and a chair in the middle of the lawn.

Ina said: 'I didn't know we were sitting for another photo-graph.'

'It won't take long, Ina dear. Look, I have a broom handle for you to use so that your arm won't get tired.' As he was talking, he pushed the children gently towards the furniture. 'I want you to pretend to feed Alice some cherries.'

Mary knew of photographs of adults, but not of children, especially without their parents, especially out here in the open, on the lawn. 'Why would you want to photograph the children?'

'Why, are children not the most perfect beings? They are so recently lent from God. Far more perfect than us adults, grown away from Him and racked with sin.'

Children did not make good subjects as far as she knew; they were too fidgety. 'Will Mrs Liddell mind?'

'Mr Dodgson has taken our photographs a great many times,' said Alice. 'I think I am very good at having my likeness taken.'

Mary's lips tightened further. 'It is not a skill, Alice. You merely need to sit.'

Mary had had her own photograph taken last year, in one of the little studios that had sprung up in Bear Street. It had been a whim of her father's. She had found herself placed stiffly on a chair with her corset pulled tight and the monstrous eye of the camera trained upon her, each moment brought into unbearable focus. Every part of her exposed face prickled with a new and horrible awareness, pushed in on and made worse by the cheery banter of the photographer, who managed to convey, by the number of his requests, that she was not making an attractive picture. Although when she had got the results back, her father had professed himself pleased. And when she looked at the photograph herself, to her surprise she had looked really quite ordinary.

'How were your lessons this morning?' Mr Dodgson asked.

'I have been doing "Harriet and the Matches",' said Ina.

'I know it well,' said Mr Dodgson. 'It is a little like the poem I wrote for my sisters when I was a child. Would you like to hear it?

'I have a fairy by my side
Which says I must not sleep
When once in pain I loudly cried
It said, "You must not weep."

'If, full of mirth, I smile and grin
It says, "You must not laugh."
When once I wished to drink some gin
It said, "You must not quaff."

'"What may I do?" at length I cried,
Tired of the painful task.
The fairy quietly replied,
And said, "You must not ask."'

'I don't see that it has anything to do with "Harriet and the Matches",' said Mary, staring at the polish of Mr Dodgson's shoe, solid against the grass. '"Harriet and the Matches" is a useful poem.'

She watched as Mr Dodgson took off his hat and allowed himself a shake of the head; his curls bounced gently in the slanted sunlight that sporadically took hold of the lawn. Air meeting hair; he longed for it, she could see, to feel the breeze drifting through follicles like a replenishing gust through a stagnant forest.

But after a moment Mr Dodgson's fingers tightened on the brim and with his other hand he smoothed down his curls. Quickly he pushed his hat more firmly on to his head.

'Nothing at all to do with it,' he said. 'I wrote that when I was a boy, at the Rectory, years ago. Only I cannot bear moralizing!'

Mary nodded, though she kept her eyes on his shoes. Weren't morals a useful tool? She had always been taught they were. Her mother had raised her on moral sayings: *Elbows off the table, hands in laps. Don't speak until spoken to. Eat your greens or you'll get warts.* And her mother's favourite: *How sharper than a serpent's tooth it is to have a thankless child.* They were the coat-hanger on which she hung all her moral fibres.

'Edith, you sit on the table. You, Ina, stand with your back to her, facing Alice. Good!'

Mr Dodgson handed Edith the bag of cherries to hold and gave one to Ina to dangle above Alice's mouth. Alice was to open her mouth as if in the process of receiving it. Then he disappeared into the darkroom that he had set up in the Deanery's broom cupboard, and reappeared carrying a glass plate, which he pushed into the back of the camera. It did seem magical, thought Mary, to be able to crystallize the exact image of a thing on to a photographic plate, as if spirits had got in.

The camera was in front of Mary on its three spindly legs, its great eye staring at the cathedral. Mr Dodgson stooped and pulled the hood over his shoulders, then reached round and pulled off the cap.

His bent-over shape, his buttocks, pointed straight at Mary's face.

Should she object? But then she would be drawing attention to it . . . Better to say nothing. A grey flannel trouser, and a bone, two bones, clearly visible behind.

Mary slid her eyes over to a tree, its leaves just coming out. She slid her eyes further, on to the cathedral. What a peaceful building! She wished she were in it, underneath the arches, sitting on a pew, asking God to have mercy upon her. Just the act of asking Him, in amongst all the others – the old lady with the lace cap, the luxuriantly bearded man with such an air of purpose – comforted her. Apes for ancestors, fornicating and frolicking in the jungle, had no place there, could not in fact exist in the same reality. One was so much more real than the other, there in front of her: a cathedral. Jesus, on a cross.

Mr Dodgson fidgeted and stepped from foot to foot, each movement sending a minute ripple down his trouser legs.

How many seconds did it take to make a photograph? Time beat in a slow pulse at her temples.

It seemed unfair that thinness, while perfectly acceptable in a man, was judged so harshly on a woman.

Mr Dodgson's buttocks were reversing. Mary leaned back as far as she dared. But he was only straightening up to replace the cap.

✦

It seemed it was usual to follow Mr Dodgson into the broom cupboard to see the photograph being brought to life, but when she went in, Mary found the place unrecognizable. It still smelt of dust, but in front of that now there was a tang of something else, a sharper smell. The brooms had been cleared away and glass funnels and trays stacked in their place. The skylight had been covered with a black square of material and a subterranean gloom hung over the room, in which Mr Dodgson moved with an urgency and fluidity Mary had not noticed before. He reached up and poured a strong-smelling liquid into one basin and quickly thrust the glass plate into it.

'I muh-muh-must think of a way to make the time pass more quickly in front of the camera – a story, perhaps – because you know you can hurry time along if you push him very hard from behind,' Mr Dodgson was saying as he agitated a tray full of chemicals.

'I should like that during lessons!' said Alice.

'Lessons are not meant to be interesting,' said Mary. 'They are meant to be educational.'

'I quite agree,' said Mr Dodgson. 'Though it does not make me popular in college.'

Mary looked at him in surprise. His poem seemed to say the opposite. She would have imagined him the most whimsical tutor.

They all stared down into the basin. Slowly something began to emerge, a light patch in the middle of the plate.

'Oh look, here come my teeth!' said Alice.

'That is not your teeth, Alice, that is your hair. Your teeth and dress will be black, and your lips and hair white. It is all reversed – negative into positive, positive into negative.'

'Is that why the plate is called a glass negative?' asked Ina.

'Exactly so, yes. When I make a print from it, it is all turned round back to normal.'

Slowly the children's image came into being. Even in the spectral version Mary could see there was a symmetry to Alice's face, a rightness to it, that she had not noticed in the real Alice. And yet, as the image swam up at her into sharpness, there was something . . . Even in the negative she could see it: the tilt of her head and the pout of her mouth. Something aggravating.

'We have something here, I think,' said Mr Dodgson. 'This will make a fine photograph. Excellent even. A story, entire and complete.' He leant down and kissed Alice on the top of her head, then Ina, then Edith. 'For once to have achieved what I set out to do in the morning is most satisfying.'

'You could not have done it without me,' said Alice.

Ina turned away and pushed open the door into the garden. When Mary came outside, blinking, she found her sitting alone on the farthest bench.

'I do not see why I should have to be photographed. I don't like it.'

Mary put her arm round her shoulder. 'You all looked very pretty. Your father will like to see it.'

'All that holding still. It is stupid.'

'I will give a very good report of you to your mother today – shall we see if she is back?'

'She *is* back, look, there she is.'

Mrs Liddell was indeed sailing over the lawn towards them in a sweep of satin and lace. Her hoops flattened grass and disturbed shrubbery; even from this distance Mary could hear the jangle of gold bracelets outside her gloves.

'My darling Ina!' Mrs Liddell stretched out her arms and sent a noisy kiss over her eldest daughter's head. 'Where are the others?'

'In the darkroom,' said Ina.

'Oh yes, with Mr Dodgson. Was he here again?'

'He took our photograph.'

'Really?' Mrs Liddell inclined to the side.

'He said you had allowed it.'

'Alice said she had been photographed before, many times,' said Mary.

'And so she has. Nevertheless, this time I was out. I do not remember giving permission.'

'I am sorry, Mrs Liddell, he was quite persuasive.' Mary flushed.

'Mr Dodgson said he would come on Monday to try for another photograph of us, if you were agreeable,' said Ina.

'*Am* I agreeable, Miss Prickett?'

The question hung in the air. Mary struggled to formulate a reply, conscious that she was blushing. She did not know if she was being mocked, or punished for letting Mr Dodgson take the children's photograph. Any answer sounded too familiar.

'Well, my friends say I am, if my governess does not!' Mrs Liddell laughed, letting her mouth open. Mary could see her teeth, very white, and her tongue in a point behind.

Mary stretched her own mouth towards the corners of her face, her lips sticking on her teeth. She was attempting a smile but she felt as if she was not making a good job of it.

Mr Dodgson and Alice came out into the garden, still talking.

'Mr Dodgson. I see you are photographing my children again,' said Mrs Liddell.

'Yes, I think I succeeded in a good image. You may like an imprint—'

'And yet I have no recollection of the appointment.'

'I am sure . . .' Mr Dodgson smiled; Mary saw the tendons in his neck.

'Did you know my husband is a very good artist?' Mrs Liddell cut in. 'Mr Ruskin says so. His blotting-paper sketches are quite prized. Usually executed during some dreary meeting or another, I dare say.' She laughed again. 'Can photography be called art, do you think?'

'There is some skill in photography perhaps.' Mr Dodgson rocked back and forth on the soles of his shoes. 'For one thing the collodion must be quite right, and then the timing—'

'But that seems to me a scientific skill, not an artistic one. The Dean, on the other hand, is very keen on photography, as well as art. He tells me that I cannot appreciate the science of it, and I dare say he's right. After all, a mere woman could not be expected to understand.' Mrs Liddell flashed out a smile to Mary.

'No, a woman's understanding is in general far below a man's,' said Mary.

'Yes, on most things, Miss Prickett, but perhaps not all.'

Mrs Liddell turned to go, but halfway across the lawn she stopped and turned back to Mr Dodgson, still smiling.

'The Dean tells me you have been having troubles with your lectures.'

Mr Dodgson flushed.

'Students can be so lazy, but I dare say now that my husband has had a talk with them they will turn up. They do seem to be in awe of Mr Liddell, I can't think why.'

Mr Dodgson stood very still, his fingers worrying at a loose thread on his trouser leg.

'I suppose that is a skill that some men have.' She smiled again, broader than ever, and then turned again towards the house, pushing her children in front of her.

◆

They stood there together for a moment, united by the stirring of awkwardness that Mrs Liddell had created.

'Students can be lazy,' said Mary.

It was the wrong thing to have said. Two angry spots appeared on Mr Dodgson's cheeks.

Mary rushed to fill the silence with more words. 'Not that I have had as much experience as you!' She had surmised that Mr Dodgson was a tutor of some kind at Christ Church. 'I have only taught the girls, of course . . .'

Mr Dodgson worried at the lawn with his foot. 'If I only had girls I think I would be much better off. It is lazy young men that afflict me. But I am afraid that is the problem with modern life. Everybody affects boredom.'

Mary had not come across modern life before. 'Yes,' she said.

'I am afraid no one is interested in serious thought, or difficulty.'

'No,' said Mary. Mr Dodgson looked very solemn, but at the same time quizzical somehow. She imagined his mouth could quickly change from stern to amused, and back again. The wisp of breath coming out of it smelt faintly of cloves.

Alice's laugh floated across the lawn, and a shriek from Edith.

'Oh, to be a child once more!' said Mr Dodgson. 'I find I long to be a child again, the further away from it I become. But we all grow older, do we not, every day!'

Mr Dodgson did not look old, thought Mary. His skin was clear and unlined. Though perhaps his body seemed older, in the way that he carried it.

At twenty-eight the line between her eyes was beginning to shape itself into a permanent furrow. 'We do grow older every day, that is true,' she said, frowning even as she spoke.

'Though of course ladies age much more slowly than men,' said Mr Dodgson.

Mary blushed. Was he paying her a compliment or was he speaking in generalities? She could not tell from his face, which was still turned to the Deanery.

Mary had not much practice with gallantry. The best way forward, she thought hotly, was to ignore it. 'Good afternoon to you then!' she said, though she thought she felt his eyes on her all the way back across the lawn.

CHAPTER 3

$\mathcal{M}$ARY'S CHILDHOOD HAD BEEN SPENT IN A LARGE town house on Beaumont Street belonging to her grandmother, but when her grandmother died the family had been forced to sell up and move to a smaller one on Folly Bridge. Mary had not been back to it since she moved to the Deanery, and now that she was here again, the rooms seemed to have shrunk even further. The whole house was filled with steam. Her mother's servant was boiling a pig's trotter on the stove, and Mary could hear the sound of the bone clacking against the sides of the saucepan as if it had been brought back to life and was trying to get out.

Mary, her mother and her mother's friend Mrs Chitterworth sat in the parlour, between them a pile of hats like awkwardly landed birds.

'You know what they say, of course: "I am the Dean, this Mrs Liddell./ She plays first, I, second fiddle./ She is the Broad, I am the High/Together we are the University!"'

When Mary's mother, Mrs Prickett, hinged open her jaw to make *University* rhyme with *High*, Mary could see the sticky pink powder gathered in the crevices of her face.

'I have heard that,' said Mary. 'Though of course if you said *University* the right way, it would not work so well.' Her head throbbed just above her eyes; she took up a straw hat and began to attack it with her scissors.

Her mother could not sew; it hurt her fingers, she said. But she did not want to waste money on a new hat every year when the old ones could just as well be updated. So Mary was called in, to change a feather for ribbons, wilting silk roses for bows.

'And I suppose her position is unassailable now. Your father said that the whole of Oxford was there hoping to catch a glimpse of the royal carriage,' said Mrs Prickett.

'And I was there waiting just at the gates,' said Mrs Chitterworth. 'I wouldn't have missed it. Though I did get cold and have a very sore throat this morning. I have already been to the pharmacy.'

'You spend your life at that pharmacy, dear,' said Mary's mother.

'You are clever, Mary, with your needle. My fingers could never manage it!' Mrs Chitterworth leaned towards Mary. 'But what of the party? I am *desperate* to hear.'

'The party was very grand,' said Mary. 'I saw the Queen up close and Ina presented her with a posy—'

Her mother interrupted. 'Yes, yes, but you, did you hold up?'

A nub of silk, where the flower had been sewn on, remained

clinging to the felt. Mary stabbed at it with the tip of her scissors. She was damaging the material round it; a small hole was starting to blossom.

'Oh, let her finish, do!' said Mrs Chitterworth. 'I must hear about it all; I cannot wait.'

Her mother blew air out of her nostrils – not a snort, nothing that Mary could argue with. But air rushing through a mother's nasal cavities can be open to many filial interpretations, which Mary now ran through:

Her mother did not trust her. She did not think she had 'held up', as she put it.

Her mother thought her a figure of fun.

Her mother was conveying her amused derision that Mary had not yet managed to find a husband and had to go out to work for a living.

Or her mother's nose had become inflamed.

She could settle on that.

'Who was there? And what about the royal family, and was the Queen magnificent?' asked Mrs Chitterworth. (Mrs Chitterworth was a woman who had reacted to the difficulties in her own upbringing by refusing to look inwards. Thus she spent her whole life in gossip, although her body hatched all sorts of ailments in protest.)

So Mary had to give out every name of every person she could remember from the party, and who talked to whom, until her mouth was dry. As she spoke, she remembered the wine stain. It would be discovered by now, even if she hadn't heard anything about it. A red wine stain might never come out. But the stain could have come from anyone's glass. Alice could have been clumsy and bumped into someone herself.

'It went off very well,' Mary repeated.

'I heard the most amazing news! Lady Malmesbury's daughter has eloped and she is only fourteen. Can you imagine?' said Mrs Chitterworth. 'The poor woman.'

'At least the girl is married, or will be,' said Mrs Prickett.

Mary stabbed her needle into the felt. 'I need more ribbon.'

'That reminds me. Sidney Wilton came to call last week. I told him you lived in Christ Church now. He wanted to know how you were getting along.'

'What did you tell him?'

'Fine, I said.'

Mary wanted to tell her mother that she was doing more than fine; she was doing very well at the Deanery; she was now moving in a circle that her mother could have nothing to do with. She might have scooped up more of the pieces from the party and dropped them into her mother's lap to force out of her some spurt of accidental admiration. But her head was aching, her finger was throbbing where she had stabbed it, and now her mother had brought up the topic of Mr Wilton.

Mr Wilton – he had called for her, just for her. For her he had come to the house in his large overcoat, his cheeks reddened by wind and embarrassment, his black hair curling out beneath his hat. For her he had loitered awkwardly on the step while he was told that she had moved away.

'Did you ask him in?'

'He said he wouldn't stay.'

'Did you tell him I was living with the Liddells now?'

'I did, Mary, what do you take me for?'

He must have been impressed, thought Mary. 'What did he say?'

'He said he would call for you there.'

'When?'

'He didn't name a date.'

He'll send a note, thought Mary. She had last seen Mr Wilton sitting on her mother's sofa in the living room, buttoned tightly into a suit. His father had worked with hers at Trinity College: Mr Wilton's father was another of the college's household servants and the two had struck up a friendship. Mr Wilton's father had been a farmer; he owned some land at Binsley, just outside Oxford, where some of Mary's family still lived. But his herd of milking cows had come down with consumption and he had been forced to take a job at the college. The etiquette demanded by the dining hall had bewildered the older Mr Wilton, and Mary's father had taken pity on him, often staying after his own work was done to help the other man, to Mrs Prickett's dissatisfaction.

So Sidney Wilton had come to the house with his father to pay a visit. The last time Mary had seen him he had talked about Elliston & Cavell. It was the finest store in the town, he said; its front took up six windows on Magdalen Street. Only the best people visited, he said. He had a new delivery of buttons, he said, made from ivory and carved by hand in Ealing. And a fine roll of braid, which Mrs Sinclair had ordered for her husband's uniform. He was particularly pleased with the colour of the blue ribbon that had arrived from Sheffield.

He paused. Mary wondered what kind of blue it was.

What kind? It was blue, dark blue, Mr Wilton replied. He could not think to describe it any other way; he was not good with words.

But he sat with his knee pointing towards hers, which signified more than words perhaps. Mary thought she read some kind of intent in his kneecap. Twice, when he leaned forward to retrieve a biscuit from the table, he had angled it into her own knee, rather hard, and had not apologized nor moved away. The motion had been curiously at odds with the way he consumed his biscuit: fastidiously, raking his thick sideburns with his nails afterwards in a way that Mary could only assume was a grooming for crumbs.

She had put the idea of him at the back of her head during the turmoil of moving and taking up her new position, but now that she had discovered that Mr Wilton had called for her at home, without his father, she found that the image of him quickly grew to fill up the whole of her mind.

'I hear Agnes Briars has had another child,' said her mother. 'That makes four, and she is not yet twenty-five!'

Mary had watched her school friends become engaged, married and producers of red-faced babies, one by one. They disappeared into their confinement and when they reappeared they had replicated.

They were all holders of the same secret that she had not the key to. There was something about the making of babies, something that married women knew and would never tell. Surrender seemed to be required. She had learnt from a girl at school that babies went in and came out through the navel, which opened up like an enormous mouth. Women were supposed to want children more than anything else, Mary knew.

Perhaps when she had her own she would feel the same way, though she could not imagine it. As far as she could see, children were like savages and it was her purpose to try to tame them until they could fit into the civilized world like everybody else.

When she was married, she would have a house of her own. Bigger than her mother's, with more than one servant.

When she was married, she would leave this body behind and grow big enough to fill up a house in Park Town with its bulging red bricks and puffed-out cheeks and long-eyed windows.

When she was married, she would have tradesmen coming to her door, her heavy black door, and the tradesmen would lay out silver trinkets from India on her dining table and she would bend low, so low that she could see her reflection in the polished surface and smell the incense that still clung to the interior of a little silver box from Rajasthan. She would pick each piece up and weigh it gently in her hand before choosing the very best to display in her hall to the guests who came for dinner, and her taste – impeccable, but with a hint of daring – would be admired by all.

CHAPTER 4

*T*HE RAILWAY ENSURED THAT OXFORD WAS CONNECTED to the vast web of communication that stretched the length of the country, and it brought, in its belching horseless carriages, the very latest of everything. Tradesmen vied with each other, with their displays which reached far into the street, and their advertising posters that hung brashly in their windows. *Oranges and nuts very cheap*, read the sheet tacked in the front of the confectioner. *Try our celebrated 4d mixtures, the best ever offered at the price. Guaranteed absolutely pure!*

The Oxford Drug Company had gone further and advertised in bold type attached to the side of a dog cart, which trotted about town: *Vaseline, glycerine jelly, pectoral balsam for coughs, linseed, and liquorice, most popular and efficacious.*

The Liddells' carriage swung out to avoid it, causing Mary to lurch hard on to Ina's shoulder. The girl's face showed pain, but she said nothing. Mary herself was suffering from motion sickness, as she often did when she travelled backwards. Behind her head, separated only by the thin partition of the carriage wall, was the immense jodhpured rump of Bultitude in his yellow livery, one hand bunched round the reins, the other cracking the whip.

Mary was hemmed in on the other side by Alice, whose full white dress and hoops she could feel pressing against her own black sleeves. Her elbows were pinned to her sides; her bones scraped against the children's ribs with every jolt of the carriage. Her hipbones jarred. Her ribcage was filled up by the beating of her heart.

On the opposite side Mrs Liddell had the whole bench to herself.

They jangled into Magdalen Street, overtaking the crossing sweeper and slowing to swing out round the cheap bookseller, who had spilled all his wares on to the street. On the corner, Mary could see the reason why. She stood laughing in a way a woman would not usually do: her head thrown back, her neck an invitation, her bosom pushed forward and out by the stance of her chin.

'What a strange dress,' said Alice.

The dress was made of satin, scalloped each in a different shade of red. Her jacket was made of orange velvet. The effect was somehow intestinal, as if what should be inside was out, and outside was in.

Mrs Liddell followed their gaze. 'Alice, look away!' she said sharply.

'Oh, why?'

'Because I said so. Because we will be there in a minute and you ought to get your gloves on.'

'But my gloves are on!'

Behind her the woman had stopped laughing and was rearranging her hat in a frank manner (a combination of all the colours of her outfit, topped off by a peacock's feather), wiping her mouth and settling her lips into what Mary could see was their habitual shape: a smirking invitation that could not erase the shadow of derision that lay behind.

Mrs Liddell leaned over and grabbed Alice's chin with her hand, forcing her to look out of the other window. Above them Bultitude shouted extravagantly at the horses to slow down and then brought them up sharply outside Elliston & Cavell.

Mary did not want to see Mr Wilton at his place of work. They would be trapped animals, observed. She worried she would seem rude and artificial.

'Good afternoon, Mrs Liddell!' The doorman swung open the door. Mary watched the rest of the attendants bow before Mrs Liddell, no doubt noticing the emeralds hanging from her ears, the rich silk balloons of her sleeves, the heavy rings on her fingers. Her thick brown hair was barely contained by her bonnet, her gold chain heavy around her neck.

The shop was suffused with a whispering industry: the rustle of silk on parquet, the attentive murmur of employee to customer, the susurration of paper enfolding a new purchase. Mary kept her eyes on the silks. They were too dazzling, she decided. 'I have an acquaintance at the haberdashery department, I think.'

'Oh?' said Mrs Liddell, pausing to let her hands drift over the plush surface of a looped towel.

'Yes, a friend of my parents. I mean, the son of a friend.' She tried to keep her voice casual.

'A friend of yours works here?' said Alice. She grinned.

'In haberdashery, I believe,' said Mary. She gazed ahead at the uneven towers of damasks and chintzes.

'He works here?'

'Yes.'

'*Here*, in Elliston and Cavell?'

'Alice, are you deaf?' said Mrs Liddell.

Mary straightened her back, made herself rigid – she had a sudden shameful sense that she was shrinking.

Mrs Liddell swept on through the drawing room of a fashionable house, done up to show off the department store's fabrics. A sofa, an embroidered footstool, and yellow curtains held back over two painted windows.

All was gleaming, soft, a rich glow. How unlike Mary's room at the Deanery. When she was mistress of her own house she would come here, order curtains, bed linen, napkins; the thousand different things that made up a home.

'Why are there birds through that painted window?' said Alice.

'Because there are birds through real windows, I expect,' said Mrs Liddell. 'My dear Miss Prickett – are you well? You look terribly hot.'

'No, I am well, thank you! Not hot at all.'

'But why are there birds through real windows?' said Edith.

'Because God put them there,' said Ina.

Sweat crawled its way from Mary's armpits towards her bodice. Let it not stain.

'But why did God put them there?' said Alice.

'Darling, let us not descend from the problem of a painted window into the problem of existence in less than a minute,' said Mrs Liddell. 'I don't think I can bear it.'

◆

Haberdashery was the busiest and brightest corner of the store. To the ceiling stretched a thousand open-fronted drawers of sewing silks, each thread bound over card and folded. On the counter were buttons, bed laces, bodkins, bobbins and carpet bindings, and below it larger compartments containing gloves, linens and handkerchiefs.

Behind the counter stood Mr Wilton, his hands resting on top of the glass counter and his fingertips extending towards the perimeter of his universe. Mary saw him before he saw her: his gaze was unswerving and straight ahead.

Mr Wilton, thought Mary, *did* look just how men were supposed to look, at least in books. His shoulders were broad, his brow was dark. His hair was thick, his eyebrows were uncontrollable, their tentacles reaching down towards his eyelids.

But he was out of context. He jarred. He seemed not proud of his nature. His fingertips were crescented not by the mud of a Yorkshire moor but by short clean nails. And the hairs that poured out of his shirtsleeves wore a slick look of shame. He had trussed himself into a rigorous suit and held himself stiffly in it; his collar was punishingly high and Mary could see a red patch on the underside of his chin, even though it was darkened by stubble.

'Good afternoon,' said Mrs Liddell. 'I am looking for lace trimmings, and some ribbon, and I dare say some buttons too, mother-of-pearl, and, let me see . . .'

Mr Wilton hurried out from behind the counter. 'Good afternoon, Mrs Liddell. Miss Prickett.'

Mary opened her eyes. 'How do you know my name?' said Mrs Liddell, looking at him for the first time. 'Though I dare say everyone does!'

'It is Mr Wilton and I who have met,' said Mary. Her heart gave a small and surprising twist.

'Ah yes, I remember now. Oxford is a small place, as I always say,' said Mrs Liddell, pointing at the display behind the glass. 'That ribbon there, the thick one, how much is that? And the red, that is very pretty, though perhaps blue might go better.'

Mr Wilton stroked his sideburns. He told Mrs Liddell the price of the ribbons. He seemed mesmerized by her rings, which gleamed right under his nose; her hands, which fluttered with the excitement of purchase. She did have elegant hands, long and tapered and uncalloused.

'I'll take that one, the blue velvet, six lengths, and some of that cream ribbon too, the narrower of the two. And I need more handkerchiefs; I had better take a dozen, and a half-dozen pairs of gloves, for I am almost run out. And some lace; what would you recommend? It is to run round the hem of a skirt, and the cuffs, and some other ruffles too perhaps.'

Mr Wilton smoothed his smooth hair and, with a similar motion, spread out all the things Mrs Liddell had asked for on the counter. She bent down to look, circled by shop assistants who had materialized from the rustlings of the shop floor, servile and admiring.

Mary turned to Mr Wilton. 'My mother told me you had paid me a call and I am sorry not to have returned it. As you can see . . .' Mary gestured to the children, Edith staying close to her mother's skirts, Ina running the tip of her finger over a length of white ribbon.

Only Alice was staring back at them both, her head angled, smiling insolently. Mary thought about castigating her, but to do so would only draw attention to the awkwardness of the whole situation. Better to pretend the child was not staring so rudely – she was only a child, after all, she did not matter! Though in spite of herself Mary felt a flush spreading down her cheeks, towards her neck and her collarbones.

She turned her body away, as she might have from a too-hot fire, and angled her head to try to deflect Alice's gaze. Alice's curiosity impinged upon her as a solid thing, making her unnatural.

'I am glad to see you here looking so well.'

From the corner of her eye she could see that Alice was smirking. Mary turned away more, forcing Mr Wilton to step to the side to follow her. She started off on a description of her visit to her mother's house, just to fill up the air between them, with no real purpose. But Mr Wilton didn't seem to mind. He put his hands behind his back, a gesture that he must have picked up from addressing customers, to solve the problem of his arms perhaps: they were too long. But forcing them behind him pushed forward his chest and strained the buttons of his jacket.

'And the fashion in hats changes so quickly, do you find?' she finished, her hand flying up to her own black bonnet, at least three years out of date.

'What lace have you here?' said Mrs Liddell.

Mr Wilton turned. 'We have the Honiton lace; we are pleased to have it. It is made by hand in an area of thirty miles along the Devonshire coast. The handwork is very fine, as you can see.'

'Anything better?' said Mrs Liddell.

'You are thinking of Belgian lace,' said Mr Wilton.

'Yes, I will have – let's see, four lengths of that. Put it on my account.' Mrs Liddell motioned to Mary to pick up the smaller packages. Larger ones were being wrapped.

Mr Wilton turned to Mary quickly. 'Could I pay you a visit one day, perhaps, at the Deanery? We have more to talk about, I'm sure.'

Mary noticed the sides of his nose, greasy, open-pored. 'A visit?'

'Yes, if . . .'

The inside of Mary's head felt stretched and light. 'Yes, of course you may visit, if . . . if Mrs Liddell has no objection, that is.'

She turned to Mrs Liddell, solid and richly coloured in the gloom of the department store.

'Visit? From – this man?' Clearly Mrs Liddell had forgotten Mr Wilton's name. 'Do you wish it, Mary?' Amusement smirked at her lips.

Mary was glad of the packages rustling against her chest. She cradled them and smiled too, to signify that this exchange was unimportant. 'We are friends – I knew him before.'

Mr Wilton was smiling also, an endlessly pleasant smile that took in the buttons and braids and Mary and Alice and Mrs Liddell and thought nothing of it.

'Of course he may. You know where the tradesmen's entrance is to the Deanery? At the back of the house. Good day to you then.'

◆

In the carriage on the way home Mary tried to think about Mr Wilton and his impending visit. But her mind would only arrange itself blankly when it turned towards him, perhaps because of the high drum of the horses' hooves and the lean and swing of the carriage as it rattled towards Christ Church.

'How do you know Mr Wilton?' Mrs Liddell asked. It was hard to see her face under her bonnet, crammed with a romantic swoon of flowers on the brim.

'My father works with his,' said Mary.

'Oh, he works at Trinity?'

Mary nodded.

Mary had grown up with her father's constant presence during vacations and abrupt and endless absences during term-time. When he disappeared to work she believed she had had something to do with it, that he had gone away from her in disappointment.

She tried to gain an inch of space by shifting her hips up from the seat, but when she attempted to settle again Alice complained. 'I can feel your bones digging into mine!'

Mrs Liddell gazed outside at a woman and her baby, both dirty.

Mary flushed and tried to ease away from Alice towards Ina. The woman wore a vacant expression on her face, as if everything that passed her was a mirage.

Thinness such as Mary's, her mother said, made for bad blood. Thinness was unengaging. (Mary wondered how to engage. She imagined a seed pushing hooks out of its surface, catching hold of things.) Thinness such as Mary's denoted a shrewish character that no husband would want.

Mary must eat more. Her mother put her on a course of suet puddings, plum duff, rice milk. And for dinner: tripe and onions, Spanish stew, stewed steak. She put each plate down on the table with a clattering challenge that Mary failed to meet – her arms did not ripen, her hips did not swell, her bosom did not luxuriate.

Fried sweetbreads and swede mashed with dripping. Pork loin served with ropes of fat. Lamb's head. Mary had seen it one morning lying on the side in the kitchen, skinned and looking more like a reptile than a sheep. She had backed out of the room but its lidless eye, its long row of revealed teeth, followed through the day. She knew that her mother had left it there for her to see – she had sent Mary into the kitchen to pick up a jam jar, when she knew Mary was squeamish about dead animals. For Mary was sentimental about animals, especially lambs. She got this sentimentality, perhaps, from the fiction she read, which did not tend to deal with meat and the getting of it but only the gambolling of lambs and their woolly white curls, as a backdrop for romance.

Dinnertime came. Mary faced her mother across the surface of the dining-room table, darkly shining and sparse. The head of the lamb was browned and collapsed in on itself from a day spent in the oven, but still recognizably reptilian. Its eyes were misshapen with fat, which must have bubbled up from the recesses of its skull. Her mother – for there were only two of them at the table – carved up the cheek. Red grease pooled around the base of the head. Mary's throat rose up. She felt suddenly that she was going to cry.

'Mary, plenty of fat for you,' said her mother.

Half the head lay on her plate, a pile of potatoes steaming gently to the side.

She stared at her mother across the table, sawing hard at a cheek. She stared back down at her own plate, at the nubby cartilage between the jigsaw of the nose bone.

A curl of shame tugged at her stomach. She pushed her chair back. 'I am not hungry.'

'You are always hungry!'

'I am not hungry,' Mary said again.

'Sit there till you have finished it. It's been all day cooking and it's not to waste.'

Mary grabbed the back of her chair and scraped the legs across the stone floor. Now her mother did look up and Mary was glad to see surprise on her face.

'I will not eat it. There is no point, Mother, and stop trying!'

'Trying what, Mary?'

But Mary could not say for what her mother was trying; she could not form the words out loud unless it was an admission of defeat.

◆

A few months after that, Mary had got her job with the Liddells, and in between times she decided that God had made her thin to test her fortitude and strengthen her in the face of people's judgement. She knew very well that she was considered unwomanly, untrustworthy, spiteful, by anyone who cared to vouch an opinion, and they could tell all this just by passing her in the street and without ever having talked to her. But she had as much soul as them – and full as much heart!

CHAPTER 5

$\mathscr{A}$LICE AND INA WERE WEARING MATCHING DRESSES of black and white checked organza, with two large black velvet bows at the neck and the chest; Mary had seen the same on much older girls.

'What are we getting dressed up for?' said Alice.

'Your mother is having a small tea party,' said Mary.

'But she always has people to tea! Why are Ina and I to come?'

'Don't ask questions,' said Mary again. She didn't know the answer, or why she was to take such care preparing them. She bent over Alice's face and scratched something off it with her fingernail.

'Do not flinch. You were dirty. I don't know how, when your face was just washed.' Mary took hold of Alice's chin in her hand and rubbed at her face with a licked thumb.

'I don't see how spit is cleaner than dirt,' said Alice. 'You said spit *was* dirt, I'm sure of it!'

'Don't ask questions,' said Mary, giving Alice's cheek three extra rubs with her thumb. Then she took the brush and swept it down over Alice's hair. The image of Mr Wilton came into her mind. She wondered when he would come for his visit. He could drop in at any moment – she ought to tidy those books, and the beading had come loose from the overhang of the tablecloth. And her socks needed darning. And she should ask the house-maid to scrub the stain out of her sleeve.

The longer she stayed at the Deanery, the larger the suspicion grew that it was not her life that was important to the world generally, but the children's. She was a shadowy presence behind their white glare. Their need for fresh air, their knowledge of Prussia, their laces being undone.

'Miss Prickett, you are brushing my ears!' Alice twisted her head away.

Mary looked down. The tips of the child's ears were red but she kept on until she could see strands of hair flying up towards the brush and others clinging to Alice's forehead.

She couldn't bring Mr Wilton to mind, not the whole of him, only his shape with its solid middle, and his darkly furred hands. His eyes she could not see; his face was indistinct even though she thought about him, the idea of him, very often. She wondered when he would come.

Mary released Alice and turned to Ina, tweaked at her lace collar and smoothed down the wiry hair that sprang up from her parting. Ina puffed out her cheeks and stared hard at the floor but said nothing.

Mary led the children out from the schoolroom, down the narrow stairs and on to the landing. On down the Lexicon staircase (bought with the profits made from the Dean's Greek Lexicon) with its large wooden panels and lions that stood sentinel on each corner. Through the drawing room, almost stumbling over the skin of a tiger, its head thrust upwards and its teeth bared, shot by one of the Dean's ancestors. Past the table with the silver enamelled box from India picked up by Mrs Liddell at the Great Exhibition, past the embroidered scenes, done by Mrs Liddell during the long winter evenings, that hung on the wall, until finally they were out on the terrace.

Mrs Liddell sat talking with a young undergraduate in the spring sunshine, his thin legs stuck out in front of him, leaning back on his chair. The hat he had thrown down beside him had a gold tassel on it. An aristocrat, then.

'My dear Francis, it will be a tragedy if the ball does not go ahead. A tragedy!' Mrs Liddell leaned towards him.

'It looks like it will not.'

'The naysayers!' said Mrs Liddell. 'And led by Mr Dodgson! He who comes over most days to drink our tea. It was the same when we came here. The Dean got all sorts of complaints. He was thought a modernizer, dangerously progressive. And Mr Dodgson was at the forefront of that too, as far as I remember. It certainly didn't stop him ingratiating himself.'

In front of her, Alice stood very still. Mary could tell she wanted to speak but held herself back. Her mother had not yet seen them.

'It is not as if curfew will be broken *every* night.'

'I quite agree, my dear Francis. Quite. To listen to them, you would think we were proposing a night in hell rather than a ball.'

Mary's shoes pinched where she had rushed to lace them. She wondered where she ought to stand. But just then Mrs Liddell saw them and beckoned them over. Her fingers were clustered with rings; she looked like an enormous shellfish festooned with diamond limpets.

'I am pleased to introduce my eldest girls, Ina and Alice. Girls, this is Lord Newry. Why don't you come and sit down?'

They went, Ina puce.

'Not over there, Ina, here.' She motioned to a seat near Lord Newry. 'Where we can all see you.'

Mary could feel Ina's embarrassment in the handling of her cup as she brought it to her mouth, in the sweep of her eyelashes as she fixed her gaze on the linen tablecloth, and the clumsy angle her body made with the table. Nobody else seemed to notice. Lord Newry flicked away a fly from the side of his plate. 'I suppose Nature, in her sphere, must include flies, but I do not know why.'

'For birds, dear Francis, that is why,' said Mrs Liddell.

'But Mama, birds could survive on worms. They are nicer,' said Ina.

'Nicer? Worms are nicer?' Lord Newry put an amused finger up to the corner of his mouth, where he had correctly divined there was a stray crumb. 'Than flies, you mean. Though perhaps that point is up for debate.'

Ina pinked again and folded her arms around her waist. Mary, looking down at her, noticed they had a new plumpness. From her bird's-eye view she saw that Ina's nose had started to pimple and she had a conical red spot to the side of her forehead near her hairline. And when Ina had been putting on her dress, Mary had noticed the buds of her breasts for the first time.

'Worms live below ground, that is why they are nicer,' said Alice.

'Well, I live above it,' said Mrs Liddell. 'I don't know anyone who lives below.'

'That reminds me, have you ridden on the new Metropolitan railway line in London?' said Lord Newry. 'There is a frightful crush in the mornings, and again in the evenings. I have experienced it, just for fun, and I must say one is pressed up against people quite as if there was no society left.'

Mary had seen young men like him around Oxford many times, but this was the first time she had been up close. It was just as she had expected. The sneering shape of Lord Newry's mouth as seen from a distance did indeed bring forth words intended to put others down when you could hear them. They dropped out of his constricted throat in a thin, high stream; perhaps the tightening of the throat developed when the aristocracy tightened their grip on the land and separated themselves from the rest of society.

'Oh, you are brave, my dear Francis!' Mrs Liddell put the palm of her hand on his knee. 'I shouldn't like to try it one bit. Travelling underground seems most unnatural.'

'I suppose you have read Spencer?'

'I have heard of him, yes.'

'Travelling on the Met puts me in mind of him. He has coined a term for Mr Darwin's theories: "survival of the fittest". And I must say, jammed into one of those carriages I am inclined to agree.'

Mary thought of the woman in the shades of red, with the peacock feather in her hat. She had had a vitality that the aristocrat lacked.

'Whatever do you mean, Francis?'

'The lower forms of society ought not to procreate, for the good of the higher. There are some ghastly people around.'

Mary's face burned. Even though she had not been in service long, she knew already to divide the world into two categories: those who noticed her and those who didn't. Lord Newry fell into the second category.

She wondered what he would have done. Sterilization perhaps. Would his plan extend to governesses? Surely not. Just the lady in orange and her sisters. But not to the men who visited them – that would take out half of Christ Church's undergraduates.

The talk travelled on. Alice was young enough to think her opinions counted for something, and Lord Newry was encouraging her by asking questions and letting off laughter that rattled like a woodpecker on a tree.

'I don't like tea very much, I'm afraid,' Alice said.

'Oh?'

'It tastes like leather shoes.'

The avian laughter. 'I daresay it does if you are – what age are you?'

'Ten years old, Lord Newry.'

'Precisely. But perhaps you will one day,' said Lord Newry. 'I should hope so at least, otherwise you will find it difficult to pay house visits.'

'Ina is growing up so fast, she will soon be making house visits of her own,' said Mrs Liddell.

Ina stared down at her teacup.

'How old are you now, Ina?' asked the aristocrat.

'Thirteen, Lord Newry.'

'Ah, thirteen, yes. I knew a girl of fourteen engaged to be married, so I dare say house visits are nothing to that.'

Mary noticed Ina's ears burned bright red. And they *were* talking about her, and thus the origin of the phrase.

'Fourteen is *rather* young, but I shan't say anything against eighteen, Lord Newry, or seventeen at a push!'

Lord Newry reddened now, though he hid it by yawning with his hand over his face.

The girls were young, but perhaps never too young to be acquainted with the right sort of possibility, thought Mary.

Standing behind the party as she was, Mary was the first to see Mr Dodgson come round the corner of the house, with his hands held out in front like an illustration of a sleepwalker. They were stained, or dirty, Mary saw straight away. Had he been digging with them? They were not uniformly black, but darker on the palms. Splotched. Like Alice's copybook.

How had she not noticed before? But – perhaps he always wore gloves. Yes, perhaps he did, though she hadn't thought it strange at the time.

Mary saw Mr Dodgson take in the nobleman, the teacups half empty, Alice and Ina in their best dresses pressed in on him on either side.

The colour in his cheeks spread up to his forehead and down

towards his neck. He passed a hand over his face. He looked back at Mrs Liddell, his mouth a disbelieving smile.

Lord Newry took a final bite of fruit cake. Not for him the possibility of crumbs, of too much or too little saliva, or gum-sticking mulch. Just one small bite, masticated neatly beneath a quivering moustache.

'Oh look, it is Mr Dodgson. Hullo, Mr Dodgson!' said Alice.

Mr Dodgson's face changed again. He bowed and then turned his palms up in a gesture of surrender. 'I am afa-afa-afraid . . . I didn't think to meet anyone today. I left off my gloves.'

'Oh, Mr Dodgson! Are you in the broom cupboard again?' said Mrs Liddell, drawing out the word *broom* into two rising syllables. 'You must be more in the Deanery than in your own rooms.'

'I have been atta-atta-attempting a view out of the garden,' he said, dropping his hands back down to his sides and pressing his palms on to the outside of his legs.

'That's why they call it the dark art,' said Lord Newry. 'I never put it together before now.'

'Why do they call it what?' said Alice.

'Photography. Because of the chemicals. They stain.'

An undergraduate shouted somewhere in the quadrangle, his voice neutralized through the sandstone walls.

'You know Lord Newry,' said Mrs Liddell.

'Yes, Lord Newry. Good afternoon.' Mr Dodgson stood unevenly, one shoulder higher than the other. 'I think you were up for a lecture of mine once.'

'Possibly.' Lord Newry hadn't moved; his hands were still behind his head, though Mary saw his lips twitch. 'Did I go?'

'No.'

Mrs Liddell smiled.

Mr Dodgson pressed his lips together; he looked fussy. Mary wondered if he meant to or if it was something he could not help. She had noticed this primness about him before. He was fastidious in matters of dress – his own and even the children's. It was not unknown for him to kneel down by Alice and rub off a piece of dirt on her collar with his thumb.

'Before I go . . . I did mean to ask. This may not be the best time, only I did promise.'

'Promise what?' Mrs Liddell rattled her teacup into its saucer.

'I met the Acland children on the way here. I wondered, if you were agreeable, if I may take their photograph along with your own children at the Deanery. Would you allow it?'

Mrs Liddell's smile reminded Mary of the head of the tiger-skin rug in the drawing room, its teeth bared. 'Oh, Mr Dodgson, I am flattered that you wish to spend so much of your time in photographing my children when you are so busy, not to mention the considerable expense of meeting the cost of chemicals and so on.'

Mr Dodgson bowed and turned to go. He had taken her answer as a yes, Mary saw. But Mrs Liddell glanced at Lord Newry and added: 'I think I saw you out of doors last night. It must have been around nine o'clock.'

Mr Dodgson turned round again. 'I like to walk; the evening air refreshes me.'

'Yes, the evening air refreshes me too. I always think the occasional late night does wonders for one's health. Do you agree, Lord Newry?'

Lord Newry smirked. 'Quite, Mrs Liddell.'

'What do you think, Mr Dodgson?'

Mr Dodgson's eyes were fixed on the flagstones. 'It might depend on what it, on what it en-en-en-en, on what it en-tailed.' He brought out the word with a stamp of his tongue on the T.

'Precisely. It would depend on what it entailed. A night of drinking and carousing would *not* be good, but I expect a night of general enjoyment, such as Lord Newry's ball, might lift one's spirits significantly. I know you enjoy many such nights, and in the Deanery too.'

'But your ball, as you know, would entail breaking college rules.'

'I don't see what you have against young people enjoying themselves. I dare say even you must have been young once!' said Lord Newry.

Mr Dodgson looked as if someone had stuck a broom handle up the back of his jacket to keep him still. Discomfort radiated from him.

Mary felt a surprising stab of pity.

'I have nothing against enjoyment, as you know, Mrs Liddell. But the rules of college curfew have been in place for hundreds of years, and if you, if you, if you were to break them once . . . then, then, then they could be broken again. And again, and they would become meaningless.'

Rules, yes, that was what Mary was always trying to impart

to the children. So she was surprised at what Mrs Liddell said next: 'And if they are broken for one night? I suppose civilization would end!'

Mary opened her mouth in surprise; out of habit, she nearly spoke, but she was a governess now. She closed her lips again and put her hand up to scratch her chin, to mask her expression.

'But don't let us keep you from your work!' Mrs Liddell said, turning back to Lord Newry. 'I should hate to be the cause of the failure of an artistic endeavour.'

Mr Dodgson's smile, as he was dismissed, was full of difficulty.

◆

As dusk was falling, Mary went out for a walk in the garden. Now that it was almost summer, she preferred to be out of doors than in her little room with its high window and pipe running through it that ticked and stamped into the early hours. She was surprised to see Mr Dodgson still there. 'Have you had any success?' she asked him.

'What?'

'Your photography.'

'Ah – some. Trees are better at standing still than children.' He stood up from the wheelbarrow that he was filling with his photographic apparatus. 'Has Lord Newry gone?'

He had, hours ago.

'Is he here often?'

'I have not met him before,' said Mary. 'But I believe him to be a favourite of Mrs Liddell's.'

'Ah, Mrs Liddell, the kingfisher. Bold and bright . . . and a fisher of kings.' Mr Dodgson threw his funnels and trays into the wheelbarrow noisily.

'Fisher of kings?' Mary echoed.

Mrs Liddell was ambitious, Mary knew that. She had once overheard an argument between Mrs Liddell and the Dean; he had been offered another position it seemed, that of the Queen's chaplain. Mrs Liddell had been so ecstatic that Mary had heard her voice from the other side of the house. The Dean had not been so happy. 'We shall have even more cares, troubles, business and all sorts of things to interfere with our arrangements!' Then Mrs Liddell, in pleading tones, pointing out the merits. Then the Dean, sterner: 'Be not ambitious, Lorina. Desire not a higher place for me. If ever I was serious, I am here – on this point.' Then a door being slammed, and sobs.

The air was colder now and midges jumped about in it.

'Do the children like him?' asked Mr Dodgson.

'Who?'

'Lord Newry.'

'I don't know. Alice prattles on to anybody, as you know.'

'Yes, and is the more charming for it. She still retains her innocence! Dear Alice. My sisters were the same as children. I miss them.'

'Do you have many?'

'Seven. I am used to entertaining them,' said Mr Dodgson, standing up and gazing past Mary at the elm tree.

'Goodness, your mother must be busy.'

'My mother, alas, is dead,' said Mr Dodgson.

'Oh dear. I am sorry to hear it. The loss must be hard to bear.' Mary stood awkwardly, half turned towards him, half turned away.

'I was never happier than when I was a boy and my dear mother was alive!' He still looked up and Mary thought she saw tears in his eyes.

'Mothers.' Mary turned away. She thought of her own. 'Yes. May I help you with your equipment?'

'Oh no. But there is one thing you could do for me – the Aclands,' said Mr Dodgson. 'I would be very grateful if you could warn their governess in advance so that we can all arrive on time. Punctuality is a good start to the day.'

'That is what I always tell the children,' said Mary.

The more she saw of Mr Dodgson, the more she realized there were many things on which they agreed.

CHAPTER 6

*W*HEN MR WILTON'S NOTE CAME, MARY READ IT twice over and folded it carefully away beside her bag of lavender in the top of her drawer. The note was short; it proposed a visit together to Mr Ruskin's Science Museum. He did not mind taking the children, he said, and although Mary had somehow forgotten to include the children in her imaginings of the day, they could not be helped, as it was not her afternoon off.

She started her preparations early, just after lunch, brushing out her hair and making one thick plait with it, which she wound over the top of her head so that it resembled the first layer of a hat. But somehow she had got it in the wrong place and her bonnet over the top was too sharply angled. So she tried again, and again, but it would not come right. By this time the children had been ready for half an hour, and had torn their own bonnets off. So she had to go out unhappy, and with aching wrists.

Mr Wilton was waiting for them outside the door of the Deanery. She had not remembered the sagging of his jawline, the collapsing flesh at his chin criss-crossed with lines that suggested the future direction of his face. His flesh looked almost womanly in spite of his stubble; Mary shut her eyes – the feel of it pierced her. When she opened them, she saw only his smile, wide with no trace of anything behind it.

'Hullo!' he said in his deep voice. Mary hurried over to him, the children behind her, and they set off.

The children were in a wild mood. On the way to the museum they ran on ahead down the pavement, even Ina, her heavy-booted feet stamping at the edges of puddles. Edith seemed to want to nearly throw herself under the wheel of every passing carriage. Mary could not concentrate on Mr Wilton's conversation at all.

'. . . that it comes from as far afield as Africa and is really as fine an example as you will find anywhere of such a thing.' Mr Wilton stopped and looked at her expectantly.

'What does?'

'The ivory, as I said.'

'Alice – get back here AT ONCE!'

'Do you like dresses very much, Mr Wilton?' said Alice, still ten feet away.

'Alice!' said Mary.

'But I was only asking! I should think it very interesting to work at a haberdasher's.'

Mary looked hard at the child. But she only wore an expression of curiosity, her neat little head cocked to one side.

'Not dresses so much as what goes on them. Buttons and braid and such. Very interesting.'

'Go off now,' said Mary, with a squirm of shame, even though she had only just told Alice to come back.

By the time they reached the museum, all of Mary's careful preparations for Mr Wilton's visit had been lost. The cooling and refreshing effects of the Rowlands' Kalydor lotion she had patted on her cheeks had been outdone by the anxiety of keeping the girls in sight; the two patches of scent she had dabbed under her chin had been overcome by the smells of the street: horse manure, distantly roasting meat.

Inside the tall domed building, Mr Wilton's voice continued in its implacable way, talking on about fabrics and flannels, twill and tweed, bouncing from the stone floor on to the displays of animal skeletons and up into the ceiling. Mary imagined his words clustering up there and growing ever more populous until they joined together and fell back down as rain.

The children had stopped in front of the remains of Buckland's Giant Lizard, standing up on its hind legs. Ina hung behind. 'Dinosaurs give me nightmares,' she said.

Mary nodded. She had always thought them the very worst combination of bird and lizard.

'Strange to think that they were walking around here. Even on this very spot!' said Alice.

'Were they as big as a house, or bigger?' said Edith, in her precise way. 'Or smaller? Some ought to be smaller, I think.'

Mr Wilton turned to the children. His hands were in his pockets. 'Perhaps you would like to hear this. Most of these bones were found by a Mr Chapman, a watchmaker, on a botanizing expedition. As the first bone came into sight, he found the foreman, stopped the digging, then telegraphed Mr Phillips, Professor of Geology, who oversaw their removal to this place here, as you see.'

'You know a great deal about this, Mr Wilton,' said Mary.

'May we go now, please?' said Ina.

'I have some interest, yes. But I prefer not to parade my knowledge about. There is no better attribute than modesty. Ambition is the curse of the age, I always say.'

Did he look approvingly at her black dress and its high collar as he spoke? Mary blushed. Though perhaps there was something not modest about the way he was looking at her. His eyes narrowed and roved about over her body until she felt his gaze had a weight to it, and a heat. His mouth below hung slightly open, his lips wet.

'*Please* may we go?'

She turned to Ina. 'Yes, go,' she said. She put a hand up to her cheek.

The next exhibit was a large bone which was at first thought to be the thigh bone of the large humans mentioned in the Bible but was now known to be an animal's. As Mary walked towards it she was conscious of the movements of her own bones: the way her hip bones swivelled in their sockets, the way her shoulders rotated as she moved, her wrists as she lifted her hands away from her sides.

'Did people and dinosaurs get along together?' asked Edith.

'Some did, some didn't,' said Mr Wilton. 'I dare say people weren't too fond of the Tyrannosaurus rex.'

'Certainly,' said Mary. 'But there is some new evidence to suggest—'

Before she could finish, Alice cut her off. 'Why are dinosaurs extinct?'

'Because God ordered it so,' said Mr Wilton.

Survival of the fittest, thought Mary. Though of course that was not true, as Mr Wilton said, when applied to animals. But when applied to humans, to *her* . . . The prettiest girls all married early and had two or more children. Except for the few who had died in childbirth. Perhaps they were meant to die, if God ordered it. But that seemed harsh, to leave children without mothers . . . Mary shook her head and tried to recapture her original thought:

She was unmarried. Therefore unfit.

'But why would He do a thing like that?' said Edith. She looked up at Mr Wilton, worried.

'We don't know the mind of God,' he said. 'But I imagine He wanted Mankind to be safe from dinosaurs.'

There was still time to put it right.

She turned to Mr Wilton. 'So you are not a believer in this theory of Mr Lyell's, that the earth developed slowly over millions of years?'

'I am not.'

'But he has some geological evidence, layers of rock . . .' Mary stopped. She had read something about it but hadn't understood all. She did not want to seem a fool.

'The earth developed as it says in the Bible. Six thousand years is a very long time. That's what I was taught and I don't think my teacher, old Mr Scammell, would lie to his pupils. He was most definite on the matter. No, I dare say we won't be hearing much more about the so-called Theory of Evolution! It is just not right – does not seem right and therefore cannot be. Thinking too hard leads to strange results.'

The Dean thought a great deal and was not happier for it, or healthier. Mary could not help thinking, though perhaps her type of thinking was not as dangerous, not being in Ancient Greek or somesuch. She thought about the same things often, running on their thousand legs down the same paths in her brain: the purpose of her life, the appearance of someone to save her, the possibility of marriage. She sometimes felt as if she had ants in her skull.

'I quite agree! Mr Darwin and his acolytes ought to be sent somewhere far away so that they can stop poisoning the minds of the general population. And children!'

'Quite, quite, Miss Prickett,' said Mr Wilton, looking her over again.

Mary looked away, blushing. His low brow and broad shoulders, his hair that pushed out beneath his cuffs, all left an uncomfortable imprint on her retinas. She said with more force than usual: 'I have never seen an ape give birth to a human, or heard of it. And nowhere else in nature does one animal turn into another.'

'You have read up on it, I see,' said Mr Wilton.

Mary nodded. There was a further thing: if Mr Darwin was right, there could not be a God, at least in the way that she understood Him. And there was most certainly a God, at the end of life, to divide the sheep from the goats. That was the purpose of a good life. Her struggle must, in the end, be acknowledged. Otherwise Mary could let her thoughts run on into the night, full of petty resentments and jealousies, and on certain occasions hatred. For it was so easy to hate! Sometimes she just had to walk down the street to see a man she hated for no more than the way his eyes flickered over her face and away again, or a woman stepping out of a carriage in a pair of calfskin boots, or a child being luxuriously embraced by its mother.

But she hacked these thoughts off at the stem, when she caught them, for fear that God might be listening. God knows everything, as her mother always said. He can see what you do alone in your room, He can see into your bed at night. Mary had the idea, when she was a child, that God would like her to sleep very straight in bed, with her legs and arms directly up and down. When she woke in the morning to find herself on her side and her limbs crooked, she always felt as if she had failed Him.

But she must try to be good, and try to make the children good, even if it was a struggle against human nature.

'Perhaps you would like to come to my church?' said Mr Wilton.

They had left the museum and were walking home. Mary squinted up at Tom Tower; it looked as if it had been pulled upwards by celestial fingers.

'Your church?'

'Yes, it is on the outskirts of Oxford. I could meet you here and we could go on together.'

'Which church is it?'

'A Christian church. God's own church, I believe.' Mr Wilton was walking quickly but his head was turned towards her and his eyebrows were raised. 'I think you would find it enlightening.' He smiled. 'In view of our recent conversation.'

Mary could see Mrs Chitterworth approaching from the opposite direction. She smiled back at him with a thrum high up in her chest. 'Yes, Mr Wilton. I would be pleased to accompany you.'

'You look exceedingly happy, Mr Wilton,' said Mrs Chitterworth. 'What has happened?'

Mr Wilton coloured. 'Nothing. I mean – not nothing. We are . . .' He trailed off.

Mrs Chitterworth cocked her head and shook her ringlets, like a spaniel with water in its ear.

'We are just returning from the Science Museum,' said Mary.

'Oh, that place! Nothing in there of any interest, I'll be bound. And these must be your charges.' Mrs Chitterworth nodded at the children without seeing them. 'But you have caught me on my way to the pharmacist; I have an inflammation of the eyelid. Do you see?'

'It does look red,' said Mary.

'Have you seen Lady Tetbury at the Deanery? She has grown very thin, they say on account of unhappiness.'

'I have not,' said Mary. 'Why is she unhappy?'

Mr Wilton shifted beside her.

'They say on account of her husband.' Mrs Chitterworth leaned closer. 'I wouldn't like to speculate on him. But they say he is never at home, always in London. Still. I dare say she has brought it on herself. Her home is not one you want to go into, by all accounts. Not well managed, and dreary. Who can blame him for leaving occasionally? But I must go on, Mary. I must get to the pharmacy, for relief. Good day to you, Mr Wilton, and to you, Miss Prickett. I am glad to see you out together.'

'Friday next, then,' said Mr Wilton, as they were near to the gates of Christ Church now. His bow to her was a tree trunk bending in half.

CHAPTER 7

$\mathcal{N}$ANNY FLETCHER, A WOMAN SHAPED LIKE A SKITTLE, often spoke about the dangers of educating girls, especially as they grew older. If Mary tried to argue, Nanny liked to quote a Mr Renishaw, a man of science, who had done experiments to prove it and had concluded that the power of women's brains was severely diminished by growing breast tissue, and that any other strain on them would put their health in peril.

'Lessons are over for today,' said Nanny. 'Far better to fill the children's heads with fresh air. Let nature take its course.'

'I don't know what you mean by nature,' said Mary. 'I should think nature ought to be suppressed, and replaced by civilization.'

'Fresh air is good for them,' Nanny replied, bending down to pick up a cardigan.

Mary had caught a cold from somewhere, the children probably, even though it was nearly summer. She was fighting a constant urge to sneeze. 'Well, they are being photographed today, with the Acland children.'

'They are not!' Nanny smiled. 'Mr Bultitude is waiting in the carriage now.'

'The carriage?' said Mary stupidly. 'But I spoke with their governess only yesterday.'

'A change of plan.'

'Ah, yes.' Mary nodded, as if she had forgotten. As if she had been told.

Mrs Liddell came in, dressed to go out, and called to the children. 'It is such a lovely afternoon, I thought we would all go to Nuneham Park. Hurry now, Bultitude is ready outside with the carriage.'

'But I thought Mr Dodgson was taking our photograph,' said Alice.

'Hurry up,' said Mrs Liddell. 'Miss Prickett, please help the children into their boots.'

By the time they were all seated in the carriage, Mary thought she must have had the wrong day; there had been no mention of Mr Dodgson's visit by Mrs Liddell and she felt too awkward and congested to bring it up. Perhaps Mrs Liddell or Mr Dodgson had cancelled and forgotten to tell her. Bultitude whipped up the horses and the carriage jolted forward. Mary hoped she would not feel sick as she usually did.

But as they were turning out of the quadrangle, Mary lurching over to the side, she saw him through the window. Mr Dodgson, heading towards them, his extra equipment piled into the wheelbarrow.

Mary looked at Mrs Liddell in confusion, but she was staring out of the other window, her mouth curved upwards into a slight smile. Mary just had time to fix Mr Dodgson's surprised eyes with her own before the carriage spun out of sight.

◆

'Mama – that was Mr Dodgson!' said Alice.

'Was it?'

'Yes, it was! He was coming to make a photograph. Why did we leave him?'

Mrs Liddell stared through the window. She had not meant Mr Dodgson to see them leaving, but now that he had, she could not help feel the tiniest bit pleased. How startled he looked, just like a lopsided bird fallen out of its nest. 'If he thought I had agreed to another photograph, and to his using the Deanery as his studio whenever he pleased, he was wrong. I never agreed to it. The plan for today had always been to go to the park.'

The carriage was passing those uncomfortable houses which a city seemed nowadays to cough up: neither smart enough to be in town nor attractive enough to be in the country. Dull-looking women loitered at their front gates, with children clinging to their arms. As the carriage passed, they turned to stare. Mrs Liddell tilted her head up so that her gaze fell only upon the trees. She kept it there until they were in the country-side. Most were still bare, but there was a row of copper beeches that had unfurled brand-new leaves already and they shone dully in the sun. Like coins.

Mary took her damp handkerchief from her sleeve and inserted her nose into it. The nose felt as if it had been grafted on, with its own heartbeat, radiating out over the rest of her head.

A misunderstanding, then. She was not to blame. She had told the Aclands' governess as Mr Dodgson had asked, but Mrs Liddell had made other plans.

Mary shut her eyes. She saw again the expression on Mr Dodgson's face as he realized they were driving off and leaving him, his eyes following them in mute surprise, a smile of embarrassment.

Mrs Liddell turned to her daughter. 'Alice, dear, perhaps you are growing rather old for Mr Dodgson.'

'Whatever do you mean?' Her frown left no trace; her skin was a material that could be puckered and lined as often as it liked but smoothed out afterwards to leave an impeccable surface.

'I mean that he has been your friend for a long time, since you were, what, four years old. But now that you are nearly eleven, you may want to . . .' Mrs Liddell squinted up at the leaves. 'You may want to move on.'

'Move on to what?'

Mrs Liddell sighed. 'I mean he is a good companion for children. But for young ladies he is not.'

'He knows lots of young ladies! He always says that his child friends are quite often by now grown into young ladies. Besides, I am not a young lady.'

'No, but you soon will be. He is fond of you, fond of you all, I know. But I don't want him coming over to the Deanery. These last few months he has practically lived here.'

'But I like him! I like him coming over,' said Alice.

'Just do as I say. I don't want to see that strange face every morning when I wake up and every evening before I go to bed. It's too tiring!'

'I still want to see him,' said Alice. 'We are friends.' She set her face out of the window; she looked just like her mother.

CHAPTER 8

𝒥T WAS MARY'S SECOND VISIT TO CHURCH THAT DAY, having been to hear the Dean preach at Christ Church with the children earlier. From the outside this church looked similar, if smaller. And the people inside looked much like any other congregation: women with ringlets, bonnets; men darkly dressed and sombre.

The scripture was read by one of them, followed by a psalm read by another. And then the first difference: the man who took to the pulpit to preach the sermon was unlike any man Mary had seen in God's service before.

'Thank you, God, ye chose in your wisdom to work through us, unimportant members, low as we are, plain as we are, but who are sustained by love.'

He ought not to have included himself alongside his congregation. The pastor was not plain. He was tall and dark, his face was startlingly symmetrical, his hair swept down past his ears.

'You have put in our hearts a longing for the day when the whole world will come to an end.'

Beside her Mr Wilton nodded and whispered: 'The day of the Lord is near, even at our door.'

Mr Wilton, a millenarian? Mary had not known it. She nodded back at him in confusion. That meant . . . would there be time . . . well, how soon was the world to end? She listened out for a date in the preacher's sermon but she could not get one.

No set date. That was a good thing: if he meant to ask her to marry him, there was still time before the apocalypse.

'The day of the Lord will come like a thief. The heavens will disappear with a roar; the elements will be destroyed by fire, and the earth and everything in it will be laid bare,' said the pastor.

Around the church feathers shook, birds' wings bobbed as women nodded their heads.

A great wind was coming, he said – the trees in Christ Church meadow flattened like twigs, their roots torn up and dripping with soil. The roofs blown off all the colleges and a hand coming down and plucking out the inhabitants one by one, flinging them first to one side and then the other.

Mary found herself smiling. The unbelievers in their finery lifted and twirled about, their topcoats flapping up helplessly, and cast into the fiery pit for all eternity. A great voice booming down from the heavens: *Mary Prickett, come!* And being lifted up, straight up, into a golden glow, warmth flooding her body.

The pastor's voice rose and rose until it itself was a hurricane that filled the church, and filled her. His vibrations got inside her ribcage and melted back out through her bodice.

They must not stand idle, he thundered, waiting for the coming of Jesus! They must, in their greatest efforts, bring *God* to the *world*, just as the apostles had done at Pentecost, when they baptized three thousand souls and brought many more to the Lord!

Mary's cheeks were hot, burning. Beside her Mr Wilton got to his feet. In front of her the pastor elevated his hands, his long, pale fingers issuing out of a velvet coat. He was the admiral of a doomed but brave ship, his cape spread out fearlessly behind. The rest of the congregation stood too, as if drawn up by the raising of his arms, and Mary with them, as if her body belonged to him.

He opened his arms and spread his hands. Mr Wilton did the same.

'Let the Holy Spirit well up within. We calleth to you, O Jesus, send down your Holy Spirit as you did at Pentecost! Come down and fill us with your spirit!'

Mary spread her arms out as the others were doing. Her heart was exposed; her breasts were exposed too, now that she had opened her arms, and pointing heavenwards.

Somewhere ahead a member of the congregation started to make noises. Mary stiffened. But it was not a madman; they were not hurried from the church or hushed up. No . . . and even another person started to make the same sounds:

'*Haw haw haw kasheya. Rrabayya cattya rrrrrabya kotosho.*'

Mary looked to the pastor. In a tone of thrilling depth he exhorted the people:

'Jesus, pour out your Holy Spirit! Open ye your mouths and let the Spirit pour forth! God will not speak unless you open your mouths!'

Another deep voice to her left. Mr Wilton, with his eyes closed, his mouth open, started first to hum, then to chant: '*Karreya shon shon magarr che che che che.*'

'Speak to Jesus. He who sits on the Throne!'

The pastor had come forward from his pulpit, in his trousers of rippling black silk, his shoes with a velvet bow, and both his arms raised to the ceiling as if he were about to be taken up to heaven. His eyes were dark but piercingly bright.

'Close your eyes!' he said, closing his own.

Mary closed her eyes. She let the sounds, spoken in an ancient language, whirl around her. In the black space in front of her eyes she saw, in a vision, Jesus, sitting on his throne. He too wore velvet robes; His hair too was dark and long; He too held out His arms to her.

'Let your mouth open and speak. The Lord cannot speak through you if you do not open your mouth!'

Mary opened her mouth. Jesus looked at her with love, such love in his eyes that she felt it rising up inside her, gushing like a fountain, emanating from the middle of her and flowing down her thighs and up through her heart and her chest and out through her fingers, which began to tingle with heat and cold, and her mouth. Hardly knowing what she was doing, not recognizing her own voice, she began to cry:

'*Korraamonshonddooor! Kayla la la la!*'

'The Spirit is here!' said the pastor.

Mary was talking to Jesus, discharging the longing of her heart in words that went directly to Him. No need to think, no need to mean anything, for this went beyond meaning to feeling.

Mary felt poured all over by feeling. She felt so much, she longed for so much: she yearned for Him.

The space in her chest, just below her throat, throbbed as if it were a cave that had just realized its own emptiness, at the very time it was being poured into and filled. Filled by Jesus. Plain Mary in here allowed – no, *encouraged* – to be needful. To have desires and long for release.

Mary's hips were pressed forward on to the pew in front. She closed her eyes and began to rock from side to side. The commotion whirled around her and penetrated her and the edges of her seemed to dissolve. '*Mmm mmm mmmaaaah!*' With the buzzing of her lips and the buzzing of her body, she rocked back and forth until the whole church was a ship riding on a wave from side to side, God's chosen people in the flood, and she felt a gush that started in the damp centre of her that was pressing hard on the pew and rippled outwards and upwards and left her flushed and breathless.

Mary opened her eyes. Around her people still continued to sway and chant. A child in the aisle, bent over double and convulsing. And another child, her mother's hand on her bent-over back, pulsing up and down.

'The Spirit is strong in the children. Bring them unto me! *Ma ma monna yay!*'

The pastor was touching the heads of the people, his face lit by ecstasy. He pressed with his palms the foreheads of the children. His hair had fallen forward, his cheek was flushed. Mary wondered how long she had been there, for she had lost track of time and the service showed no sign of ending.

It was dark by the time they disgorged on to the street. After the intensity of the church, Oxford was quiet, muted. There were no gas lamps in this part of town and only the clatter of distant carriage wheels to break the darkness. In the sky Mary could see clouds of different shades moving, one over another, as if being painted in by a heavenly Creator.

She shivered and wrapped her arms round herself.

'You enjoyed it, Mary. It is rare to speak in tongues your first time. I know it took me many months.'

Mary did not know what to say. She wished she were back at the Deanery, in her bed, small as it was. She found she could not make sense of what had just happened; it was still too close to see all of it. She needed to construct a narrative around it and make it fit.

'I hope this will not be your only visit.' Mr Wilton's inflection rose up at the end, making the sentence into a question.

'No, no,' said Mary. 'I should like to visit again.'

Mr Wilton's hand on her arm was warm and immutable. She felt its presence as they walked all the way down the High Street until they reached the gates of Christ Church. She still felt it as she undressed in her room at the Deanery and fell into a long, deep sleep.

CHAPTER 9

A TANGLED MASS OF ROOTS HUNG OVER THE BANK of the River Cherwell and dipped fat fingers into the water, stirring the river into a swirling brown broth. The weeds twisted and turned on their moorings of rock, the water slipped and slapped, gushed and splashed. The children ran ahead of her in the bright summer gloom, but Mary thought only of Jesus on his glowing throne. She could not help but see Him looking very like the pastor, with his dark hair curling on to his collar, his air of melancholy beauty. Then she thought of Mr Wilton's lips. The words that tumbled out of them had lent his face a different, a foreign, shape. It was hard to align the Mr Wilton who had visited her parents with the Mr Wilton who had sat next to her in church. The new image had different contours to the old, would not fit, no matter how she tried to place one over the other.

There might be a note by now, waiting for her on the tray back at the Deanery. A note folded in two, on paper as thin as skin, asking to take her to church again. Mary imagined Mr

Wilton's skin between her finger and thumb. It would not spring back into place; it would slowly collapse into repose, like the skin on a rice pudding, though he was not very old, he could not be more than thirty-five.

The gift of the Holy Spirit had opened up an emptiness inside her, just below her collarbone, that needed to be replenished. She would ask Mr Wilton to take her to his church again, if he did not suggest it. Even though, when she thought of what had happened there, who she had turned into, she was a foreigner to herself. She tried to mouth out the words she had spoken; she could remember the sound of them, sharp and ancient, but she could not bring up their form.

'Are you speaking to me, Miss Prickett?'

Alice interposed herself between Mary and her thoughts, in her yellow hat and coat.

'No, I am not. I was not speaking. What do you want?'

'Why do rivers bend?' Alice asked, her voice high against the water's gush.

'It is to do with geography,' said Mary.

'But why is it to do with geography?'

Mary stared straight ahead. The meadows were quiet at this time, a little after lunch, except for a man striding away from them at right angles, his boots muddy, his head turning first one way, and then another, as if he were looking for somebody.

'Because geography is the study of the land,' she said.

'Is it the land that makes the river bend so?'

'Yes.'

'But why?' said Alice again, breathing up at her.

'Because Y's got a tail!' said Mary, in a rush of fury. 'Now go away!'

It was beginning to rain. Mary stared up at the grey mass of the sky. When she looked down again she saw that the striding man had changed direction and was now coming towards them, rather fast. She recognized the way his hat was angled on to his head, tipped very slightly back.

Ahead of her the children were crowded round something on the ground, white and awkward. Its neck was twisted and much too long, its beak pointed impossibly back towards its neck.

'Come away, come away at once!' said Mary.

'It stinks,' said Ina.

'Then come away.'

Somebody had kicked the swan over. The whole of the underside writhed with fat white maggots, bringing the bird horribly back to life. Mary fumbled in her reticule for a handkerchief; the smell clung to the inside of her nostrils and filled up her mouth.

She stepped back and tried to pull Ina with her.

But Alice and Edith still stared in at the entrails, which curled out with a horrible intimacy. Above, it was still recognizably swan-like: clean white feathers, wings held as if they were still floating on water. It made the spillage below worse, a ghastly secret. It reminded Mary of a medical book she had once seen. This skin that held in so much sausage meat. That glistened so terribly; that was both you and not you.

'Come *away*, I said!' But Mary's voice was muffled by the handkerchief she held over her mouth. What if they got dirty –

got a disease? Disease was surely floating about in the air round where the swan lay, and they would inhale it and get sick. She must wrench them all away. She must go in and push them back from in front, using one arm for two children.

She heaved in a breath and shouldered her way in, pushing them backwards with her elbows, full of rage. Her shoe came down on something soft and marshy; she heard the high, slick sound of it. She cried out.

Mary felt a steadying hand on her elbow – Mr Dodgson's.

'Are you all right?' he asked her.

Mary nodded; she could not speak.

'Sit here, on this log.'

On a log? Women did not sit on logs. But he pressed her down, his hand on her shoulder.

'I saw you in the distance. I hoe-hope you don't mind.' His smile held traces of embarrassment. 'I thought I might join you, for a walk.'

Mr Dodgson had seen her ineptness; he had seen her lose control. Abruptly Mary wanted to cry. She nodded up at him vigorously.

'Your boot,' he said. He crouched down in front of her. Her boot had a residue of something pink and white around the rim and on the top of the toe.

'Let me,' said Mr Dodgson.

'No, please!' Mary tried to twist her foot to wipe off the matter, round and over.

But he had got up to fetch some dock leaves and was back in front of her, rubbing at her boot. Mary wanted to pull her foot away, but he had hold of her heel, and short of wrenching it out of his hand she could do nothing.

The children's faces made a semicircle behind his back. Alice was smirking. Mary looked back down at Mr Dodgson's top hat as he worked; its circle of smoothly brushed black was a solid thing to hold on to. But when he got up, she could not look at the face that revealed itself underneath, smiling solicitously.

'Shall I walk you back towards Christ Church?'

'We were going down here.' Mary indicated the direction with her chin.

'Oh – well, do you mind if I follow on for a moment?'

'Yes please, Mr Dodgson,' said Alice.

Only now did Mr Dodgson turn to the children. 'Your governess was right. Dead animals carry disease. You ought to have come away.'

'But I have only seen a swan's outsides before, never its insides,' said Alice.

'And you never need see it again, I think. It is ghoulish,' said Mr Dodgson. 'I cannot abhor cruelty to animals. I only hope it wasn't wretched town boys who killed that one. I have seen them torment a cat before now; they seemed to be completely without human feeling. I chased them half the way down the Broadwalk.'

Mary walked next to him with her eyes down. He was beside her on the small path that ran by the river, his elbow bumping into hers. She could feel his breath alongside her cheek, smelling distantly of fennel and the wine he must have drunk at lunch.

'Can I ask you something please, Mr Dodgson?' said Alice.

'Alice, you are too full of questions!'

'I assure you . . .' said Mr Dodgson.

'Why do rivers bend?'

'Alice! I told you—'

'No, Miss Prickett, it is quite all right. Without questions and answers there would be nothing at all! And I am very happy to help you out. The education of young minds is an arduous business.' He smiled at her. 'I know that myself, though the minds I have to deal with . . .' He trailed off. 'Well, they are not so young, and even more arduous. But in education we are in the same boat, both struggling to enlighten. Are we not, Miss Prickett?'

'Yes,' said Mary uncertainly. Though she would not have put it like that. The children's questions, the number and velocity of them, overpowered her, dragged her under. And their needs, for attention, for affection, for physical things – paper, ink, dolls, dolls' clothes, tin soldiers – were endless. They seemed to demand that she open herself up and pour out her own blood – she couldn't do it. Not always. Not even often.

But Mr Dodgson was answering Alice.

'Bends in rivers may have evolved,' he said. 'Young rivers go quite straight.'

'Young rivers?'

'Those high up in the mountains. They are in a dreadful hurry. But when rivers get old and far away from where they began, the land gets flatter and they meander and loop about, just as humans do.'

'But why do they need to loop?'

'They need to loop because every river needs to run into the sea and they are trying to find the best way there.'

'Thank you, Mr Do-Do-Dodgson! I'll remember it always!'

'My pleasure, Alice dearest.' As Alice ran away from them he remarked: 'I must confess, I am not fond of children who look like porcelain dolls, as so many people are. I have an idea of what makes a good photograph of a child: vitality. A look in the eye. And also good breeding. The children of the working class, who may be quite pleasing in other ways, so often have something that jars: a thick ankle, large hands. Something that betrays their roots and ruins their beauty.'

The working class did have uglier children, it was true, Mary thought. Just the other day she had been shouted at on the street by one, more monkey than child – great coarse lips, dark skin. Dirty, too. As it turned out, Mary had dropped her handkerchief and the girl was letting her know about it, but it had not sounded like that at all. The girl's voice was harsh and accented and anything that came out of her mouth sounded like an insult. Although – Mary ran over the scene again quickly, as if she were stepping over hot rocks – when she stooped to collect the fallen handkerchief, she found herself unable to meet the girl's eyes.

'Perhaps you have seen a little periodical called *The Train*, Miss Prickett?'

'Oh no, I have not. Is it widely published?'

'Very narrowly published, I should say. I have something in the current copy that I would like to show you. Not under my own name of course, it is just a poem. May I?'

Walking as he was by her side, Mary did not have to turn her head to know he was looking at her. His eyes were pale and cool and flecked with points of grey. Sea-washed stones.

The grass fell into the path, swept into disarray by the breeze.

'I would like to see it,' she said, glancing back at him. His face was all politeness, just as it had been when he made his remark about the Queen. She could not tell if underneath he was mocking her, or if he was covering up his embarrassment with good manners.

'I should like to show it to you. It is a happy coincidence that I ran into you all today.'

'It was not a coincidence!' said Ina. 'You were following us!'

Mr Dodgson blushed. 'Well, I admit it. I thought it might be pleasant to take a walk with you.' After a pause he added: 'I think I may have overstayed my welcome at the Deanery. For the time being.'

For the first time that afternoon Mary remembered Mr Dodgson's humiliated smile, the handles of his wheel-barrow dropped in dismay. She had caught his eye, and what expression had she made? She had smiled, tried to impart that it was a misunderstanding.

But if she brought it all up with him now, she would have to give a reason why Mrs Liddell cut him. Or lie and say he came on the wrong date. But it had not been a misunderstanding. Mrs Liddell wanted him kept away. Did that mean she should steer the children away now?

She shook her head and smiled, trying to signal that he was being foolish, without contradicting him.

'Well, I suppose I had better leave you here, for we are at the gate,' said Mr Dodgson. 'Before we part, I wondered . . . well, I wondered if you would like to come over to my rooms on Thursday? I could show you *The Train*; it's only a little thing, as I say, but you may like to read it. I hope one day to write something of note, in the field of mathematics perhaps. I do write, as often as I can. It is good to have ambitions, I think. It may drive one on to do something one otherwise would not have achieved.'

Ambition was a good thing in a man, as long as it was not for fame. Mary thought of Mr Wilton with his bear-like hands on the glass countertop, and his disparagement of ambition, though he did work in a haberdashery.

Of course there was nothing wrong with a haberdashery.

'Bring the children too,' said Mr Dodgson. 'They may find something to amuse them.'

Mrs Liddell had said that she did not want Mr Dodgson at the Deanery. But she had not said that the children were not to see him at all.

'Mr Dodgson's rooms! Oh, let us go,' said Alice. 'There is so much in them, I should never be bored.'

'I would like to,' said Mary. There could be no harm in it.

As they were turning to go, Mr Dodgson called out: 'No need to trouble Mrs Liddell about it! I have troubled her enough. The vacation is only two weeks away. I am sure she is busy, and we ought to keep out of her way.'

CHAPTER 10

THE NOTE *HAD* BEEN THERE, ON A SILVER PLATTER IN the hall, when Mary and the children returned from their walk. It had suggested a walk around the meadows. Mary had written another note to suggest that perhaps, instead of taking a walk, they might visit Mr Wilton's church again as she had '*very* much enjoyed it last time'. But perhaps she sounded too keen. She crossed out the word *very*, but it could still be read. She cross-hatched it, but now it looked as if an earwig had landed on the word.

She started again, this time making no mention of enjoyment.

Mr Wilton wrote back to say he would be happy to take her again, the following Sunday, if she liked.

◆

The light filtered quite brightly through the diagonal panes of the church and fell on the gleaming shoulders of the pastor, and on those of Mr Wilton, illuminating the specks of dust or skin that speckled below his collar.

As Mary knelt to take Communion, she felt the firm palm of

the pastor on her shoulder. He seemed to press all the air from her lungs and she felt, in her last whisper, the tendrils of the words *I'm sorry* wisp from her lips. *I'm sorry, I'm sorry*, and as she breathed it she struggled to find out what for, though the words were a relief to say. They swept through her with a soft brush, cleaning out her mouth and the back of her throat.

But afterwards she found herself unable to speak in tongues, though most around her did. The pastor seemed to glide over her, as if he knew.

Outside in the spring glare, Mr Wilton assured her that the gift would come back. She had been lucky, he said again, bending over her close enough that she could see the two black hairs that sprang from the depths of his ears.

Mary nodded. She desired it, she told him, very much.

She must wait for the gift to fall, he said, but next time she must open her mouth to let it in.

❧

The sound of tongues was like an ancient language, unlearned, dredged up from the soul. Mary could hear it still as she and the children walked across the quadrangle towards Mr Dodgson's rooms a few afternoons later.

One of his nonsense poems came back to her:
*'Twas brillig, and the slithy toves/Did gyre and gimble in
    the wabe.*
Ta kennita kanardi.
Both seemed to signify something deeper, to have some meaning, but she could not fathom what. She put her hands

up and rubbed her ears. The fleshy buds of the lobes were a comfort; they assured her that she was there.

After the service, she and Mr Wilton had seen Mrs Chitterworth. There seemed to be no place in Oxford that the woman did not go. She had looked at the couple and then at the church in a pointed fashion. Unasked, Mr Wilton had volunteered the information that they had just come out of a service there; had she been?

Mrs Chitterworth had stepped back with what Mary later thought of as needless drama, her hand to her mouth. 'Is it respectable?' she had asked.

Mr Wilton's smile was easy. 'Very,' he'd assured her.

She dropped her voice. 'But I heard stories of *the devil* being heard in there.'

'Nothing of the kind, Mrs Chitterworth. God's voice may be heard, that is all: "For he that speaketh in an unknown tongue speaketh not unto men, but unto God, for no man understandeth him, however it may be that in the spirit he speaketh mysteries." That is from Corinthians, Mrs Chitterworth, as I am sure you know.'

Mrs Chitterworth had pulled herself up. 'I do know the scriptures, thank you, Mr Wilton.' And she had bade them good day with pursed lips.

◆

Mr Dodgson had seemed to want her advice, or her judgement. Mrs Liddell had not said that Mary should not see him, merely that he ought not to come to the house.

The feeling of being a fugitive, hurrying towards Mr Dodgson, was not unpleasant.

Although whenever she thought about Mr Dodgson and the swan, she experienced a curl of shame. She had read no book in which the hero wiped entrails from the toe of the heroine's shoe.

But of course, Mr Dodgson was not the hero of this book.

The sticky pink intimacy, smeared across the leather; even when he expunged it, it left a darker slick that Mary could see now. But he had saved her, in a manner of speaking. He might not have ridden to her aid, but the white horse was a matter of semantics.

They had reached Mr Dodgson's corridor and were admitted inside. The walls were damp and the air smelt of the river. When he opened the door to his rooms, it was darker still, cluttered with piles of books and other objects Mary could not make out.

'Mr Dodgson! Will you forget me while we are gone?' said Alice, pushing forward.

'Yes, Alice, I am afraid I might, for you will grow so much over these next two months, and I have been taking lessons in forgetting, at half a crown a lesson.'

'Rather expensive lessons,' said Ina.

'Yes, but well worth the price. After three lessons I forgot my own name, and I forgot to go to the next lesson. The Professor said I was getting on very well, but he hoped I wouldn't forget to pay him. I said that depended on how good he was.'

'How good was he?' asked Alice.

'The last lesson was so good that I forgot everything! I forgot who I was, I forgot to eat my dinner, and so far I've forgotten to pay the man.'

'But you won't forget me,' said Alice. She shook her fringe out of her eyes. 'Even though it is the vacation.'

'I won't forget any of you.'

Mary found she was clutching her bonnet to her chest. Mr Dodgson gently shook it from her fingers and put it on a pile of books, smiling his lopsided smile. The cheek that turned towards her was very smooth.

'Are you looking at the mousetrap, Ina?'

'Oh, is that what it is?'

'It is a live trap, it is my own invention. You see, he enters here,' said Mr Dodgson, pointing at a wooden flap, 'and arrives at the bottom, where he has his final meal of cheese. I slide this wire compartment shut – of course there is no mouse in it at present – so that when I take it and plunge it into the water there is no chance of the mouse struggling on the surface and prolonging its death. Animal cruelty, as I said,' he turned to Mary, 'is horrible to me.'

'But Dinah might like to play with the mouse,' said Alice.

'He would not like to play with Dinah, I am sure. I quite believe that the time will come, in England at any rate, when the death of animals, when it must occur, will be quite painless.'

Mary thought of the sheep's head. And of Mr Dodgson's steering her away from the swan. 'Do you think so?'

'Not yet, I am afraid. There is something,' he dropped his voice so that the children could not hear, 'that I abhor.

Vivisection on live animals, in the name of scientific progress. It must stop. I am writing pamphlets to that effect.'

Mary had seen a baboon once that had been tied on to a pony's back in the name of sport. Half human, half monster, but full of recognizable desperation. And the laughter of the men who stood around, taking bets.

Mr Dodgson's face was clear and clean, unencumbered by hair. Vivisection must be stopped, Mary found herself thinking, for the first time. Rabbits cut open when they were alive, writhing and pinned.

'Look at me!' said Alice. She was staring at her reflection in the looking glass. Her head was squashed up like the round end of a hammer and her arms dangled down from somewhere above her ears. Her shins were so elongated that her knees were up where her hips ought to be.

'How do you find yourself, Alice?' said Mr Dodgson.

She moved her chin down and now her face was one hideous roar. 'I can't find myself!'

'And isn't that a most interesting place to be!'

Mary went to the sofa; she did not want to commit to sitting in the seat of it and chose the arm, but only one foot could comfortably reach the ground, while the other swung into the air like a child's. So she sat down on the seat, which turned out to be even lower than she thought. She fell back and back, her haunches sunk into its recesses while her knees were brought up against her breasts.

And there was Mr Dodgson, with a slice of Victoria sponge cake, which he held out.

Mary struggled forward, on to the edge of the sofa, its forward rib against her thigh bone. 'Cake?'

'Yes, today's. I had my scout bring it up.'

Mary took the plate and balanced it on the cushion next to her. The cake tipped on to its side, the leading edge hanging over the plate. He had not provided a fork and it was too big to pick up whole. She broke off a bottom section, the sticky yellow icing clinging to her fingers. The clods of it stuck in her throat. He was watching her eat. Mary smiled, unconvincingly. She hated to be watched while she was masticating. She had caught a glimpse once of herself at the dinner table. The bones in her jaw could be clearly seen as they hinged and slid. 'Very nice, thank you,' she said.

At last, he went. Ina was fondling a clockwork bear.

No choice but to lick her fingertips clean; she could not see a napkin. Though even after she had used her tongue, a residue of sugar remained. She stuck her hand flat under her dress. He would not notice a smear on his sofa, what with everything else in the room.

The shelf nearest her held a microscope housed in a mahogany travelling case marked CLD GLASS WITH CARE, a telescope, a pair of field glasses, what looked like a human skull, a modified typewriter, a number of musical boxes and a collection of watches. On the lowest shelf was something that looked like a silver pen, only it had no nib, and both ends were splayed.

Mr Dodgson had returned. 'I see you are looking at my Ammoniaphone, Miss Prickett. The air inside it is supposed to resemble the soft, balmy atmosphere of the Italian peninsula. I believe its inventor analysed the air there and found a quantity of ammonia and peroxide of hydrogen unique to the area. It is supposed to produce a melodious and rich voice, much like the Italian voice, I suppose. Would you like to try it?'

'Oh no, I have never been to Italy!'

'You will not need to, if the claims for this are to be believed.' He came towards her. 'Press the end valves and place your lips tightly over the entrance.'

He could not be coming to put it between her lips. Mary smiled to try to signify that it was normal, this coming towards her, this insertion of an Ammoniaphone in her mouth, but at the last moment Mr Dodgson allowed her to reach for the thing herself and guide it between her teeth, only the sides of their smallest fingers brushing each other.

Mary felt, but did not admit to herself until later, a small shrink of disappointment.

'Breathe in, slowly but deeply.'

Mary breathed in as she was told, fastening her eyes on the ruched black buttons that punctuated his sofa. Mr Wilton would like the material: practical, without being cheap. The Ammoniaphone tasted of peppermint and something else sharper – ammonia, she supposed. As she inhaled, a popular song drifted into her mind:

I've found a friend, oh, such a friend!
He loved me ere I knew Him;
He drew me with the cords of love,
And thus He bound me to Him.

'There now – speak to me, let me hear if you are improved.'

'What shall I say?' asked Mary.

'Ah, you see, it has done not a whit of good; you sound just the same as you did before. I knew it! I shall send it back to its maker at once.'

She must think of something clever to say. But nothing came. 'What should I sound like?'

'You should sound just exactly as you do, Miss Prickett.'

Mary blushed. She still felt his eyes on her. She turned her head away.

'I had hoped it would help me in the speaking of my sermon next Sunday, but now I do not hold out much hope.'

She turned to look at him again. His face was so smooth, so different from Mr Wilton's. So untroubled by hair.

'I should hate to have an attack,' he said.

'An attack?'

'Of my affliction. My hesitation.' He sat down beside her, quite close. He was still smiling, but now it seemed to Mary that she saw behind to the sadness that lay there.

She said impulsively: 'Perhaps the Holy Spirit could help you.'

'I pray to the Holy Spirit every night. Alas, my hesitation is still with me.'

'I mean tongues. The gift of tongues.'

Mr Dodgson, who had been resting his hands on his knees, sat back. 'You mean glossolalia?'

'Yes! It is marvellous. Jesus and the apostles at Pentecost, of course . . .' But something in Mr Dodgson's face stopped her from explaining more. Her hand went to her lip and started worrying at it.

'To have Jesus in one's life is a blessed thing, Miss Prickett,' he said, with his head on one side. His smile looked as if it had slid down correspondingly.

'I am bored. Tell me a story. Please!' said Alice.

They looked up. Alice was standing at Mr Dodgson's letter-writing table. 'Who is Effie?'

'One of my child friends. Why are you reading my letters? That is very interfering of you. You didn't think you were my only friend, did you?'

'No!' said Alice. But she pouted.

'Although Effie is not strictly a *child* any more, being eighteen. But we are still friends, I think.'

'That's what I told Mama!'

'Told her what?'

'I am sure Mr Dodgson does not want to be troubled telling you a story,' Mary said quickly.

'No, Alice. Maybe next time.'

'But it *is* next time. Because you said that last time!'

'When was last time?'

'I don't know! Last week. But *do*, please. Otherwise we shan't come to your rooms again.'

'Alice!'

'And must I be susceptible to blackmail?' Mr Dodgson sighed, though not crossly. 'Very well. A short one. What shall it be about?'

'Me,' said Alice.

'Sit down then, with your sisters.'

'Where will you sit?'

'I will sit here, next to Miss Prickett.'

Mr Dodgson settled himself, crossed one thigh over the other. The space was not quite big enough for two: it was a love seat upholstered in pink velvet. Mary could feel the reverberations of his foot as it joggled; she could see his hipbone protruding beneath his twill trousers. He started on a story about an enormous puppy, the size of a house, which had appeared in Oxford.

She looked over at the children. Alice and Ina had curled their legs under them and were leaning against each other on the sofa. Alice's shoelace had come untied and hung down over the edge, her skirt ruffled up to her knees.

'Did Mama and Papa not see anything?' asked Alice.

'They did not; they were so absorbed in their ham and eggs that they did not notice a thing.'

Mr Dodgson talked on, about Alice escaping from a game with a stick, how she ran back indoors and into the nursery.

As he told the story, Mary felt the quadrangle to be animated by the gigantic dog, its eyes level with hers as it peered into their room, its nose the size of a plate.

'What happened to the puppy afterwards?' asked Ina.

'He blundered through the doors of Elliston and Cavell, where they did not know what to make of him at all, and all of the men gathered up brooms and pushed him out again.'

Mary felt sure Alice would say that perhaps he would see Mr Wilton, and she started to speak just in case she did, to drown it out. She did not want to talk about Mr Wilton to

Mr Dodgson; heat rose up her face at the thought of it, but Mr Dodgson spoke instead.

'*That* is the expression I want to capture in a photograph. I have my camera set up just downstairs; what do you say we run down there and make a photograph?'

Mary looked in surprise, but he – of course – meant the children.

Mr Dodgson hurried the three girls outside and sat them on a sofa with a backdrop rigged behind it. He heaped them up together, Ina in the middle, Alice and Edith leaning in on either side. It was easy to see that the children's heads were still filled with giant gambolling puppies, and they all sat still.

Mary thought fleetingly of Mrs Liddell. If the photograph came out well, the detail of the sofa would be magnificent: pale silk with brown tendrils curling all over the front and back.

CHAPTER 11

$\mathcal{M}$R DODGSON HAD NOT MADE ANY ATTEMPT TO show her a copy of *The Train*. The realization nagged at her. Possibly he had forgotten, even though that had been the reason given for the visit. Or he had realized that she would not make a good critic.

Mary thought again about the Ammoniaphone: the silver gleaming tube, the bud-like protuberances at either end, the hard feel of it inserted into her mouth. And of Mr Dodgson's face as he came towards her. Smiling, playful. And what else, behind the crystalline orbs of his eyes?

She went to get a copy of *The Train* from town. There was no poem in it written by Mr Dodgson. Only after she had read through the whole thing did Mary remember that he had said something about a nom de plume. She looked again. A poem called 'Solitude' seemed the likeliest, written by a Mr Lewis Carroll; its several melancholic verses ended with:

> *I'd give all wealth that years have piled,*
> *The slow result of Life's decay,*
> *To be once more a little child*
> *For one bright summer-day.*

But Mr Dodgson was not old! His face was unlined. Although, she thought again, perhaps there was something elderly in the way he walked: the peculiar gait, the stiffness. Mary was glad he had not asked her for her opinion of the poem; she would not have known what to say.

She would not want to return to her own childhood, not for anything.

✦

In the evening, as Mary was looking through *The Train* once again, there was a knock on her door. She started, and closed the periodical. She stood up and smoothed her dress. 'Come in!'

It was the housemaid. 'The Dean would like to see you before dinner,' she said, her thin face betraying nothing.

The Dean! The Dean had not asked to see Mary once, not since she had taken up residence. Perhaps he wanted to hear about the progress of the children's education. Yesterday she had made Alice write out the line *I will not question my governess so much, otherwise I will end up in no good fashion*, thirty times. Had it been enough?

She swallowed. 'What time?'

'Six o' clock, he says.'

Without looking Mary in the eye, the housemaid closed

the door. It was as long a conversation as Mary had ever had with her.

❧

Mary was surprised at the untidiness of the Dean's study: books and papers toppled over every surface, candles oozed wax all over the desk. The Dean sat behind the desk, Mrs Liddell stood.

'It has come to our attention,' said the Dean from behind a steeple of fingers, as soon as the door was shut, 'that you have been visiting the church on Cheevney Lane.'

'The church? Yes,' said Mary distractedly. She wondered what the church had to do with anything.

'Are they habitual, your visits there?' he said.

'I have been twice,' said Mary. Perhaps he wanted her to take the children next time she went.

But the Dean drew in his breath. 'Miss Prickett, I'm afraid that church is not the kind of place we wish to have associated with one of our employees.'

'Our employees?' Mary said stupidly.

'Surely you know what is said about the place, Miss Prickett!' Mrs Liddell leaned forward on the desk. Her gold chain fell away from her neck and hung straight down, the locket at the bottom swinging from side to side.

Mary took a quick breath in and pulled at her collar. It was too tight. She remembered Mrs Chitterworth, after the service. 'But, I beg your pardon, Mrs Liddell, what is *said* is wrong!'

'It doesn't matter if it is wrong or right. Oxford is full of rumours, as you know. If something is talked about as fact, it is fact. And we cannot have you going about to that place, especially when the Dean takes the services here in Christ Church.'

Mr Liddell's nose was very imposing from this closeness. He took out a handkerchief the size of a dinner plate and buried his nose in it. After a moment he said: 'It reflects badly on us. I'm sure you understand.'

Mary felt like a child brought before the headmaster. Which, of course, the Dean was, or had been when he was at Westminster School for all those years. The boys had been terrified of him, Ina always said.

She had not considered that her visits to Mr Wilton's church would bring the family into disrepute, but now that the Dean had chastised her, she saw that he was right. 'I'm . . . I'm sorry. I will only attend the cathedral services in future. I'm sorry to have caused a disturbance.'

The Dean nodded. 'You may like to take the children there on Sunday next. Mr Dodgson is preaching, I believe.'

Mary nodded also and stared at the floor. The Dean signalled, by opening up the heavy book on his desk and starting to leaf through it, that the meeting was at an end.

CHAPTER 12

MR WILTON HAD SENT MARY A NOTE ASKING IF HE might visit her at her mother's. The note revealed nothing, except perhaps an unwillingness to see the children again. As their parents were friends it would be proper, and pleasant to see Mrs Prickett, as well as Miss Prickett, he wrote.

Mary did not look forward to sitting in her mother's front room with Mr Wilton on her only free afternoon of the week, perched on one of those wooden-backed chairs with the creaky legs, balancing a cup and saucer on her knee, trying to find a moment to tell him without her mother overhearing that she could no longer accompany him to church. But she could not easily refuse.

So she set off, on the appointed day, across town. Carriages clattered past, spraying up mud. Mary clutched her reticule to her breast, her knuckles sharp on her collarbones. She drew her coat tighter around her. She was cold, she had always been told, because she had not enough flesh on her. The tips of her middle toes were splayed with chilblains. Her knuckles were purple. Her legs, when she unrolled her stockings, were mottled, just like the inside of her arms. She alone had a map of the inner workings of her body, delineated in purple veins. The tip of her nose, her forerunner into the world, was chilly.

But as she turned into the High Street Mary saw Mr Wilton, and her heart surprised her by twisting in her ribcage. She had not expected to see him so soon.

She began to walk parallel to him on the other side of the street, staring over, about to call to him. He was on his way to meet her, obviously. His face, absorbed, was quite different from the one he wore at the haberdashery and at church. Heavier, looser. The heft of him, the weight of his shoes struck her. His chin pushing out through the crowd.

He stopped. Mary stopped. She thought something had caught his eye. But instead he pushed his index finger deep into his ear. He closed his eyes and agitated his finger, his elbow stuck out at right angles to his head, a look of contentment on his face. The vibration shook his whole arm. It was familiar, this action; Mary must have seen him do it before, but not noticed in the same way. It was obviously a habit.

Mr Wilton pulled his fingertip from its waxy recess. He stopped walking to peer down at whatever was on the end of it. He looked back up, still standing still, rolling the tip of his finger against the tip of his thumb, a faraway look in his eyes. Then he flicked the residue on to the pavement.

A couple with a poodle walked by, Mary expected them to see it and to step over it with disgust etched on their faces, but they did not. She turned away, intending to walk the other way for a moment so that she could lose Mr Wilton in the crowd; it would be better to arrive five minutes after him anyway. But he saw her.

'Miss Prickett!'

'Mr Wilton!' As she spoke, she tried to push away his vibrating elbow, the bit of him that lay on the ground near his shoe. To leave the moment behind.

Mr Wilton's face had changed again: his full lips turned up towards his moustache, whose tips were waxed. 'Well. We have met early.'

'Are you going to my mother's?' Of course he was. It was just to fill the air that she said it.

'Yes. Shall we go on together?'

'I enjoyed myself at the Science Museum.'

'And I.'

'The bones were fascinating. The children do like dinosaurs.'

'They certainly seem to. Are the children well?'

'Yes.'

Mr Wilton took this in with a nod. Mary thought she might bring up her visit to Mr Dodgson's rooms but for some reason she decided against it.

'And your mother?'

'Yes. She came down with a cold last week, which was strange considering the season. But she is better now.'

'I am glad to hear it. Spring colds are not pleasant.'

'How is *your* mother?' asked Mary.

'Quite well, thank you.'

Conversation would be even harder when they arrived at her

parents' house in Folly Bridge, stuck on chairs, inside four walls. She must try to find an opening to bring up the church before they arrived.

'How is your father?' she asked. Father to church – perhaps it could be one of those games of which Mr Dodgson was so fond: doublets. Changing head to tail by the replacement of one letter by another.

'He is settling in, I think, thanks to yours. It is difficult to take up a new position so late in life.'

Mary blushed and looked at Mr Wilton. But he had not meant anything; his face showed no embarrassment.

How was it now? Head. Heal. Teal. He had shown her only the other day . . .

'How is *your* father?' asked Mr Wilton.

They would soon have drunk dry all news from relatives and would be standing in a conversational desert. Into which Mary – but how? – could introduce a new trickle of conversation.

Teal to tell. Tell to tall. It was remarkable how something could be transformed to its opposite just by incremental changes that by themselves seemed to signify nothing.

'I have not seen my father recently, he works so hard.'

'But it is the Easter Vacation soon.'

'And I will be away with the Liddells.'

'Ah yes.'

'In Wales.'

And then from tall it was easy: tail!

'You are smiling, Miss Prickett, are you looking forward to going?'

'Oh no! It's just—' Mary did not see the woman approaching her from the opposite direction until she felt a blow on the outer edge of her arm.

'Watch it!' The woman's voice was too close to her ear. Mary could smell alcohol.

'I'm sorry,' she said, drawing her reticule close to her chest. 'Excuse me, please.'

'You nearly took my arm off.' The woman's nose looked as if it had been grafted on from the insides of another animal: pullulating and red.

'I don't think that is quite right.' Mary did not know what else to say. She hoped the woman would accept her apology and let her pass, but she stood there balefully.

Mr Wilton stepped in front of her. 'Move on,' he said.

The woman took him in.

'Move on, or you'll be sorry,' he said, making his voice lower, more like a growl.

The woman snorted. 'If you say so.' Even though her words were still provocative, Mary saw that her shoulders had dropped and her chin receded back towards her neck.

Mr Wilton, on the other hand, had made himself bigger. His shirtfront was pushed out, with muscle and hair. Hair that must also matt between his thighs.

Mary caught a tang of sharpness, the smell of sebum, sweat.

The woman turned away, muttering. Mr Wilton pivoted round to follow her.

When she had gone, Mary was surprised to see that she was trembling.

'Are you all right?' Mr Wilton was still puffed up, his face full of blood.

'Oh yes, thank you, you're very kind.'

He had his hand on her shoulder; she could see, even from her vantage point, that between his second and third knuckle more hair sprouted.

She looked away, into the window of a pharmacy. *Brandreth's pills are a tonic purgative for ragged feelings.*

'The streets are full of vice and depredation,' Mr Wilton said. 'It is a good thing that the End of Days is approaching and we will be cleared of all this.'

'Yes,' said Mary. She turned to face him. 'Mr Wilton – I must tell you. I am afraid I can no longer accompany you to church.'

'Why not?'

'Because . . .' She had not rehearsed this. Because she had been told not to was the answer. But to say it would make her sound pitiful.

'Is it Mrs Chitterworth?'

'Mrs Chitterworth? No!' Although, of course, that must be how the Dean found out. Her next words came out sullenly. 'My visits there reflect badly on the Liddells, I am told.'

'Badly how?'

'The rumours, the devil . . .'

Around them people passed by on all sides. A man in a top hat apologized as he brushed Mr Wilton's arm with his own. Mr Wilton still had his hand on her shoulder and he now pushed her back towards the side street that ran off behind them, where fewer people walked.

'The devil has nothing to do with it!'

'I know! I told them as much. But I have been forbidden.'

The news seemed to affect Mr Wilton greatly. His cheeks were flushed a deeper purple. He gripped her shoulder to the bone and pushed her against the railings. 'But you enjoyed it, Mary. I have not seen you like that, like you were in there.'

Mary flushed. 'I *did* enjoy it, Mr Wilton, but there is nothing I can do.'

'This means I will see less of you.' His voice had dropped again.

'No!'

'I will see less of you at the church.'

'But I can see you at other times.'

Mr Wilton was standing close to her without looking at her face. He brought his free hand to one of her breasts and ran his palm over it in a circular motion. Mary gasped. He spread his fingers and engulfed it easily, first one scrap of flesh, then the other. She felt a heat rise from them to her cheeks and up into her scalp. She tried to pull away but he was strong and held her easily against the railings.

She stared over his shoulder at the window opposite. It was opaque and held many panes. She counted them. Nine panes.

'You may write me a note,' she said.

In her peripheral vision she could see his knuckles rising and falling, his fingertips dragging upwards and together.

'And I will see you.' Her breath was coming from very high up in her throat; her panting brought her bosom in closer contact with his hand.

And now she heard the sound of boots striking on pavement. Down the street someone was approaching. 'Mr Wilton. Somebody is coming. Let us go on to the bigger street.'

He turned his head, his hand continuing its kneading motion as he ascertained her claim.

The footsteps drew nearer; there seemed to be nothing in the world except the strike of feet on the pavement and the motion of his hand on her breast.

Then with a grunt he stepped back. The railings ground against her backbone and the breath was forced out of her.

He turned away, his hands in his coat pockets pressing something down at the front of him. His breath was heavy.

The woman walking was upon them now and she went quickly by, staring at the ground, her reticule gripped hard in her hand.

'Shall we go?' Mr Wilton asked, after a moment. 'Your mother will be expecting us.'

Mary straightened her coat. She turned to face the High Street. Ahead of them a panorama of people streamed by; none of them turned their heads to look down at them.

Mary's mouth was dry. She found herself longing to be in her mother's parlour, in possession of a cup of tea.

CHAPTER 13

*G*OD HAD SEEN FIT TO TEST HER IN STRANGE AND unusual ways. To pour out His grace so liberally in one church, only to torture one of his creatures in another – but this time by withholding His grace, or stopping it up like a cork in the wine at Cana – did not seem fair.

Mr Dodgson had ascended the pulpit of Christ Church Cathedral in a white surplice, and started to speak. Mary, who was sitting in the front row with the children, had not seen Mr Dodgson in a surplice before. Chapel was as full of people, packed into every pew, as the game the children played: *Here's the church, here's the steeple*, turning over their fingers to represent the people stacked in the pews.

He had been talking for a few minutes, his hands gripped on either side of the lectern, his eyes staring down seriously at the Bible, when he embarked on the phrase from St Matthew that Mary knew by heart: *Enter ye in at the straight gate, for wide is the gate and broad is the way that leadeth to destruction.*

Only he got stuck on the first *straight*.

Stah-stah-stah-staaaah-staaaahhh . . .

The congregation grew still.

He tried again. But it was worse: *sssssaaaaah-sssssaaaaahh*. He had dropped a letter. Mary could see his cheeks quivering on either side of his open mouth with the effort of trying to reclaim it.

He closed his mouth. His smile seemed to be trying to signify his own stupidity. Mary leaned forward and gripped the pew in front of her with both hands.

Straight!

'What's wrong with him?' a child asked in a clear voice.

Shhhhhh!

Mr Dodgson closed his eyes. He opened his mouth again. He opened his eyes and looked straight at Mary. His gaze had got hooked on her face. She was all eyes; she hardly noticed that she was mouthing the word straight for him.

Sahhhh-shahhhh.

A red rash mottled his exposed neck. Because of the acoustics of the place, she was sure she could hear the bones of his jaw clicking.

Sssaahh-sssahh-staaa-staaa!

Mary's face burned – for him. She had heard him mock his own affliction, but he would never mock the Bible in this parody of tongues. Perhaps this was why she had never heard him preach before.

Mr Dodgson swallowed again and then, from deep within himself he spat out: *STRA*.

He paused, keeping his head down. *EIGHT*.

Mary sat back in her pew, struck by the force of it.

As soon as the service ended, Edith ran up to him. 'You've got your white gown on and you read in chapel!'

Mr Dodgson's neck was still mottled. 'I'm afraid I didn't do it particularly well.'

'Oh no,' said Mary quickly. 'I thought you read admirably.'

She saw that he could not look at her now. His eyes, when he had held her gaze, had been full of terror.

'My stammer is my mortal enemy. Most of us Dodgsons stammer. It drives my father mad. It is a curse of the family.'

'I enjoyed the subject of your reading! We must all be on guard, very well chosen. It is so easy to stray from the path.'

'My doctor, whom I visit every week in his consulting room at Hastings, tells me that stammering can be cured by appealing to the reason and the will. Oh, we are so full of sin, are we not?' He looked, abruptly, as if he might cry. 'All of us except children. Alice, what did you think of my lesson? Could you understand it at all?'

'Not really, I'm afraid, Mr Dodgson.'

'It was about how hard it is to be good,' said Mary.

'That is right. But I don't think God minds childish naughtiness – at least He won't keep you out of heaven for it. It is rather adult sins that He cares about, I think.'

When the time came to say goodbye, the children clung to Mr Dodgson and would not let him go. They made him promise to write every day during the vacation, even though Mary told them he would not have the time.

'Twice a day!' said Alice. She hung round his neck and kissed him on the cheek, on her tiptoes. She clung on so long that she was obviously causing Mr Dodgson discomfort, and Mary stepped forward to rescue him.

'Goodbye, Mr Dodgson.'

'Goodbye, Miss Prickett!'

He was flustered, she could see, which made her flustered, so she bade him goodbye still without looking him in the eye. Although as she walked home she reflected that she had never met a person – man or woman, mother or father – who had such a way with children.

◆

The vacation began tomorrow. Mary was to spend it with the Liddells in North Wales, at Penmorfa, their holiday home, which the Dean had built just below the Great Orme. The people were bound to be different up in Wales. Shorter, stouter. Strangely shaped heads. The suitcases were even now stacked downstairs in the hall. Mrs Liddell demanded new shoes, new hats, new shawls, a walking outfit and a new bathing costume, just in case it was warm enough to swim. Mr Liddell demanded his volumes of Aristotle, Xenophon, Kant, Locke and Hutcheson; they sat in brown paper next to Mrs Liddell's luggage.

Mary's own suitcase was small and still in her room. Two dresses, and literature consisting of the latest copy of *Aunt Judy's Magazine* and a book by Mary Braddon called *Lady Audley's*

Secret. The Welsh were all low-browed, she had heard tell, though she had never been there. She would have to consult her phrenology chart – she had a feeling it was base instincts.

It was not early enough to go to bed. There was nothing to do now except read, and she was not in the mood for reading; or write a letter, and she was not in the mood for writing either.

She gazed at the little picture of Jesus hanging on his Cross, his head falling to one side. Mr Dodgson's stutter, the sound of it as clear as music with its rhythm and staccato crochets falling down the scale, sang its way into her head. Crew-crew-crucified! The thorns that dug into Jesus's head were very clearly painted. She could see his hair matted with blood, and a drop of blood on his forehead, round and lascivious, as if juice was being squeezed from a very pale and large berry.

The back of her thighs were numb. She pushed herself up from her chair and went to the small cupboard in the corner. She moved the books aside and took out the bottle she kept behind them, half full of liquid, which had, she reflected, the same depth to it as the berry juice on Christ's forehead. She swallowed it quickly – she had not poured herself enough. Outside it was still light. A walk, a respite from her room; that was what she needed. Although it might be chilly out there – just a little more, to warm her. She went back to her cupboard, opened it again, and poured herself a larger measure, waiting until she could feel the warmth begin to curl upwards from her stomach.

Outside the air was cold and crepuscular. A thrush still sang its complicated trill; it sounded grating, unknowable. She walked across the Quadrangle and into Christ Church Meadow. Her nose itched, as it often did on spring evenings. Perhaps she ought to turn back, else she would start to sneeze and her eyes water. But it was peaceful in the meadows, the trees overcome with heavy stillness, nearly empty of people, the light diffuse and darkening.

She walked for a while along the path. She thought at one moment she heard footsteps behind her, but when she turned round she could not see anybody. Mr Wilton's moustache floated in front of her, though she could not bring the rest of his face to mind. His hands she would always see: broad-knuckled, kneading. She closed her eyes. She felt again the railings against her spine, the rhythm of his hand, in and out, up and down, as if it were the only rhythm in the world. The sickening pulling at the tips of her and the sudden strange connection to her groin.

But there *were* footsteps behind, growing closer now. Her chest writhed as if she had a living thing behind her breastbone. She quickened her pace. There was a bench, just over there, within sight of the river, but not too near. She would sit down and let the man pass her by.

The branches snapped alongside the path on which Mary had just trodden – whoever he was, he was in a hurry. Mary stared in the opposite direction, trying to calm her breathing. She was not afraid; she had no interest in the man and his movements at all.

He was upon her now. She heard the voice first, and then saw the man. 'Miss Prickett, what a surprise!'

It was Mr Dodgson, leaning over her in the half-light. 'I often take a walk here in the evening, but I have never seen you.'

'Oh!' Now that she was called on to talk, her tongue was thick in her mouth. 'I wondered who it was. Whom it was.'

He was even paler than usual, his eyes pinpricks in the dimness. 'It was I.' He smiled; his lips were dry and had white specks at the corners.

'I thought I would catch a last breath of air before my journey tomorrow.'

'Quite.' Mr Dodgson stood back up, his hands in his pockets, a scarf bound tightly round his neck. 'But when you arrive, North Wales will be invigorating, I have no doubt. The country is so different up there. It's strange, isn't it, how nature, when revealed at her wildest, should be the most soothing to behold.

> 'Though the torrents from their fountains
> Roar down many a craggy steep,
> Yet they find among the mountains
> Resting-places calm and deep.'

His words came out easily, as swiftly as the river.

'Did you write that yourself, Mr Dodgson?'

'Oh no! That is Wordsworth,' he said.

She was glad it was nearly dark so that he could not see her face. 'Yes, of course.'

'Do you mind if I sit for a moment? I have a back complaint.'

He sat down carefully, his hands poised just above his waistband.

'My father had a similar problem. He found laudanum the only cure,' said Mary.

'I am taking it. It certainly numbs the pain, but the only cure is time, I think. It helps me sleep, too, at least in the earlier part of the night. Otherwise I am afraid my sleepless nights are becoming a recurring theme. I thought I might write out some of the mathematical problems I devise whilst I am tossing from one side to another. I might call it something like *Pillow Problems*.'

He stared at the tree ahead of them for so long that Mary began to feel uncomfortable. But Mr Dodgson seemed not to feel it.

'That is a good name,' said Mary.

At last he started up again. 'There are sceptical thoughts, which seem to uproot the firmest faith; there are blasphemous thoughts, which dart unbidden into the most reverent souls; there are unholy thoughts, which torture, with their hateful presence, the fancy that would fain be pure.'

He lapsed into silence. A thrush grated out its noisy night-time song.

It was Mary's fault. She had nothing to say now that Mr Dodgson was here beside her, though plenty to say to him when he was not. 'Will you publish these one day?'

'I hope to, yes.' He leant back on the bench. Without looking at her he asked: 'Do you have trouble sleeping?'

'Not really.'

'You are lucky indeed. If I could drop off quickly every night I would be very grateful.'

Mary thought of the picture of Jesus hanging in her room. 'Sometimes perhaps I struggle,' she added.

'My early childhood was very happy. It started at school, I think, at Rugby.'

Mr Dodgson made no move to go, even though the evening had lost all light. Mary remembered his open mouth, a tap from which no water came, the rabbit-in-a-snare look of his eyes. She wondered whether to say something, to commiserate and comfort, though perhaps to remind him would be worse. But he spoke again; he had no problems in that direction now. In fact he seemed particularly garrulous.

'I do not look back on my life at a public school with any pleasure. Three years, but an eternity to me.' The edges of his face blurred in the dimness. He looked straight ahead, at the branches fast turning into skeletons in the dark, but he seemed to see only that of which he spoke.

Mary shivered. She had not expected his confidence, especially here, especially now, but now that she had it, she was glad. 'Was it so terrible, then?' she asked him softly.

'Terrible . . . yes. It was terrible to leave the loving arms of my mother to go to that *place*.'

Mary had always thought public school a privileged place. No man had ever confided otherwise.

'I was always hungry. Always cold. There was never enough food to go round. I remember coming into my den once to find everything turned upside down. Everything! Table and chairs hung from the ceiling, my books were turned the wrong way up, my bed had been turned over and my clothes pressed in a heap under it. My tormentors even glued my pen and inkpot to the roof!' His face was full of still new astonishment. 'If they could have just put the thought into their studies that they put into tormenting me! They hid behind the door to watch my face as I discovered it.'

'Oh dear,' was all Mary said, but she did not mean it in the normal way.

Mr Dodgson's voice dropped very low. 'But if I could have been secure from annoyance at night, the hardships of the daily life would have been comparative trifles to bear.' His face crumpled. He looked like a child again.

What had happened to him at night? Was that why he could not now sleep?

The back of Mary's neck tingled and she felt tears at her eyes. She blinked them away. That he should be confiding this to her!

'I too had an unhappy childhood,' she said. She was surprised to hear the words coming out of her mouth. She had never said it, even to herself. 'My school was nothing like Rugby, of course, but the teacher was cruel. In the winter she would beat our knuckles with a ruler for a wrong answer, and we were freezing. On cold days now I still feel it, here.' She stuck out her two longest fingers, which were without gloves – she had not thought to meet anyone.

Mr Dodgson took one of her fingers up in his gloved hand and looked. Mary felt a freezing heat running up her hands.

'It does not look bad,' said Mr Dodgson, 'but then we all carry scars that no one can see.'

Still holding her finger he added: 'I should like to make you a small gift, before you go.'

'A gift?' Mary said in confusion. 'Why?'

'I thought you might like it. I think it is too late to collect from my rooms now, but I will leave it for you at the Deanery tomorrow morning.'

He released her finger and Mary made a fist with her hand and hurried it back into her pocket.

'What is it?'

'Let it be a surprise, Miss Prickett. Gifts are better that way.' She could see his smile gleaming through the darkness.

When they parted at the door of the Deanery, he bowed and thanked her. For what? Mary almost asked, but didn't. She thought she knew – but if she asked him, it might signal that she thought that nothing out of the ordinary had happened.

CHAPTER 14

*W*HAT GIFTS DID MEN GIVE TO WOMEN? WHAT DID
an Oxford tutor give to a governess? A pen-wiper, a fan perhaps,
or a pincushion? Mary had seen a pincushion in the shape of
a strawberry last time she had been in town, and had wanted
it. Or a needle case, embroidered perhaps, though Mr Dodgson
would not himself have done the embroidery, but perhaps they
had the cases in Elliston & Cavell. Perhaps he had gone to
Mr Wilton for something! But they did not know each other,
Mary was sure.

But Mr Dodgson *had* carried her in his mind. He had left his
rooms, walked purposefully to the stationer's, or the haberdasher, or the bookshop, thinking of her. He had retrieved his
wallet from his pocket and taken out his coins, still thinking of
her, and carried the parcel wrapped in its brown paper home, his
fingers pushed underneath its string.

Or perhaps he had gone to the jeweller's. Mary had seen
a pair of emerald earrings in the window, just small, nothing
like Mrs Liddell's, but she had experienced a sharp pang of

covetousness for their blaze of colour, their promise of life.

She must not think of jewellery, though. But of the intimacy that a gift suggested, she could not help but think. Mr Dodgson had said the word *gift* with such tenderness, had he not, there in the darkness?

Mary's school friends had provided intimacy of a general kind, but up till now she had only had real access to her own inner life. She had always assumed other people were generally as they told her they were. Even her own mother gave no indication of having an inner life, unless feelings of irritation and impatience could be counted. But even the revelation that another human being struggled, as she did, experienced unhappiness, as she did, would not bring forth emeralds. But it was so unexpected, and one unexpected thing could easily lead to another . . .

She would get up. A little light was edging round the curtains, enough to go downstairs. The maids had been up for some time and would have been able to answer the door, if he had come.

She pulled on her dressing gown and trod carefully out of her room. The wooden stairs under her bare feet gave way to carpets below, and below that, the cold flagstones of the hall. Mary saw long before she got down that he had not brought jewellery, but she would not be disappointed. There was still a package, flat and regular-shaped, on the table by the door.

She snatched it up and shoved it under her arm, the sharp corners of it poking into her skin. She did not open it until she was back in the safety of her room, tearing off the three sheets of brown paper.

It was revealed to be a photograph of the Deanery, taken from the garden. The three miniature girls were seated in front of an open window. Mary had not remembered Mr Dodgson taking it; perhaps it had been done before she arrived.

She brought the photograph close to her face. It smelt of nothing. The girls each held croquet mallets. They had tiny balls at their feet. The Deanery was covered in ivy; it looked massive, its great windows bulging. She could read no expression on the girls' faces. She would need to study the photograph further to try to extract a meaning from it.

She opened her case and quickly angled the photograph inside. She would take it to Wales; it would be a comfort to have it there, even though she was not over-fond of the Deanery. She could keep it in her room, but it would do well to let nobody else see, in case of awkward questions.

◆

Mary's only holiday as a child had been spent in Dorset, where the land unfolded like a shaken-out rug. North Wales was a land of crags and pinnacles, and Penmorfa was a gothic pile with turrets and crenellations that merged with the countryside in a gloomy way.

The house was damp and dark and the light was filtered by the lead windows that dominated the front side. Even with the fires going all day, Mary's knuckles and wrists were chilly and the pad of her big toe was often numb.

The children quarrelled more than in Oxford, perhaps because they had not got Mr Dodgson to amuse them. Ina said that Alice took everything of hers; Alice denied it. Ina could not even bear to see Alice with her old doll, which she had long out-grown, and snatched it away.

One afternoon Ina was sitting reading a booklet she had acquired about etiquette, with the old doll on her lap.

'You are too old for a doll. I don't see why you are bother-ing to learn about how to be a lady when you still want the doll,' Alice said. She took the doll and sat her on the table; Kitty's pan-taloons splayed out from her skirts like two chicken drumsticks.

'Give me the doll!'

Alice grabbed Kitty's arms with each of her hands. 'Miss Prickett,' she said, pretending it was the doll who spoke, 'why have you got a photograph of Mr Dodgson's?'

Mary stood still, her chest very cold. 'Have you been in my room?'

'Yes, you told me to get my mittens.'

Mary had told her that, it was true. 'How do you know it is Mr Dodgson's?'

'Because he is the only one who takes photographs of the Deanery.'

'I am not speaking to a doll, Alice. Use your usual voice and give Kitty back to your sister.'

Alice did not give the doll back. In the same grating voice she read, over Ina's shoulder: '"A gentle, deferential manner will disarm even the most discerning. Steer a course" – I can't see, and how will I ever learn if I can't see – "between silence and the twittering of a canary, and remember that gentlemen do not want to be told what to think."'

'Give it me!' Ina got up and made a grab for Kitty.

'I won't! Not until Miss Prickett tells me why she has a photograph of Mr Dodgson's in her room.'

Mary found herself at Alice's side. She grabbed the doll from her and threw it to the floor, its porcelain head hammering on to the floorboards, its blue eyes blinking. 'It is none of your business, Alice. You ought not to ask so many questions! You would know that, if you read more of that booklet on etiquette.'

In three strides she was at the drawer where the ruler was kept. She could already feel its smooth wooden sides, the snug way it fitted into her palm. She had not yet used it as a weapon – only for measuring – but now something pushed at her behind her collarbone: light and expanding rage.

'Alice, hold out your hand. You can see what it is like to have a taste of your own medicine.'

Alice would not hold out her hand.

Mary went over and pulled her arm up by the sleeve. 'Turn the palm to me!'

'Why is it a taste of my own medicine? I have not hit anybody!' Alice's wrist bone wriggled in her grip; an animal trying to escape a trap.

Mary held on harder and brought the ruler down on Alice's palm.

She had expected to feel relief as the crack rang out. But instead she felt abruptly as if she might cry.

She turned her head to the window and squeezed her eyes shut. Three birds fell, as if they had been dropped behind the window pane. She must punish Alice; it was for her own good.

She could hear her mother saying the same words to her as she brought the ruler down on Mary's hand. The harder the better, as her mother said; the lesson would be learnt. And it *had* been for her own good. She had learnt her lesson. She had been quiet and taken her slaps as she was meant to, without making a fuss.

Not like Alice, who was cradling her hurt hand with an exaggeration of rebuke, her eyes blinking just like the doll on the floor.

Alice was not authentic. Her sadness showed on her face as desolation, her cheerlessness as devastation. Her aim was to suck sympathy towards herself and to discredit Mary.

'Mr Dodgson says I may ask as many questions as I like. I wish he was here!' cried Alice.

'Mr Dodgson does not mean you to ask *impertinent* questions. The other palm, please.'

Again Mary had to force out Alice's other hand herself. Again she brought the ruler down. But again she had to hold back the tears that threatened to spill out as if a tap had suddenly been unblocked.

Her mother had sometimes given her three slaps – it was the second one on the same hand that punished the most, of course – if she had refused to finish her supper, say, or if she had been caught running down the corridor, something her mother could not abide. Or if she had spoken out of turn, as Alice had.

But Mary had lost the taste for punishment. She hardly noticed that Alice's eyes at last filled with tears and her bottom lip trembled. She turned away again towards the window, letting the ruler clatter down on the table.

In the afternoon it rained, gently but persistently, pricking the sea with pin marks. Shrimping was cancelled and the children and Mary were kept indoors. Mary found herself aiming all her diversions at Alice. Would she like to play the piano? She would not. Would she like to practise her watercolour painting? Or perhaps a collage? She said nothing to this, but Alice usually enjoyed collage, so Mary started one up, of the Angel Gabriel. They had not even started on the wings when Alice said she needed to use the water closet.

'I thought you just went?'

'But it is so pretty. I want to see the picture of Pan on the bowl, and the water rushing through!' Alice looked at her for the first time that afternoon, and smiled.

The water closet was new, and it was exciting, Mary concurred. Of course she may!

But fifteen minutes later Alice had not returned. Mary, unwilling to bellow into the echoing hall, set off after her.

Alice was no longer in the water closet, which stood alone over its dominion of white tiles, if she ever had been. Nor was she behind the damask curtains in the hall, nor behind the new pine door into the morning room, which still smelt of the sun slanting through a green forest, nor behind the canary-yellow sofa.

Alice was hiding from her, she must be!

The scheming, conniving little girl had looked her in the face and smiled, and all the time she'd been planning to trick her. Humiliate her in front of her family, where Alice was the worm buried inside the apple and she, Mary, was a wasp crawling on the surface, trying to get in.

Or perhaps – and this was worse – she was not being wicked, she was afraid. Afraid of Mary, and that was why she hid.

Or perhaps Mary was imagining it all and Alice was back with her sisters now, carrying on with the collage.

But as she was hurrying back through the hall she came upon Mrs Liddell sauntering the other way. 'Miss Prickett! What a pity about the rain.'

Mary nodded, caught on the edges of her feet.

'Have you found some entertainment for the children?'

'We are making collages. I should get back.'

'How dear. I will come and see.'

Mary swallowed. 'Yes.'

Mrs Liddell followed her through the hall; Mary could hear her skirts slipping over the uneven surface of the flagstones, could feel her perfumed breath on the back of her neck as they turned into the corridor towards the nursery.

But when they arrived, there was Ina, jumping up to show her mama the angel's gilded wings, and there was Edith, but no Alice.

'She went . . . Alice felt the call of nature and became distracted, I believe,' said Mary.

'Oh, is she upstairs?'

'I . . . She may be. I will find her for you.'

Now Mrs Liddell would see that Mary could not keep control of her children. She would see that Mary could lose one of them, even in the house! She thought of Alice's neat little nose and the swing of her hair; her hands, large for a ten-year-old, their knuckles like a full-grown woman's.

'I expect she is playing a game,' said Mary.

'I hope she hasn't gone outside.' Mrs Liddell frowned through the window at the rain. 'I can't think why she would have.'

Perhaps Alice had gone out into the sea; perhaps she had come to some harm, her thin, pale body washed up on the beach. It would be Mary's fault. 'I will look for her.'

'I will come with you. Some exercise will do me good.'

They set off together into the house once more. But even though Mrs Liddell started out gay, calling out Alice's name, to Mary the search soon took on the aspect of a nightmare. Crouching under tablecloths, opening up obscure cupboards, the idea of Alice growing and growing between them the longer she was lost.

Mary thought about saying sorry to Mrs Liddell, but she could not bear to, so even though apologies rose continuously to her lips, she swallowed them down. She moved through the house self-consciously, much too big and at the same time as if she wasn't there. Mrs Liddell often had that effect on her.

After what seemed like hours, but may have only been minutes, they heard a sob coming from the boot room. Alice's polished foot stuck out from underneath a mass of hanging coats. Mary had been there twice before and not discovered her.

She felt a rush of relief that was immediately overcome by anger. 'You are a very disobedient child! You shall be punished. We have been looking for you for hours.'

Alice escaped Mary's outstretched hands and ran to her mother. Tears and mucus slid down her face. She clasped her mother's skirts and pressed her cheek against them. But her look, when it met Mary's, she was sure, had triumph in it.

'We have been searching for you for a long time. I am quite cross. We were worried.' Mrs Liddell put a jewelled hand on her cheek.

Alice kept crying.

'Whatever made you hide like that, Alice?'

'I will take her now,' said Mary roughly. She would hit her again, once she was back in the nursery.

'I was upset.'

'Whatever for?'

'Miss Prickett hit me, with a ruler!'

'I dare say you deserved it.'

'I did not! I did nothing at all!'

It was on Mary's lips to say that Alice had been impertinent, and prying, although she could not explain to the child's mother the true depth of her irritation because it was unfathomable, ran too low, somewhere beneath reason.

'I only asked her about the photograph Mr Dodgson had given her.'

Mary's face, already flushed, burnt itself a deep crimson. She stared down at the galoshes the Dean had had made, as dark and glossy as tar.

'Ah yes, the photograph. He does seem to be liberal with them.' Mrs Liddell put her arm round Alice's shoulders.

Why would Alice tell her mother about her photograph?

There could only be one reason: to embarrass Mary, to humiliate her. Well, she would not be humiliated. But she stayed staring down at the floor so that they would not see the colour of her cheeks. A woodlouse was trying to bury itself underneath Ina's boot.

Mrs Liddell was staring at Mary with one eyebrow raised.

'It was a gift. Mr Dodgson is liberal with them, as you say. That was not the reason why I punished Alice, however. It was for taking something that belonged to her sister.'

'But I wonder, if I may, why Mr Dodgson is giving a gift to my governess?' Mrs Liddell's voice was sharp with excessive politeness.

Because he had followed her in the dark and they had sat on a bench together – she could not say that. Because she had heard him talk as she had never heard a man talk – she could not say that either.

Because he was paying court to her – she certainly could not say that.

'I don't know, Mrs Liddell. He gives his photographs to everyone, as you say.' Mary kept her tone even. She knew he did not give his photographs to *everyone*.

'And you have brought yours up here, on a perilous journey to Wales.'

Mary swallowed. The room was small and smelt of damp tweed and galoshes. It was crowded with oilskins and umbrellas, ranked in their stand like curious birds. 'I had not the time to look at it before.'

It only took a moment to look at a photograph, especially of the Deanery. Everyone knew that. 'Alice, let us go!' said Mary quickly. 'We have troubled your mother enough.'

'No,' said Mrs Liddell, tightening her hand round Alice's shoulder. 'I think I will keep her. She may like to see her father.'

◆

One other thing happened while Mary was in Penmorfa, that at the time she did not consider important. She happened to glance at a letter Mr Dodgson had written to Alice, which Alice had left carelessly open on the side table in the hall.

My dear Alice,

I liked your letter better than anything I have had for some time. I may as well just tell you a few of the things that I like, and then, whenever you want to give me a birthday present (my birthday comes once every seven years, on the fifth Tuesday in April), you will know what to give me. Well, I like, very much indeed, a little mustard with a bit of beef spread thinly under it, and I like brown sugar – only it should have some apple pudding mixed with it to keep it from being too sweet; but perhaps what I like best of all is salt, with some soup poured over it. The use of soup is to hinder the salt from being too dry, and it helps to melt it. And I like two or three handfuls of hair; only they should always have a little girl's head beneath them to grow on, or else whenever you open the door they get blown all over the room, and then they get lost, you know.

Mary could not help but compare the letter, whose images poked her in the eye like awkward elbows, with the one Mr Wilton had written to her. Mr Wilton's letter told her about the visits he'd paid (Mrs Storing, old Mr Flumy, Mrs Mull), the weather (better in Oxford than in Wales) and news of a horse that had gone lame.

But he was not good with words, as he often said. That did not mean anything. The tone, however, suggested domesticity. And domesticity suggested marriage.

Mary tried to imagine kissing the red lips that were pointed to so sumptuously by his sideburns, in front of the altar, in her wedding dress. But she got snagged on the texture of him; his lips would be moist, flaky. His sideburns like stroking a glossy bear.

His hands, blossoming with dark hair. The railings at her back.

Did the gift of a photograph suggest marriage too?

A sharp rush through Mary's chest made her fold up Mr Wilton's letter and put it away.

CHAPTER 15

$\mathscr{M}$ARY HAD NOT BEEN BACK IN OXFORD LONG WHEN Mr Wilton came to visit. He had put on extra pomade for her; his hair smelt strongly of soap and candles, and was greased back from his temples in a way that probably suited his work at the haberdashery.

They had the schoolroom to themselves. The children were next door, arguing; their voices could be clearly heard. 'What is the point of a book without any pictures?' said Alice.

'You are a baby,' said Ina.

'I am not! Yours are dull.'

'Why is whatever I like dull?' said Ina.

'Tea, Mr Wilton?' said Mary, pushing a cup towards him.

'Children,' said Mr Wilton. 'I suppose to be childish is in their nature.'

'I am going to read my book,' said Alice.

'But I thought we were going to read together!'

Mary got up and went next door. 'Alice. Read together as you promised, then you may read on your own.'

'But it's boring!'

'Do as I ask.'

'But I can do what I want, you said so!'

'I certainly never said so! You do what I want, that is the end of it.'

Mr Wilton was sitting with a hand cupped over each knee. In each fingernail there was a crescent, as polished and white as a new moon.

Mary shut the door. She smiled. 'Well.'

Mr Wilton shifted on to one haunch and brought out something from his pocket: a square of folded tissue paper. He held it out to her. It was light, insubstantial.

She unwrapped it in silence, the leaves of tissue papers shuffling away from her fingers; she tore a hole in them getting to what was inside.

A length of Belgian lace, so delicate she could not at first make it out against the tissue. It was beautiful. Flowers so fine their stamen could be clearly seen, berries with bulging seeds, leaves made to show even their veins – the world remade in black and white. It reminded her of one of Mr Dodgson's glass negatives.

She held it up draped between her fingertips, a spider's web. She was aware of Mr Wilton watching her.

'It is beautiful. Thank you.'

'When Mrs Liddell bought some, I thought you ought to have some too.'

'Yes,' said Mary, staring down at it.

'One day you may have a dress to put it on,' he said.

Was he criticizing her clothes? 'I already have a dress, only . . .' Mary was about to add that the lace was far too beautiful to attach to it when his meaning caught at her.

He was smiling at her, or had been, and now was absorbed at scratching dirt from his trouser leg, waves of embarrassment rolling from him.

Belgian lace was used for weddings.

Or perhaps it had many uses that only Mr Wilton knew about. 'It came to the store only yesterday,' he said at last. 'From Belgium. I thought of you.'

'You are very kind. It won't fit my usual dresses. Much too fine!' She stared down at the floorboards.

Now she had brought up the subject of the dress. But there didn't seem to be any other conversational alleys. She sounded as if she were waiting for a proposal, or at the least as if she were too poor to own a nice dress.

'It would do very well on a handkerchief,' she said.

❧

It was only later, when Mary was wrapping the lace back up and putting it in the drawer next to her bed, that she remembered the full story of Belgian lace. It was made by old ladies in Flanders in rooms made deliberately dark, to preserve the quality of the lace. But the quality of the old ladies' eyes was not taken into account. As they laboured in their dark rooms, beautiful gossamer webs blossoming on their laps, their eyes grew ever weaker and more clouded, until in the end they were rendered totally blind.

CHAPTER 16

$\mathscr{M}$ARY RAN INTO THE GARDEN, ON TO THE EMERALD
carpet of the lawn. She had heard Edith scream; she dreaded
something happening to the children, especially after Penmorfa.

But it was Villikens who lay on the grass in the brightness of
the day, his white and tan fur ruffling in the breeze, his lips
frozen in a final snarl, blood crusted round his mouth.

Alice exploded into tears, as if she had been waiting her entire
life for this moment.

The cat, whose bony spine Mary had run her hand over so
often, was unnaturally stiffened and arched.

Ina started to cry in gulps. 'Oh, Miss Prickett! What happened to him? Why is he dead?'

'It looks like poison,' said Mary. She had seen the gardener
putting it down in the shed.

'We all loved him so much, I don't understand why he
had to die!'

Ina wrapped her arms around herself and rocked. Mary
started to go to her, holding back her own tears; she wanted to

comfort her in her loneliness. But she had never got close to the girl like that before – Ina was almost grown up and she had something contained about her, unlike Alice, who seemed to sprawl. Even as Mary went towards her, Ina put her arms back by her sides. Mary wished that she could have more of Mr Dodgson's easy familiarity with the children. When she got to Ina, she rested one hand on her starched shoulder and palpated it. She could feel the bones beneath her dress.

'We still have Dinah,' she said.

'But we have lost Villikens! Oh dear!' said Alice. She stared down, tears falling off her chin, her face swollen and red and not inviting comfort.

'We should come away. The gardener will bury him at the bottom of the graveyard.' Mary thought of the swan, the maggots, Mr Dodgson.

'Will he be in heaven by now?'

There was no provision in the scriptures for cats. 'I don't know.'

Mr Dodgson would know what to do. He had a limitless supply of knowledge about animals, dead or alive. She wanted to see his face with its clear skin; she wanted to rest in his cool eyes. And she wanted to thank him for her photograph and to tell him she had found a place for it, just above her bed. 'Let's pay a visit to Mr Dodgson's rooms,' she said. 'He will cheer us up.'

◆

Mary let the children run ahead; she had not had time to send him a note, but children could traverse social barriers usefully.

When she came into his room, he was still standing at his writing desk, silhouetted against the window. She had an impression of movement even so, of wavy hair and lips curled up. He was different from the man she had seen in her mind all through the holidays and it took a few moments to readjust the images, to see that his features were just as pleasant as she had thought.

'I missed you all! How was your vacation?' he said.

Alice ran into his arms and started to cry again.

'Something is wrong. What is it?'

'Villikens is dead,' said Ina.

'Who is dead?' said Mr Dodgson

'Villikens. The gardener found him poisoned,' said Ina.

The children started to cry again.

'Oh, I don't know why he went into the shed in the first place! Silly cat!'

Mr Dodgson sat down and motioned for all three children to sit within the boundaries of his arms. 'Poor dear cat. I do so hate pain and suffering.'

Mary remembered the bench in the darkness, Mr Dodgson's grief.

'But why, why did he die, Mr Dodgson?' said Alice.

'Well, we must all die some time, and it just happened that today was Villikens' day. And Dinah, are you sure she did not eat the poison?'

'I don't think so,' said Alice. 'Only Villikens was in the shed.'

'But why today?' said Ina.

'Because God wanted him to come to heaven today. But lucky Villikens, who will never know the pain of growing old and grey and stiff with every friend gone. He will always be a kitten, full of play, up in cat heaven.'

'Is there such a place?' asked Alice.

'There is. Each cat has its own enormous ball of wool, never taken away by a human for their knitting. Sardines for breakfast, salmon for tea and any number of mice in between.'

Alice looked at him. 'I shouldn't think mice are happy in cat heaven.'

'No, indeed they are not. But they are quite happy if they think they are somewhere else. Swan heaven, for example. They are in no danger there.'

Alice said: 'I don't think Dinah would eat mice for fun, although I have seen her with a dead mouse, I'm sure.'

'It is in their nature to eat mice for fun. Just as it is in your nature to like bread and jam. A cat cannot change that,' said Mr Dodgson.

'Oh, *poor* Villikens, I will miss him.'

'Did you get my note I wrote to you all? I wrote it on your first day back.'

'I don't think so,' said Ina. 'Mama did not mention it.'

'Perhaps she has been too busy unpacking,' said Mr Dodgson, turning to look out of the window. 'But come, we need something to cheer us up. I have an idea: what do you say to a play?'

'A play?' said Mary. 'At the theatre?'

'No, no, perhaps the children are too young for that. I meant the performance of a play, here in my rooms. *Away With Melancholy* is my favourite. It is a sort of farce. The title seems particularly apt today. If Mrs Liddell can spare you.'

'Mama likes plays. She often goes to the theatre,' said Edith.

Mrs Liddell could not mind if it was to enliven the children, and if it was to be performed in Mr Dodgson's rooms. She knew the children still saw him, and he had been a part of the Liddells' life for so long.

'Who will put it on?' said Mary.

'I will, I have performed it quite often.'

'What is it about?'

'About love lost and gained.'

'Oh, will you not perform it for us?' asked Alice.

Mr Dodgson looked at Mary.

'I don't see the harm in it,' she said.

'Of course . . .' said Mr Dodgson. He smiled at her with such charm, his head slightly at an angle, his eyes gazing at her, that she could not meet it.

'Of course?'

'It would go off so much better if you could take one of the roles.'

'One of the roles?' said Mary stupidly.

'Otherwise, you see, I have to run back and forth across the stage pretending to be everyone, male and female, and I get quite exhausted.'

'But I am no good at that sort of thing.'

'I am sure you are better than you think.'

'I am not!' said Mary, colouring.

'Miss Prickett, it would not make you an actress if you were to put on a performance for the children.' She glanced at him. He was still smiling. Had not stopped looking at her.

Her cheeks were hotter, as if his gaze was some kind of grill.

'Oh do, please say you will, Miss Prickett,' said Ina.

'There is a role, Mrs Maynard, that would suit you very well. The last time I read the play I thought of it for you.'

Thought of it for her. How did he see her, through what prism?

'In London I went to see *The Tempest*. The scenic effects surpassed anything I had seen before: the shipwreck of the first scene seemed to feature a real ship heaving about on huge waves, finally ruined, to my delight, under a cliff that reached up into the roof. Shakespeare reminds me of my nobler aspirations.'

'Shakespeare,' Mary repeated.

'And as I sat there in the darkness of the stalls it seemed to me to be the embodiment of the place between waking and dreaming, a fantastical world made real. Theatre can be a force for the good, I think. Shakespeare and, to a lesser extent, the modern plays are uplifting and educational. But I am afraid to say that my favourite type of play is a modern farce, just like *Away With Melancholy*, because they have no moral at all! I could bring over a copy of the play this evening. Perhaps you could look at it before you refuse absolutely.'

◆

Later that evening, Mary crept downstairs to the hall. There on the table was the volume of the play, as Mr Dodgson had promised. Nothing on the cover to suggest impropriety. It was a slim book; there could not be too much harm in reading it, surely. She clamped it under her arm and made her way quietly back upstairs. It would be hard to explain if one of the servants should see her. The book grew hotter with every step until she felt sure that the print had come off on her dress.

But no, when she reached her room, Mary had the same colourless dress on as ever. She unhooked her bodice and slipped off her shoes and sat down heavily on her bed. Her arms were thin and pale; her bones moved sharply about underneath her skin as she reached up and took out her hairpins.

Mary's hair was thick, though nobody but her own reflection ever saw it brushed out in its auburn mass. Usually she sat brushing it until she was hypnotized, one hundred strokes, as her mother had taught her. But tonight she did not sit in front of the looking glass. Her two heavy plaits fell down on her shoulders and she let them lie there.

While they had been visiting, Alice had asked Mr Dodgson about the photograph. She had not even thought to ask in a low voice, but kept to her usual insolent tone, while Mary's face burned away nearby. Mr Dodgson had replied quite calmly and openly that it was a gift. Then he had turned to her and smiled.

Mary opened the book.

Mrs Maynard, Mr Dodgson had said. She began to skim the text.

She saw at once that Mrs Maynard had a large speaking part. At first she was supposed to be droll but melancholy. Then there was a verse she was to sing.

But she, Mary Prickett, could not sing. If she took part, she would make a fool of herself. The children would laugh at her.

After the singing, she was supposed to be happy. Because she was in love with Mr Windsor. Mr Windsor – that must be Mr Dodgson's part.

Mary closed the book quickly, and shut her eyes. A pulse beat behind her eyelids.

A love story. Had he chosen the play specially? Was it a message to her? He had never asked her to put on a play with him before. It must be a message, then. A glow began in Mary's chest. She could not do it, of course, but the fact that he had chosen it for them to do together was enough.

She opened the book again and let her eyes roam across the pages. They had no scenes together at the start, it was true. But eventually Mrs Maynard was reunited with her lost love and they had plenty. They had to saunter, sing, and sway. She saw them on stage together, darkness all around, locked together in a single beam of light.

At the end, she could see, Mr Windsor made Mrs Maynard a passionate proposal of marriage.

Mary buried her face in her hands. She was glad she was in the sanctuary of her little room, hidden away at the top of the house.

What would Mrs Liddell think? Mrs Liddell did like the theatre, she often went, but that was not the same as having her governess perform. Though she would not be performing as such, merely reading.

Still.

She would make a fool of herself, never having been to the theatre, not knowing what people did there.

The children would laugh at her. She would be exposed. All her outside would be rubbed away and just the raw nub would be left: a slug on a toothpick. Even the children would see into her.

Mary smoothed the pages back down, closed the book and got into bed. She would say no, but she would say it regretfully; she would try to communicate to him that she understood why he had suggested it, but without using words.

CHAPTER 17

$\mathcal{M}$R WILTON WROTE AGAIN. IT WAS AGREED THAT they would visit a new exhibition (without the children this time): a pictorial representation of local farming methods, the new ways and the old. It was several weeks before Mary could escape, however – the children had so many pressing needs that she could not easily get away.

He took hold of her arm on the way to the gallery, talking of new deliveries at Elliston & Cavell, of new customers, in his usual way: running over the surface of things. Underneath his grip, sweat blossomed.

They stopped to admire a charcoal drawing of a horse labouring in front of a plough. The horse's neck looked as if it could crush a man with one swipe. The plough seemed to be hooked up on a clod and the effort that the horse was making was magnificent. Mary's eyes were caught by the bulge of its shanks as they strained: tight and curvaceous.

'I think it was Lady Arndale, though I could not be sure, but the finest muslins were ordered, for her daughter I believe,' said Mr Wilton.

'Lady Arndale?' said Mary. Even in charcoal she could see the gleam on the horse's coat.

They moved on to a photograph of the new steam plough. It looked like the front of a train, waylaid in a field.

Mary was expecting the flow of conversation to continue all the way round; that she need not listen to it. Was expecting to be able to carry on underneath with her own private existence. But Mr Wilton had stopped talking and was standing in front of this new photograph, a look of unexplainable anger on his face.

'I can't abide it,' he burst out.

'Can't abide what?' Mary's mind was still on Lady Arndale; perhaps she had done something egregious, or perhaps Mary had. Mr Wilton's jowls had darkened. She thought of the church, of her refusal, and what came after.

'That! That monstrosity can do the work of twenty horses. And what then? What becomes of them all, and of the labourers?'

Mary wriggled free from his grip and rubbed her arm. She wished she could roll her sleeve up and expose her skin to the air. But even undoing the buttons would not allow her sleeve, so tight at the wrist and at the elbow, to let the air in. 'The steam plough?' she said.

'And look at that!' Mr Wilton shifted his weight round to an etching of a pallet on wheels. 'One man and two horses pulling that reaper-binder could do the same amount of work in one mere hour that would take a scytheman *all day*.'

'Is that wrong?' Mary spoke timidly. This sudden change unnerved her.

'It is going against God's time. It is forcing Mankind's will over the earth. It is a relief, a blessed relief, I say, that the End of Days is coming.'

Mary wondered if it were a relief. For one thing, she did not dare ask herself whether she would be with the sheep or the goats. She did try to be good. And in daylight hours she was certain that she was. But if she were lying awake at night, she was gripped by the certainty that she was not.

It would be hot in hell, of course, and there was bound to be moaning and people hanging in chains. Or perhaps it was as George MacDonald said: no fire, no devil, just the cold withdrawal of God's love.

She glanced at Mr Wilton, his face mottled purple, standing with his legs apart, the polish of his shoes and the polish of the floor reflecting the same shine. She wished that Mr Dodgson was there with her instead, with his cheeks as cool as a drink of water. Mr Dodgson, whose contraptions were all so devotedly on the side of life.

And how to tell which was a good and which a bad angel? In pictures they looked much the same, luxuriantly winged and robed.

They moved on finally. Mr Dodgson hovered in front of Mary, imitating in his teasing way the voices of the horses, and the dogs; perhaps even the hay bales. Ina would object that hay bales didn't have voices, and Mr Dodgson would reply that, on the contrary, they often cried out, *Please don't cut me, I don't want to be food for a horse. Surely you must all have heard that when you went for a walk!*

'What is your opinion about the theatre?' said Mary.

'I have never been,' said Mr Wilton.

'Nor I. But what do you think of it in principle?'

'I think it may lower moral standards. The theatre is filled with rowdiness and cigar smoke. I don't think it can be quite right to dress up as someone else every night of the week. Why, are you thinking of going to the theatre?' he said.

'Not going, not me. I—'

'Would you like to go?' said Mr Wilton, turning away as he said it.

Mary hurried on, unsure if he had just sacrificed his beliefs about the theatre on the altar for her; unsure if it was an invitation.

'Oh no, I don't . . . It's . . .' She trailed off.

She could not bring up *Away With Melancholy*. She found she did not want to mention Mr Dodgson's name. Even if she did, Mr Wilton was bound to tell her she shouldn't take part. Which she was not going to in any case. So there was no need.

But he still seemed to be waiting for an answer.

'Oh no, I don't think I should like the theatre, as you said.'

Mr Wilton walked away, but she saw his face. It was a mixture of embarrassment and regret.

'You are quite right,' she said again. 'About the theatre. As a place for moral decay.'

CHAPTER 18

$\mathcal{W}$HEN MARY CAME INTO MR DODGSON'S ROOMS, she saw that somebody had sewn a large white cloud on to a black square of felt for the backdrop, and painted a board blue to approximate the sea. He had gone to so much effort! And he looked so pleased to see her, too.

'Mr Dodgson. Good afternoon! I had a look at the play.' She searched for his eyes. 'But I think in this case . . . Oh, you have hats!'

'Yes, and I chose this one specially for you.' Mr Dodgson placed one of the hats, a bright one twitching with feathers, gently on her head. 'It fits perfectly! See in the looking glass.'

He put his hand on her shoulder. She felt the heat of it burn through the stiff material of her dress and on to her skin.

He gently turned her round.

The hat did suit her. It lent an angularity to her cheekbones and a depth to her eyes. She looked like a different person.

Mr Dodgson spoke to her reflection, more boldly than he usually did. 'You must do it, Miss Prickett. Don't you see?'

He brought his other hand to join the first upon her shoulder.

They stared at each other in the looking glass.

She did see.

'The hat suits you so well, it's as if you were made for the part.'

Made for the part. The part of marriage. She had never felt made for the part before: her body was too shapeless, her face too thin, and all the other things were awkward and wrong.

But now here was Mr Dodgson saying that she *was* made for the part.

'And your head – it is most interestingly shaped. Your brows, they are quite the opposite to a criminal or savage kind.'

'My brows?' She looked at her reflection again. She had never paid much attention to her brows before: they were thin, and straggled along in a haphazard way above her eyes. But perhaps they were something that should be admired. Perhaps she ought to invest in a pair of tweezers.

'In the science of phrenology,' said Mr Dodgson.

Mary tried to remember what her poster said about brows.

'I went to visit a phrenologist once,' said Mr Dodgson. 'The results were quite extraordinary. He ascertained that I had a taste for order and dress, good analogical reasoning and a strong love of children. The last is certainly so! But who cannot love children?'

She and Mr Dodgson had so much in common; she was only just beginning to realize how much. Was there a protrusion on the skull that denoted a matching love of phrenology? She was about to mention it to Mr Dodgson – she felt light-headed – he might like it. But his hands had left her shoulders and he had turned towards the stage. 'Come, Miss Prickett, your part is not taxing. You will find your main appearances are towards the beginning – when you are sad, though you pretend not to be – and the end, when you are truly happy. It is a kind of farce, I am afraid, as I said.'

'I have read it.'

'You have? Good, then, you are persuaded.'

There was a knock on the door. It was the Acland children.

'I hope you don't mind, Miss Prickett. I took the liberty of asking them. I think a crowd makes a better audience.'

He handed her a green robe – it looked Chinese, she would never have worn it usually – to put on over her dress. She raised her arms, mute. It felt supple and cool, the shimmer of its colour surprising after all that black.

'Miss Prickett, you look like a lady in the magazines,' said Alice.

'She does!' said Mr Dodgson.

'I hope not,' said the governess, her hands flying up to the hat.

'I think Alice meant it as a compliment. A lady of fashion,' said Mr Dodgson. 'Of course, if you would be more comfortable without the hat, you can leave it off.'

'No, no,' said Mary. If she took it off now, it would look as if she did not know her own mind. And he had complimented her in it, twice.

'Good. Is everyone else ready? Then let us begin.'

Mr Dodgson made a scraping bow and in a grand voice announced the play and the two players, making such stupidness of it that the children were shouting with laughter before he had even begun.

He put on his top hat.

'My name is Windsor,' he said. 'I am a man of six-and-twenty. I am as happy as can be; at least, that is what I tell people. But I have lost my only love. Shall I tell you about her?'

'Yes!' said the children.

Mary stood awkwardly, holding the script with both hands.

'My affection for her commenced at rather an early period of her existence; she was a mere child – ten next birthday – whereas I had reached the mature age of eleven and a half! Well, the course of our true love ran on smoothly enough till I was twenty-one, when I made a proposal for Julia's hand, which her father, Smith, rejected. And why? Simply because my father, Brown, who had made all his money in the soap line, had christened me Windsor! Indeed, if it hadn't been for my mother, his original intention was to have me called Best Windsor.'

The children laughed.

'How silly,' said one of the Aclands. 'Imagine not marrying someone just because they were called Windsor!'

'But it's the name of a soap,' said Ina.

'It is silly, very silly indeed. But alas, the world is silly, as you will soon find out,' said Mr Dodgson in his Windsor voice. 'Well, Julia and I separated, vowing eternal constancy. I plunged into the law and became an attorney; she rushed into matrimony.'

Mr Dodgson dropped to his knees and sank his head into his chest.

'Finding that she had become another's, I resolved to forget her! To place the wide wide ocean between us! I went to Margate: there I might be seen walking by moonlight on the jetty in my Margate slippers, singing Mrs Maynard's favourite duet all by myself.'

He wandered from side to side, swaying and clasping his hands together, and sang in a high voice:

> 'Away with melancholy,
> Nor doleful changes ring
> For grieving is a folly,
> Then merrily merrily sing.'

Then he conducted the children, until they all sang along with him.

Mary looked down at her book. Hers was the next scene. She was anxious. Feeling that she ought not to be anxious added to her anxiety.

Now was the time to step forward.

'Oh, but I am so sad,' she said. 'I know not why.' Her voice did not seem to belong to her. Her cheeks were burning hot.

She had several more lines, which she spoke without lifting her head from the text.

Then she and Mr Dodgson took the stage together, supposedly reunited after many years. She felt Mr Dodgson's wiry presence close to her, swooping away and returning, his voice lifting and falling. Gradually she found her self-consciousness dropping away. All the time Mr Dodgson was there, teasing her, imploring her, making fun. Soon she was reading the lines as if she were Mrs Maynard, and Mr Dodgson Windsor.

Then she turned the page once more and came upon the final scene. The love scene.

Mr Dodgson stopped abruptly in his pacing. He hardly seemed to be looking at the script. Suddenly he turned to face her.

'I have loved you since I was eleven and a half!' he declaimed. Mary could not find her place. She stumbled, but Mr Dodgson carried on, dropping to one knee. He took her hand quite fiercely, pulling her down on to the edge of the wooden box.

'I must insist that you marry me – and I will not hear a word against it.'

Mary looked down at her script in a haze. Mr Dodgson did not seem to be following it.

'Oh, I, should I?' she said. She was present and not present, herself and someone else.

Mr Dodgson shouted: 'You should – say yes, oh do!'

'Yes, then,' said Mary. 'I will!'

For a moment she thought he would embrace her. He took her one hand in both of his and brought it to his lips. She let her hand lie in his, even though she felt the imprint of his lips as if she had been branded.

And then Mr Dodgson was up and skipping about the stage. The children clapped and cheered. Mr Dodgson went into a long speech about how all his prayers had been answered and how nobody could be more content. Mary noticed his eyes – she had read in her romance novels that eyes flashed, but until now she had never seen it. Perhaps she had never really seen anybody alive before. Bowing and taking the children's applause; now pretending they clapped him too much, now imploring them to clap more wildly. He bowed deeper and deeper until his head came down on his knees and his top hat fell off and he pretended to fall into it.

CHAPTER 19

*A*LL DAY IT HAD BEEN UNIMAGINABLY, UNSEASON-
ably hot, even though it was only the end of April.

Mary went over and over the play, her neck and chest sweat-
ing. She had always thought that if a thing had been felt and
remembered, physically remembered with a jolt in her chest, say
ten times or more, that it might lose the power to shock, but it
never seemed to.

Mr Dodgson going down on one knee. Her heart leapt in its
cage. His face coming towards hers. The smile that came up on
one side higher than the other that would be wrong on anyone
else, but that on him did not seem so at all. She had read somewhere that a truly symmetrical face, a mirror image of itself,
looked horrible. Perhaps the reverse was true: an asymmetrical
face such as his looked so pleasing. She could hardly now
remember when it had not been – she fancied now that even
when she had first seen him, when he came to photograph the
cathedral, she had thought the same.

She stared at her phrenology chart and tried to impose Mr

Dodgson's head upon it. Order and dress were not represented on her chart, though she saw conscientiousness and wit. She had never seen a love for children represented, but perhaps the phrenologist intuited it.

She imagined pressing her fingertips through his hair to feel his secrets.

Had it really been her up there? It was so unlike her. But she *had* put the emerald robe over her black dress and she *had* read those lines and (the sharp pulse again in her chest) he *had* gone down on one knee, wild-eyed, and he *had* looked as if he were about to kiss her.

All her life Mary had known, had been told it, that she had no special talents. The list of what she was not far outweighed the list of what she was.

She was not pretty, she was not plump, she could not play the piano beyond a few thumping chords.

She could not paint; she was not a conversationalist.

She could not dance.

She could not find a husband.

Possibility and yearning rushed from her chest. She threw herself down on the bed, dislodging the pile of books she usually kept there. *Jane Eyre*, its corners curled up. *Vanity Fair*. *East Lynne*, which she hid away in a cupboard, with its infidelities and children born out of wedlock.

Sweat dripped from her temple; her hair was damp and loose tendrils clung to her face. Moisture gathered around her waist, her upper lip and her wrists, where her dress clung to skin.

The sun blazed away in the middle of the cerulean blue.

There was no possibility of going out, or of anyone coming in. She would not see Mr Dodgson today, then.

Mary threw one arm over her head. It could not be hotter anywhere than it was here today. A swim in the sea would be delicious. To strip away her clothes, layer by layer, to sink into the cool water, to close her eyes and drift beneath the surface, the cool, clear water seeping into every crevice of her body . . .

She had gone to the seaside once, when she was a girl. Her mother had said it was good for the constitution, healthy, happy and wise, cleanliness next to godliness. All these things related to the sea, she said, and had let Mary swim away into it. It was cold but she had not felt it; she had loved the feeling of her limbs striding out into the water and the taste of salt biting into her mouth. When she was far away and her mother was nothing more than a black dot, she imagined she could go back to any one of the other black dots on the shoreline and become someone else.

In Oxford she had gone to a quiet part of the river, with some screeching classmates. The rocks underfoot poked blindly through the mud and she slipped and nearly fell. Her bathing costume had sewn-in weights at the hemline to prevent the dress from billowing up in the water and revealing her body. As she had struggled in, mud oozing shudderingly between her toes, the water crept up her thighs and up to her waist, but instead of the lightness she had been longing for, the weights and the heavy fabric of her bathing-suit material dragged her down the further she went in. She had only managed a few strokes, the weed's soft hair clinging to her calves, until she had lumbered out.

Mary took off her clothes and lay down on her bed. She closed her eyes and began to drift away, swim away, in the sea again, though instead of being cool, it was hot; the water clung to her like sweat. She pulled at the waistband of her drawers; it was her bathing costume she pulled at, wanted to be free of.

The sea took on an amorphous weight; it pressed down on her and lapped over her breasts, a hot and moulding pair of hands. Mr Wilton was motioning to her with a strange look on his face; she could not tell if he meant her to come or to go further away. But at once she was next to him and there was a painful feeling between her legs that needed to be rubbed, a rising point that needed to be flattened. Mr Wilton stretched his hand and burrowed into her and the pain increased in pulsating bursts until she was one throb of pain vibrating around a central point.

When she looked again, it was Mr Dodgson's face, a line between his eyebrows, his hand caught between her legs.

Mary came up to the surface with a lurch. The feeling inside her exploded and then violently dissipated.

She woke up properly then, her own palm flat between her legs, hot and damp, the picture of Jesus hanging balefully over her.

◆

A while later, after the children had been put to bed, Mary sat reading by the light of a candle in the schoolroom, as she sometimes did when the walls of her room became too oppressive.

She was not tired now.

She ought not to have slept.

She had seen a poster once, representing 'The last stage of self-pollution'. A man lay on a chaise longue in a torpor, his cheeks hollow and his eyes gazing listlessly into the distance. He was wearing a green smoking jacket and a silk burgundy waistcoat underneath that signified, somehow, his lack of agency in the world.

Although Mary had never heard of self-pollution referred to in women. Perhaps it did not exist. But she ought not to have woken up with her hand pressed into the folds of flesh and the curly black hair, so unpleasant to the touch, and some horrible moistness. Those parts that were never named.

Her eyes fell on the picture of Jesus again. He looked nothing like the pastor after all. Perhaps he looked nothing like the picture either; he was unlikely to have had blonde hair, being a Jew.

A sickness, as if she had eaten bad meat, started to spread from the point just below her breasts.

The feeling she had had at Mr Wilton's church, just as she was speaking in tongues – of ecstasy – was the same one that she had experienced now, in her dream.

The blood crawled down His arms and down the rack of His ribs. His head was twisted away from her – in disgust, Mary now saw.

She put her hand up to her chest and rubbed it; the sickness was in her neck now, making it hard to swallow.

Self-abuse led to madness. And if self-abuse led to madness, it followed that night-time emissions did too. Although she was a woman: she had no emissions to spill out and leak from her oozy soul and seep her energy away.

Exercise, a proper diet, and self-control; even – or especially – as far as dreams went. That must be possible, must it not?

CHAPTER 20

A FEW EVENINGS LATER THERE WAS A KNOCK AT the schoolroom door. The children's nanny bent her head round. 'I have lost Edith's cardigan; I thought it might be in here.'

'I have not seen it,' said Mary.

The woman walked about, the heels of her boots ticking sharply on the wooden floor. 'Have you seen Mr Dodgson today?' said the nanny, after a while.

'No, not today. Still too hot, I think,' said Mary, glancing at her.

'I suppose you must have grown used to him by now.'

Mary looked at Nanny Fletcher's face. She often disagreed with the woman, even though she was the one who was most nearly her equal. Yesterday the nanny had launched into a long story about a girl who had been foolishly allowed by her parents to wander around the library to read as much as she liked, and whose brain grew so large she fell down dead.

Most things she said seemed to be directed obliquely but critically at Mary's sphere; in general Nanny Fletcher did not stay to make conversation. But this evening she circled the room, picking up cushions and replacing them in a way that did not suggest particular urgency as to the whereabouts of the cardigan.

'I think the cardigan is not here,' said Mary. 'It may be in Edith's room; perhaps you will find it tomorrow. I had best turn in.'

Nanny Fletcher hesitated. 'It may not be my place . . . '

Mary noticed peripherally how small her feet seemed, how agile, underneath the bulk of her body.

The woman had heard something.

'It may not be my place,' Nanny Fletcher said again. 'There is gossip, around Oxford . . . I thought perhaps you ought to know.'

Mary had made a fool of herself and now she would be shamed. Discovered. In the centre of her a thing that should never see the light squirmed upwards.

Nanny Fletcher paused, and then came out with the rest of the words in a rush. 'Some say that Mr Dodgson is paying court to you; that is why you see him so much.'

Mary kept her face very still and turned away from the other woman.

'Of course they are wrong. Aren't they? But I thought you ought to know.'

She wanted to smile, was desperate to smile; she would have no choice but to let the corners of her lips turn skywards if the nanny did not leave.

She had been right.

She pressed her hand over her mouth and shook her head; she hoped it would look like disbelief.

'Thank you, Mrs Fletcher. It was good of you to bring it to my attention.'

Still with her hand over her mouth, she pushed past and rushed to her room.

❖

Mary threw the stack of books that were on her pillow on to the floor and sat down. She pressed her knuckles into her eyelids. Mr Dodgson rushed into the space behind them, the acid-sweet smell of him, his long pale fingers.

His wild look when he proposed on stage. His smile as he handed her the Ammoniaphone. His strange confession in the dark.

She got up from her bed again and paced up and down the room. She was fierce with joy, terrible with it.

She could leave this place and set up her own home. But where would they live? She sat down again, the springs squeaking.

Tutors could not marry. She had heard Mr Dodgson say that that was why he would never marry, as his father had; he would never give up his career to be the rector of an obscure parish somewhere, as he put it.

But men said plenty of things they did not mean!

The talk in Oxford irresistibly chimed with the conversation Mary had been having with herself. Every book she had ever read told her that gossip like this was never brought up just to disappear without a trace.

She would have to wait and see what Mr Dodgson wanted to

do, where he wanted to live. He had not even proposed yet! Oh, where would it be, how would he do it? In the schoolroom, or down by the river, his knee pressed into the mud? Perhaps he would invite her to a garden, with roses in it, and sit her on a bench and take her hand and press it to his lips and look into her eyes with his own fevered orbs and . . .

Her orbs were fevered too. She must rest. But rest was impossible! She must, though, if she were to see Mr Dodgson tomorrow. She might see him – she might see him tomorrow! But how could she sleep, with her heart pounding in her ears?

She took up her book again and tried to read, but could not. Sleep would come later, or not at all. It made no difference now.

◆

The only wedding Mary had previously attended was that of her classmate, Amelia. Amelia smelled of Parma violets; her skin was smooth, pale and plump. On a sunny day the sun shone straight through Amelia's pale hair on to the white scalp beneath. Her flesh was soft; it swayed beneath her upper arms and sat in self-satisfied rolls underneath her chin. If it were pressed too hard it would retain the divot, like a pillow.

Her way of clasping her hands together in front of her bosom was plump and self-contained. Her voice was high and tonally designed to soothe men's ears.

When she was eighteen, the suitors came. She encouraged them all and read their letters out loud to Mary, smiling, showing her small, sharp teeth. Sometimes she tore up a letter in front of her and let the pieces drop in the waste-paper basket.

She told Mary how one man might meet another in the hall as they came and went – when she spoke of this, her usually pale face grew flushed, but there was no sign of embarrassment in her features.

After eight months Amelia became engaged to a wealthy gentleman farmer who lived just outside Oxford. During this time Mary saw them drive by in his fine carriage, with a chaperone, close but not yet touching. Once she saw them stepping into a large house together in Summertown.

She watched the couple come back down the aisle: the beautiful bride, the handsome groom, walking on a snowfield of petals. Mary's mother, who had accompanied her, pressed a handkerchief to her eyes ostentatiously. Mary herself had smiled until her mouth was a crack that held up her face. As her old friend went by she looked in at her face, suddenly revealed by her thrown-back veil. But Amelia only glanced sideways at her husband through half-shut eyes; she had passed through to somewhere, it seemed, that could not be reached by unmarried people.

At the wedding breakfast Mary had wandered into the hallway of the house, where three cakes were lined up on a table, under a bough of heavy jasmine. The smaller two cakes represented the bride and groom, the dark one for the groom, the pale one for the bride. But the largest was decorated with elaborate orange scrolls and Amelia and her mother were busy dividing it into pieces so that while the front of it still presented a glittering facade, the back was a crumbling slope of dark devastation. The slices had been boxed up and tied with yellow ribbon, ready to give to the guests on their departure; each box contained a trinket.

> *The ring for marriage within a year;*
> *The penny for wealth, my dear;*
> *The thimble for an old maid or bachelor born;*
> *The button for sweethearts all forlorn.*

Amelia had handed Mary a box with a smile that prohibited intimacy. When Mary got home and unwrapped her box, she found a thimble.

It was hard to see how Amelia could have engineered it.

Soon Mary must write to her old friend with her news – although not now: Mr Dodgson had not proposed yet, but as soon as he did, she would write. Not boastfully, though she would mention that Mr Dodgson was a tutor at Christ Church, and that would sound much better than a farmer, no matter how rich. But it would not be the first thing she said, or the second even. The first thing would be to invite Amelia to her wedding, a simple yet elegant affair, attended by everyone important in Oxford.

A long veil attached to a coronet of orange blossoms, a long train; she had always thought that would be the thing. Short white kid gloves, silk stockings embroidered up the front. White – or cream? Silk slippers with a red bow at the instep.

But she would need to get new handkerchiefs with new initials! MD. A good name. *Mary Dodgson* spoke of the wife of a rector in a leafy parish, in Gloucestershire perhaps. A teapot on the table, a beech tree outside with leaves rustling, flagstones in the hall worn away at the edges . . .

But the housemaid was calling out her name, her old name. 'Miss Prickett!'

Mary squeezed her eyes shut. Rosa could not want her for anything urgent.

Miss Prickett!

Her name inserted itself in front of the image of the rectory, and the flagstones dissipated through the edges of her mind.

'What is it?'

'There's someone here for you,' shouted the maid, not bothering to come up.

A visitor: could it be – so quickly? She was not ready. She rushed to the looking glass. 'Who is it?' she said. Her voice was shrill.

'Mr Wilton.'

Mr Wilton!

His presence now, here, was as unwelcome as a sea lion's . . . Mary saw him lumbering up the stairs, freshly slicked. If she could put him off – but he must have heard the housemaid calling to her. He would be inside by now, and taking off his gloves.

She pushed a piece of hair behind her ear and looked in the mirror. She was surprised to see that she looked the same as she always had, with a faint air of worry or disapproval clinging to her lips.

Behind her the door opened.

'Miss Prickett?' Mr Wilton said her name as if he could not

be sure she was there, even though she was right in front of him. She turned. He seemed to hold his weight on just one foot, as if her look had frozen him. He held his smartest hat below his navel; the fingers of both hands drummed on the brim as if he were playing a difficult piece on two silent flutes.

Now that he was here, even though he had sent no warning, Mary must offer him tea, if for no other reason than to give him a teacup to stop his invisible orchestra.

But when the tea was brought, Mr Wilton would not touch it, would not sit down. He would not talk on his favourite subjects: the new Indian silks, the tweed mills of Argyll, or anything else he usually liked to discourse on at such length. He only answered Mary's enquiries in the briefest way, until at last she fell silent.

He walked to the other end of the room and chewed on his lip.

'Is there something wrong, Mr Wilton?'

'No – I mean yes. Well.' He stopped chewing and sucked in breath through his teeth.

'Is it your parents? Your health?'

'No! Nothing like that.'

He went over to the window and put his back to her. Mary stared at the silk of his jacket, the dark grey gleam, the horizontal rifts in it between his shoulders.

Why was he acting so strangely? And why would he inflict his mood on her, now, when she was such an unwilling participant?

'I see that I have started now, so I must continue.'

Behind the shadow of his beard his skin was inflamed.

Mary, looking at him, had a premonition, a shock high in her breast, and rushed to open the windows. 'It is warm in here. These windows always stick but I usually can open them. Today they are particularly difficult.' The words rushed out of her in an attempt to keep him from talking. But he was beside her now, fumbling with the fastener, reaching his arm across hers, pressing down on it. Mary could see where the edge of his collar had rubbed at his neck, a red, raw line.

He caught hold of her arm. She must have looked frightened, because he dropped it again, although he did not step back.

'You must know what I have come here for.'

'I don't!' She clung on to the last hope that she might be wrong.

Mr Wilton looked at her, waiting for some sign. When he found none, he continued.

'I have come here for some months now and have grown very fond of you – fonder than I was before.' He swallowed. 'Oh, Mary! I am not good with words. You know that. I cannot speak around the thing. I must say it plainly. I was hoping . . . that is to say, I *am* hoping, that you would do me the honour of agreeing to be my wife.'

A chaffinch hopped up the trunk of a tree, pecking at the bark as it went. It must have babies to feed.

A month ago, nothing. Now two proposals at once.

Mary felt laughter rising up, as inexorably as oxygen finding its way to the surface. It would be disastrous to greet Mr Wilton's proposal with an attack of laughter. Somehow that made the thing more funny. And when the laughter came bursting out of her mouth, Mr Wilton looked astonished, as if his chest had been struck a violent blow.

She covered her mouth with her hand, tried to push the laughter back down into her stomach. She must stop! But her mouth operated on its own: gaping, noisy. Out of the corner of one eye squeezed a tear, as hard earned as sweat.

Mr Wilton took hold of her arm and started to shake it. 'Mary! Stop laughing!'

But she could not.

'Stop it!' He put his palm on her breastbone, his thumb and forefinger making a U around the base of her neck. Still bubbles tightened in Mary's chest and rose remorselessly to the surface. Her laugh was high and constricted and sounded unlike anything she had ever uttered.

'Stop it, I said!' His hand had the effect on her neck of a stopper being pushed into a bottle.

Now a feeling of something else, more angular. Fear.

She gripped his wrist tightly with both of her own hands and took a step back.

'Mr Wilton! Please – I am sorry. I don't know – please forgive me. I didn't mean to laugh. I don't know what happened.'

Mr Wilton let his grip slacken.

'I thank you for your proposal. I am flattered, really. But I cannot marry you.' She forced his hand away and it fell down by his side.

'Cannot? Cannot?'

'I cannot marry you.'

Mr Wilton had been so clearly expecting another answer that his face still showed some trace of gladness. 'But you . . . You took my gifts. You welcomed my visits. I thought you welcomed me.'

'I did welcome you. Your visits. But I cannot marry you.' Mary pushed herself away from the window and walked into the centre of the room. 'I will admit it – I thought perhaps I could once. But not now. I do not possess the feelings towards you that a wife ought to possess for a husband – and that is all.'

Mr Wilton's face was a riot of conflicting colours and directions. 'The feelings that you gave every sign of having not two weeks ago. What has changed?'

'Nothing has changed! Or – everything has changed. I have changed, Mr Wilton, not you. It is my fault.'

'I don't understand.'

'I am sorry. I do not know what else to say.'

Mr Wilton stared into her face, his lips open and wet with spittle. She could smell his breath, the smell that had come up from the inside of him: red and sweet.

Then he took a step back with a grunt and turned on his heel. Mary watched his clothes creasing and uncreasing as he made his way heavily to the door, his hands hanging down at his sides like pink hams.

◆

That was unfortunate, thought Mary later that night. Unfortunate timing. Or perhaps, how fortunate! If Mr Wilton had proposed two weeks ago, she might have been inclined to accept him. Then she would be bound to him until the end of the world, or the end of her world, whichever came sooner.

She tried to turn her thoughts back to Mr Dodgson. But she could not recapture the rectory or its flagstones. She could only see the confusion and distress on Mr Wilton's face.

CHAPTER 21

$\mathscr{S}$HORTLY AFTERWARDS, MR DODGSON SENT MARY A note asking to see her alone. She waited for him up in the school-room, her heart battering in her ribcage.

She stood at the window, seeing nothing. She walked to the door, and back again. Movement eased the pounding a little but her limbs were too weak to walk. She sat down again but it was worse than before; her heart threatened to choke her.

This moment, and this moment, and this moment.

The future was rubbed into a white glare. She could not imagine the shape it might take. She would be completely different in it, she knew that much. As different as an ape to a human – she would not recognize the form she would take.

It was inconceivable that the trees still stood, that Bultitude still strode across the lawn, that Dinah still lazed in the shade.

While she . . .

She!

Would he get down on one knee? He would clasp her to him – the texture of his jacket, his hair, seen from above. His face, bare and open and honest. He had once said, in so many words, that they thought alike, and they did. If she was not as linguistic as him – no matter! Their morality was the same.

A knock, at last, downstairs. But she was not ready! Her heart, again. Pale motes of midges jangled about over the lawn.

Mary shivered. She could hear his footsteps approaching, muffled as they walked up the carpet on the main staircase, then striking on the wood as they moved up on to the smaller staircase that led to the schoolroom, and her, her black bustle sticking back into the room, her shoulders tensed, her face set.

Escape, if she could hide somewhere from this appalling footfall!

She let the door be pushed open before she turned round.

'Mr Dodgson!'

'Miss Prickett. How kind of you to see me.'

Mary didn't know how to respond. 'Shall I call for tea?'

'Oh no, no thank you.'

Mary was desperate for tea. Her tongue felt too big for the inside of her mouth; it stuck to the roof of it.

But tea, tea would not suit the solemnity of the occasion. Still, Mary kept envisaging the pot with its jocular sides and its pattern of pale blue dancing ladies, and wishing it might be brought to them.

'It is chilly for the time of year,' said Mr Dodgson.

'Yes. I had to wear my shawl when I went out,' said Mary. She wondered how the words came out so ordinarily. She noticed everything about him: his hair, long but contained; his soft jowls; his lips, which today seemed to blend with the rest of his face.

'I don't doubt it.'

'The cows were lying down,' said Mary. 'In the fields as I went by. That signifies rain, I think. Or is it the other way round?'

'The other way round?'

'That it will rain if they are standing up. And the sun will shine if they lie down.' She smiled, the insides of her lips catching on her teeth, to stem the flow of words. But as soon as she pulled out her smile, her jaw felt too tight.

She might break. She longed to be back upstairs in the safety of her room.

'Cows are you-you-usually to be found standing up and it you-you-sually rains,' said Mr Dodgson. 'The probability is thus on the side of standing up.'

'Yes!' Mary forced out a laugh. Too loud, it rattled off the glass. She had lost the sense of their conversation.

Mr Dodgson had sat down on the arm of a chair. The sun picked out the tiny white hairs that clung to his black jacket and black waistcoat and black bow tie. Hairs that belonged to what? A hairy white caterpillar, a whole legion of them, in every house but hidden from sight. Crawling over Mr Dodgson's jackets in the darkness of his cupboard. Mary's heart kept on, banging against its confines.

'My uncle has a farm near Binsley.' She thought of the cows there, lying down on their broad brown sides.

'Ah, Binsley. The site of the treacle well.'

'The treacle well.'

'Does its water have healing powers?'

Mary peered again into the damp mossy cool, looking for the black water. She had always imagined it smoothing thickly over boils and lesions. 'They say so.'

'St Frideswide, the site of her first miracle, is that correct?'

She wanted him. She wanted to be away from him, sitting on the edge of the treacle well with a peaceful heart. 'Yes.'

Mr Dodgson got up. 'The reason I have come here, Miss Prickett, is a particular one.'

Mary's heart resumed its pounding, an unforgiving horse.

'I wondered if I could ask . . .' and did he pause here for a moment? The space between the words was long enough for Mary to teeter on the edge of nothing, to float . . .

'. . . for your help in getting the girls to come on a boat ride with me?'

Now he seemed to be talking so fast that she couldn't follow.

'If I applied to Mrs Liddell myself she may well think of a reason why we could not go, what with, what with . . .' He smiled. 'Well, you know everything, Miss Prickett! But a boat ride at this time of year, up to Godstow perhaps, would be the *perfect* way to spend an afternoon. Don't you agree?'

A boat ride . . . That seemed to be what he was asking.

'Yes.' Mary swallowed. 'What did you need my help for?'

'If you could mention it to Mrs Liddell, I would be most grateful.'

She smiled, waiting. 'I will, of course. It's unnecessary perhaps.'

Perhaps he had more to say. Perhaps this was the preamble

to the question she hoped for. But he was getting up from his chair, moving towards the door. He was thanking her, saying he did not want to take up any more of her time.

My time? she wanted to say to him. *You take it all up. Without you I have no time at all.*

But he had gone. He would see her in a few days, he said.

Mary turned back to the window and pressed her forehead against the glass. His black figure came into view and walked diagonally up the pane until it disappeared from sight.

CHAPTER 22

*I*N THE END, MARY HAD NO NEED TO ASK MRS LIDDELL anything. The matter came up of its own accord, at breakfast.

The remains of a kipper lay crumbled in a pool of egg yolk on Mary's plate; the spine she had pushed to the side but the tail end kept intruding, finding its way into the pool of juice that extruded from her tomatoes, in a way that seemed insurmountable.

That the herring could ever have known that it would end up like this, pulled from its silvery world up on to a plate, shared with a tomato from a greenhouse and an egg laid by a chicken, impressed Mary with the force of what she might not know herself.

'I don't see why Mr Dodgson cannot come to my birthday party, when he is the only person I want there!' said Alice.

Mrs Liddell brought a coffee cup slowly towards her mouth, pursing her lips and gently sucking in air when the cup was still as low as her bosom. 'That is very rude to the rest of us, Alice.'

'But I want Mr Dodgson. If *he* cannot come, I won't have a party.'

'But it is a family occasion!' said Mrs Liddell. 'As are all the children's birthdays.'

'Let him come. The Newry business is over—' said the Dean.

'Thanks to Mr Dodgson!'

'The Newry business is over, and if we failed to let inside our house anyone who had disagreed with us we would see nobody! Oxford is a small place. But I am late.'

Mrs Liddell reached across and rubbed away a patina of dried yolk from her husband's upper lip. 'You are always late, Henry, always in a hurry, always looking at your pocket watch. People must expect it by now.'

Oxford was a small place. Had Mrs Liddell heard the gossip? Mary tried to divine the answer by looking at her eyes with their thick lashes, her eyelids with their thin purple veins crisscrossing them like ink, but they only looked at Alice.

If she had heard, she would have said something, surely.

'What do you think, Miss Prickett?' Mrs Liddell looked up and into Mary's face.

Mary grew hot. All eyes were on her now. 'I don't see any harm in it, Mrs Liddell. Mr Dodgson is good company. For the children,' she added.

'Please, Mama!' said Alice. 'I want him there!'

Dinah twisted around the table leg, her fur rubbing and smoothing against the fabric of Mary's ankle. The feel of it spread up her leg and through her waist and up to her chest, tightening round it until she felt she could hardly breathe.

'Please, Mama!'

'You know I want you to have a happy birthday, darling.'

Alice pouted. 'Then let me ask Mr Dodgson. He has been at all my other birthdays.'

'And I don't wish to be difficult.'

'Then don't be!'

'Alice, do not talk to me like that. But perhaps your father is right. We must have everyone here, good and bad, we who work together.'

'Mr Dodgson is not bad.'

'No, no, Alice, I am not saying he is. I am just saying . . . Ah well!' Mrs Liddell turned up her hands to the ceiling. 'He has been your friend for so long. You will grow out of him soon.'

'Grow *out* of him? That sounds like something Mr Dodgson would say!'

'I only want the best for you, darling.' Mrs Liddell pushed herself up out of her seat and came to kiss Alice on the forehead. 'Eleven years old. How fast the time goes. If you want Mr Dodgson here, you may have him, I suppose. He is not impor-tant to me either way. I don't want to fight about it!'

Mary pressed down on her tomato with the back of her fork. The seeds that squeezed out looked like miniature rafts. If Mr Dodgson was coming to Alice's party there was no need to ask about the boat ride. He would be allowed to take them; he could ask her himself.

◆

They gathered in the drawing room for Alice's birthday; a room Mary did not often come into. Every surface was cluttered by something of Mrs Liddell's. The occasional table had two tortoiseshell boxes in the shape of hearts, which flanked a clock with a doleful face. The larger table held up a ferret under a bell jar with its teeth bared, front paw up, on a woodland floor it would never more walk on. The two side tables by the sofa were clustered with enamel boxes, glass bowls, an ivory letter opener and a miniature of Arthur, the child who had resembled the Dean the most closely, on his deathbed. He looked as if he was sleeping, his cheeks rosy from scarlet fever, his golden hair tousled.

'I have bought you something, Mrs Liddell, a small gift,' said Mr Dodgson.

'Me? It is not *my* birthday!'

He bowed. Ever since he had arrived at the Deanery, Mr Dodgson had been more himself, if that were possible. His skin was whiter, his eyes bluer; he was both more playful and more restrained. Courteous, charming, wily.

'Nevertheless, I should like to present it!' he said, bringing out a photograph album, a presentation album, half green leather, half ochre cloth board.

'Ah, more photographs. You are quite generous with them, I see,' said Mrs Liddell.

Mr Dodgson looked over at Mary for the first time since he had arrived, his eyebrows raised. She smiled, or half smiled, back at him. She did not know whether *he* knew that the family knew about his gift to her. Whether it was supposed to be a secret.

Her jaw tightened in confusion.

But he looked away and said in an even voice, to Mrs Liddell: 'I would like you to have the album as a symbol of our friendship.'

Mrs Liddell smiled a little and took it over to the table and opened it. The first photograph was a portrait of Alice that he had sent to a professional artist on Broad Street to be coloured. Mary leaned in to have a look. The artist had brought out the blush on Alice's cheek and the velvety animal quality of her eyes.

'It is lovely,' Mrs Liddell said at last. 'You are kind to think of me. Ah well, perhaps there is something in photography after all! This certainly captures something of Alice that I thought only a mother could see.'

Mr Dodgson inclined his head. Mary could see by the faint tinge of colour to his cheeks that he was pleased.

There were more prints of Ina, Edith, of men of the college, but mostly they were of Alice.

Alice sitting on a sofa, Alice dressed as the beggar maid, Alice as Queen of the May.

Mary turned away. There was no reason on earth why Alice should be the one who was doted on. Ina was the prettier girl, neater and more presentable.

'They are very fine, Mr Dodgson, very fine,' said the Dean.

They turned to a portrait of Alice sitting sideways on a chair. Her hair was shorter, her cheeks rounder than they were now.

'Ah, she was so young!' said Mrs Liddell, leaning forward on the table with one arm.

'That is the first portrait I took of her. She was four, I believe.'

'How her face has changed!' Mrs Liddell turned to him; the flare of her nostril was translucent in the sudden piercing sun. 'I think you must understand children as well as I, Mr Dodgson.

I am so glad to be given a memorial of them all. Who knows, perhaps Alice's great-grandchildren will one day look at these pictures and know her as we know her ourselves.'

The flush on Mr Dodgson's face increased. 'I think each photograph tells a story, entire and true.'

Mrs Liddell put a hand on his arm as she turned away, and smiled. 'Well, Mr Dodgson, you are very kind. What a thoughtful gift. I am sure we shall treasure it.'

The real Alice went back and sat on the arm of Mr Dodgson's chair, one leg hanging into space. She swung it from side to side, side to side.

'Can I have my presents now?' she asked.

Her mother indicated the largest box.

Alice opened the wrapping paper with the excess of glee, thought Mary, that comes from being watched, tearing gobbets of paper off and throwing them aside. At last a doll's house was revealed, carved in wood and painted a bright green. Everything in the Deanery was replicated in the house: a sofa, a dining-room table, beds in bedrooms, miniature servants and four children. The boy had his own top hat; the girls each had a cape and fur muff.

'Oh thank you, Mama!'

Mrs Liddell held out her cheek to be kissed. 'You are not quite grown up yet, darling, and even when you are, you will have a miniature Deanery to remember us all by.'

'Except Mr Dodgson, he is not there.'

Mrs Liddell laughed. 'Neither is Miss Prickett. I thought it best to stick to family.'

'Thank you, Mama, it is beautiful.' She turned to Mr Dodgson. 'May I unwrap your present now?'

'You may.'

Mr Dodgson's present was a doll, with two round black eyes and a fringe.

'I thought she looked like you,' he said.

'I am prettier,' said Alice.

'Alice!' said Mary.

Mrs Liddell laughed.

The Dean said: 'It is no laughing matter. Humility is far more important than beauty. Whatever beauty means.'

'Even if it *were* true, it is not good manners to admit it,' said Mr Dodgson. 'If society was made up of people speaking the truth, civilization might come to an end. We need manners.'

Mary leaned in closer to Mr Dodgson. Manners were the film with which she, every day, tried to overlay the uncivilized, brutal and petty natures of the children. Manners were what society relied upon to operate, otherwise the world would be made up of people following their desires and the streets would be full of thieves, and husbands would leave wives, and they would all be no better than monkeys defecating where they sat. 'That is right. Manners are very important. I tell the children that every day.'

'I am sorry for being boastful,' Alice said. 'Sometimes my words just tumble out without my being able to do anything about them.'

'Now that you are eleven, you will have to invent some kind of blockage for that,' said Mr Dodgson. 'I suggest a sta-sta-sta-stammer.'

'I don't think that would be a good idea,' said Mrs Liddell.

'How about a heh-heh-hesitation?'

'Not that either!' said Alice. 'I shouldn't like to speak like you.'

'Alice!' said Mary again.

'Sorry, Mr Do-Do-Dodgson. He doesn't mind, do you, Mr Dodgson?'

Mr Dodgson's face was unreadable.

'Thank you for my doll,' said Alice. 'I shall give her a kiss every night.'

'Give her a kiss every night and pretend it is me,' said Mr Dodgson. 'For I do love to be kissed, you know, especially by little girls. Here.' He leant down and pointed to his cheek. Alice kissed it. 'And here,' he said, pointing to the other.

Alice kissed his cheek with a smacking sound.

'I hope you will forgive me, Mrs Liddell. The airy touch of a child's lips is worth more to me than almost anything in the world. A kiss given in innocence, and received in the same way.'

Mr Dodgson's head was cocked slightly as he spoke. His face was a perfect oval, his skin very even, almost waxy. His lips were turned up. If Mary reached out her hand to touch his cheek, it would be cool and supple.

The thought of Mr Wilton assailed her then, his hot face, his bristles. Was his proposal known all over Oxford? She wished it had not come about like that. She wished she had not caused his face to crumple and sag, or his shoulders to slump.

But she had been right to reject him! He ought not to have assumed that she would have been glad of him. She had led him to believe that she might, perhaps, if viewed from a certain angle. But had she not always had her doubts? And now her course of action had been righted. She had been saved. By Mr Dodgson.

Who now cleared his throat and said awkwardly: 'I . . . I don't know if Miss Prickett has asked you already . . .' He looked at Mary and Mary shook her head minutely. 'Whether you would lend me the children for an afternoon? I had an idea to take a boat up to Godstow and make a picnic there.'

Mrs Liddell said: 'A boat ride? What a lovely idea. Perhaps you can take them in June.'

Geniality and good will radiated from him: 'Thank you, Mrs Liddell, thank you.'

Mary smiled too. Now that Mrs Liddell had forgiven Mr Dodgson, his path would be clear. He would come to her now.

CHAPTER 23

On her way back to the deanery, Mary walked into the quadrangle, where the air was clear and still. The honey-coloured buildings had their windows propped open and voices floated through them. She was hot. She let her feet drag against the gravel, enjoying the scratch they made, and wafted her fan in front of her face. She was louche, bohemian even. She was the sort of woman Mr Dodgson might meet in London, at the theatre perhaps.

She was being watched by some unseen author. Her actions had significance in the greater scheme of things. There was a Divine guiding principle.

Oh, she sighed, it was much too hot! She might yet expire. A corridor of shade hung down from the roof along one side of the quadrangle. She moved towards it, slowing her pace even more. She could hear a group of men talking inside the college.

And then, it was a jolt to hear the name spoken aloud that she spoke so obsessively to herself.

'Have you seen Dodgson recently?'

'I hear he was consorting with the Greats.'

The voice was detached, modern, amused.

'His hobby seems to have got him into the Tennyson household. The old man has a great aversion to having his picture taken, so it seems to have been a triumph.'

'Ah, Dodgson the lionizer, it all makes sense. He does insinuate himself into the narrowest of cracks.'

'Whatever do you mean?' More laughter.

A flush, hotter than the day, spread up from Mary's chest. She should walk on, but she could not; she had a horrible compulsion to know what was coming next. It was astonishing to hear Mr Dodgson spoken of in this way. New worlds opened up, where people did things differently, dressed differently, spoke differently. There were places about which she knew nothing, where it might be possible to move through life easily, without embarrassment. Perhaps wearing a hat with the wing of a thrush pinned to it. She and Mr Dodgson at a party together: she would have a new dress of pale blue, with lace at the cuffs down to her knuckles. Mr Tennyson would be there – Mary saw him with a quill in his hand, although that would be unlikely at a party, unless he was always writing poetry. But even then it would not be a quill most likely, but a pen.

'If he is such a lionizer, he has more in common with Mrs Liddell than we think. No wonder they get along so well.'

'Or is it someone else he gets along with? There must be some reason why he spends more time at the Deanery than in his own rooms.'

It is me. Say it so that I can hear.

'I was told an excellent story the other day that brought Dodgson to mind,' continued the detached voice, and he began on a story about three men, stutterers, in a Parisian tobacconist.

'Dooo-do-doo-donnez-moi des-ci-des-ci-des-cigares.'

Still Mary strained to hear her own name.

'It so happened that the tobacconist had a terrible stutter himself. So all four men began horribly to stutter and not a word could be understood between them.'

There was a second volley of laughter. 'Like a meeting of Hottentots!'

'Now the tobacconist was furious, thinking they were mocking him. So he seized a stick and threatened them and swore at them so violently that they all fell out of the shop on to the pavement, one on top of the other.'

Nobody knew Mr Dodgson as she did. She saw again his mouth, his jaw going up and down, trying to spout out the gobbet of a word.

Someone entered the quadrangle on the other side. Without thinking, she shrank into the passage behind her; as she pressed her back against the wall, she realized that it was the entrance to a college building.

'But do you know the strangest thing of all? In his rage, the tobacconist had lost his stutter completely!'

Mary, desperate to hear, desperate not to hear, at the same moment saw who it was that was coming towards her. It was Mr Dodgson. In a few seconds he would be upon her.

He would walk by and hear them at any moment.

She must not let it happen. She stepped forward.

'Mr Dodgson,' she said, very loudly; loudly enough for the men inside to hear.

'Miss Prickett.'

Inside the voices stopped. She heard someone make a shushing sound.

Mr Dodgson halted and folded his hands across his breastbone. She could see the whole of his pupils, and his mouth was snapped together like a shut purse. 'What are you . . . I mean to say where . . . where-where . . . this is not a place for woe-woe-woe-women. *Women* are not allowed into the college buildings. College is only for tutors and undergraduates. Women are neither of those. But you know that, surely.'

From inside Mary heard the sound of laughter. 'Yes, I know, Mr Dodgson. I was just inside, inside the corridor that is, not the building.'

'But what were you doing?'

'I was looking for something.'

'The corridor is still the college building, in the statutes I believe. I would have thought that you of all people would have been inclined to follow the rules on this matter.'

Mary stepped away from the building, out into the full gaze of the quadrangle. Windows surrounded her on all sides, like eyes.

Had he softened, at the last minute, as he bade her goodbye? He was very fierce about upholding the rules: that was why she loved him. Yes, she loved him. Of course.

Mary stood outside the building for a while longer; she could not bear to make the trip across the empty quadrangle straight away, even with the force of her realization burning in her cheeks.

She could still hear the voices of the tutors through the open window.

'Ah, Dodgson, just the man. What is that you are reading? Is it Tennyson?'

She heard laugher, and she heard in Mr Dodgson's voice that he mistook the reason for their laughter as his choice of reading material.

'No. This is equally worthwhile, however.'

'*Confessions of an English Opium-Eater*?'

'Thomas De Quincey is an instructive writer. You would know that if you had read him.'

'Well, I have read Tennyson. Do tell me, is Mr Tennyson as eccentric as they say?'

'I am afraid I cannot indulge you as to his eccentricity. I merely took their photographs.'

'What for? Do you mean to sell them?'

'Oh no. I am certainly not a professional photographer, neither do I intend to be. Any photographs I take are for the pleasure of my friends.'

Mary thought of her photograph, of the Deanery. It would be nice to gaze on it again; nicer, perhaps, than being in the building itself.

CHAPTER 24

*M*ARY HAD BEEN TALKING FOR MANY MINUTES –
perhaps ten, she could not tell – but the sound of her own voice,
bright and artificial, suddenly made her stop. Then there was
only the sound of scissors snipping through paper as the children
cut out the crests from the letters their parents had received.
They were updating their crest books. The table was covered
with letters and calling cards and pots of glue.

'Who is this?' said Mr Dodgson. 'Only Mrs Heyworth. Does
anyone want Mrs Heyworth?'

Nobody did. Everybody wanted Queen Victoria or the
Empress of Russia or an earl at the least. Alice had cut out the
royal crest from one of the envelopes the Queen had sent her
parents and put it in her book. Edith had cut out another from
a different envelope. Ina was in bed with a cold.

'Where did you find the Empress of Russia?' said
Mr Dodgson.

'A friend of Papa's had a letter from her,' said Alice, snatch-
ing it from him and starting to cut. She had put the crest of

Queen Victoria on her front page, with those of other nobility behind. At the back of the book she planned to put the untitled, or lately created titles. Plain Mr and Mrs the children took very little care with, snipping off a feather here, a curlicue there.

'Do you have a coat of arms, Mr Dodgson?' asked Mary.

'Yes, though it is rather ugly. *Respice et resipisce*: look back and see reason – a better motto I suppose than "look back and see unreason", as I quite often do.'

'Oh, Mr Dodgson. There is God's hand to be found in everything.' She looked at him and smiled, but he was sifting through the envelopes with his pale fingers, holding one then another up to the light and discarding it.

'May I put your crest in my book?' asked Alice.

'Certainly, though it is not on all the little notes I write you; I am not as grand as all that. You may have it on some letters, I suppose.'

Mary had seen Alice's pile of notes and letters from Mr Dodgson downstairs on the hall table. She had been surprised at the number of them, and that the child, who was usually so careless, had kept them all. The top one was carelessly splayed and Mary had paused to read it. It was a note, it was to a child, it was there, filled with Mr Dodgson's neat purple ink, to be read.

It was, or had been, amusing.

My darling,

Do you think we will see each other soon? And that there isn't time for many more letters? Now to me it seems, oh, such a long way off! Hours and hours: 30 or

40 at least. And I should say there is plenty of time for
fifteen more letters – 4 today, 8 tomorrow and 3 on
Saturday morning. You'll get so used to hearing the
postman's knock that at last you'll just say, 'Oh, another
letter from Mr Dodgson, of course!' and when the maid
brings it in you'll only say, 'Haven't time to read it: put it
in the fire!'

No end of love and kisses to Edith and Ina. I'm afraid
there's no use saying 'and the same to you', for if I never
leave off kissing them, how in the world can I begin
on you?

Mary had a few notes from Mr Dodgson: one asked her to
meet him by the old oak tree in the meadows at three o'clock;
another wondered about the possibility of bringing the children
to his rooms. By now she also knew the times of his lectures, the
number of his dinners taken in the Great Hall, the amount
of times he had been seen in chapel, his route across the
quadrangle every morning, the variation of his ties. She stored
all this information in a tight parcel away under her ribcage.

'But if I cut your *letters*, I would destroy them,' said Alice.
'And I would not do that!'

'Do not cut them; do not cut me,' said Mr Dodgson, though
he smiled.

Alice laughed, as she always did, head up, hair shaken
back. The child felt Mr Dodgson's affection for her and grew
bolder in it like a weed in the rain. Everything about her was
designed to draw attention: his attention. The widening of her

eyes, the curling of her hair around her fingers. The wild running in the garden.

Alice got under Mary's skin and irritated it, made Mary want to pick her out.

She thought again of her favourite catastrophe: a storm that would destroy all of Oxford, all of the Liddells, all of the children. She ran her eye quickly over the houses, standing up like an ancient forest: roofs blown off, doors hanging on their hinges, the furniture inside jumbled about. Outside the dazed survivors would stagger about, their hair matted, their clothes torn, their cheeks criss-crossed with patches of dirt. Only there would not be a heavenly voice, as Mr Wilton believed. No sheep, no goats. Instead Mary would be found by Mr Dodgson wandering in the street – he would have been out all night in a desperate search, and when he found her, he would be half crazed with fear and joy. His jacket would be undone, or off, and his high collar unbuttoned, and he would fall on her neck and kiss it – her own collar would have come off too; her neck would be long and pale and uniquely inviting.

Mr Dodgson's lips would be dry, in spite of the storm, and cool. And they would inch down her neck to her shoulder, his fingers fluttering over her skin like paper. And down over her dress to her breasts like a bird, so light, like the sunlight—

'Pass me the scissors please, Miss Prickett!' Alice's voice, full of entitlement. Mary passed them, wordlessly. Her other hand was spread near to Mr Dodgson's hand. Her little finger and his were inches apart. She crept her finger until it was just a pulse away from his. Her nail was chipped, her finger long and bony.

His nail was filed into a semicircle with a small pale fleck in the centre, like a star.

She could feel heat emanating from his fingertip. She leaned forward so that her finger brushed his, still cutting with the other hand but all her attention on the quarter-inch of skin that was touching him. Mr Dodgson carried on talking. He did not move his finger away, even though he must have felt hers resting against it. When she was a child, Mary had seen her own fingertips under a magnifying glass. She had been amazed at the glistening ridges and whorls, hidden in plain sight.

She closed her eyes.

'Have you got a crest?' asked Alice. 'Are you tired?'

Mary opened her eyes. 'No.' Alice must know that. 'And no.'

'Oh,' said Alice. 'We have. Quite a nice one. Though we don't use it on our letters!'

'Is that Lord Newry's crest? I think it might do well here,' said Mr Dodgson, leafing to the end of Edith's book.

'No one will see it there,' said Alice. 'It is quite a grand one.'

'But do you expect everyone to start at the front? No, they will start at the back and go forward. Then Lord Newry's will be in the best position.'

Alice took the crest from him and stuck it in her book, at the front.

'Lord Newry is one of the new breed,' said Mary. 'He seems to me rather arrogant.'

Mr Dodgson turned his knees to her. 'I agree, Miss Prickett. Quite agree.'

Mary said: 'Monstrously arrogant, yes indeed – I did not like the look of him at all.'

Tea and a lemon sponge arrived. Mary poured and took a sip; the heat spread from her mouth down to her stomach. Mr Dodgson was still turned to her. She waited to hear what he would say next, if he would whisper it, if it would be for her ears only.

But it was about the boat trip again, in the diary for next week. Mr Duckworth would be coming, Mr Dodgson said, and she should ask the cook to roast them a chicken.

CHAPTER 25

MARY SWUNG HER FEET OUT OF BED – THERE WAS a nail on the floorboards just there that she must ask Bultitude to hammer in – and went to the mirror. Now that she was nearly thirty, the early mornings showed in her creases: a new line ran from the side of her nose to the corner of her lips. Another mole on her neck that had pushed up from somewhere. She pulled it between her thumb and finger and rolled it; it managed, she thought with a shudder, to be flaccid and springy at the same time, its nobbled innards contained in a dark skin like something the Scots ate.

She took up her comb and began to pull it through her hair, growing it and spreading it until it covered the whole of her back. In the sunshine it was the colour of polished oak. She picked up her brush and ran it over and over her hair, harder and faster, until she was burying the ends of the pigs' bristles into the skin of her skull with a noise that sounded, to her, as if an animal was trying to get in.

The boat trip was planned for today.

Mary gathered her hair together behind her and pinned it back. Then she began to replait it into a tight coil, which she looped around the outside of her head.

And on the inside, on their own loop: Mr Dodgson in the boat, next to her. His thigh alongside her thigh. His oars, rising up and down. The unevenness of his mouth as the words came out. He insinuated himself into every crevice of her mind, he thrummed constantly beneath the surface of her thoughts so that anything (the shape of a shadow, a window pane, a pair of shoes, even the wind) could spear him and bring him wriggling and silver-scaled up to the surface.

Only she saw him. Only she knew him as he really was.

His legs were thin, just like hers. They had a knee bone that pushed sharply against the fabric of his trousers and a foot at the end that constantly jiggled inside its shiny shoe. The hands were so smooth and fine and the voice wound around the mind, but only she knew that the foot beneath the table danced with its secret disease, never ceasing in its tremulous judder, like the beating wing of a trapped bird or the scurry of a boxed mouse.

Mary ran her finger down her collarbone. She squeezed her eyes almost shut. It was not her finger that caressed her, it was his. What did it feel like to be touched by another's fingertips, another's lips?

Like this, perhaps, and *this*, only – Mary opened her eyes and saw her own skin and bone – she could not, standing there in front of the looking glass, could not shake free of herself.

She turned away from the hip bones that jutted out, from the legs that hung off them, from the boy's breasts and the mottled purple skin, and let the folds of her petticoat fall down over her body. It was time to dress.

Love always triumphed in the end. The audience demanded it. Morality demanded it.

The good must have a happy end, the bad a bad one.

❧

Mr Dodgson stood in the hall with his friend Mr Duckworth, dressed in dark clothes in spite of the bright day, except for his straw boater, which he held by the brim between thumb and forefinger.

Mary and he were alike in their black garb. If they sat together on the boat, the two of them would merge into one.

'May we go out all day, until the evening?' asked Alice.

'That is entirely up to your mother,' said Mr Dodgson.

'Until the evening, yes,' said Mrs Liddell. 'It will give me a chance to finish reading my book. But be careful not to entirely ruin your dresses, for I am rather fond of these ones.'

❧

They set off and were soon at Folly Bridge. 'Prima, let me hand you down into the boat first, as befits your age.' Mr Dodgson gave Ina his arm. 'Eager Secunda, you had better hold up for a moment, else I shall not have a hand for you.'

'But Mr Dodgson, you've two hands,' said Alice, standing in the sunlight, her hair blazing.

'I meant no free hands, for a man may have sixty-six pairs of hands and not a free one amongst them. Here we are now.'

Mr Dodgson advanced upon Alice with all ten fingers and thumbs waggling. Alice gave a scream; the kind of scream, thought Mary, as she stood in the shade, that was intended to signify a feeling without actually being one.

'You are to be coxswain, are you not? You had best go in the stern.'

Ina sat in the prow and Mr Duckworth, already hot, took one oar. But Alice: every step, every movement of the boat led to a shriek and a plea for help. She was so conscious of the effect she created, every shake of her head and pout and grimace flew from her, and surrounded her with a kind of jaggedness that others might mistake for vivacity.

Mr Dodgson helped her into the boat, he held on to her elbow, he brushed a piece of grass from her skirt, he unhooked her hem from a stray nail. He kept addressing her in a mock-gallant way that drilled into Mary's ears and itched her scalp from the inside.

'Tertia, you are very quiet. Come sit in the bow with Prima,' said Mr Dodgson, reaching for Edith, who carefully stepped into the back of the boat. Mr Dodgson himself stood with one leg on the bank and the other on the boat until, at the very last minute with a great comic grappling motion he hauled himself into the prow.

Nature pushed out from every crack and cranny. It grew between bricks in the old buildings. It burst from the bank into the river, trailing green tendrils. It hovered in thick clouds over the water. Tiny insects gathered like commas between the fingers of Mary's gloves.

Perhaps the children had gone on boat trips before with Mr Dodgson and were used to it. Mary had not been on the river since she was a child. She stared over at Alice, who had pinched her gloves off and was wiggling her fingers in the air, and then letting her hand drop and waggling her fingers under the water, pretending they were four miniature fish she had caught on a line.

'Stop doing that, it may be dirty.'

Mary's voice lacked depth; Alice knew it. She didn't turn her head.

'I dare say there are fairies hiding under that hedgerow there.'

Fairies, neat little people who drank from acorn cups and ate their food off pieces of bark. Strange that they should mimic humans while the rest of Nature was so unruly. Mary had never seen them and usually she had no objection to them, but now the thought of them cringing under hedgerows, pausing in their work of extracting honey from a nettle flower and watching the boat as it drifted by, was unsettling.

She stared down at the waving weeds, which fanned out in the current like hair.

The chirruping, the rocking, the slap of water on the boat's sides.

She wished suddenly that she was alone, brushing out her own hair in front of the looking glass.

'A little to the left, I think, Mr Dodgson,' Alice said.

Alice did not seem to feel the motion of the boat at all. She was angular with movement, an elbow leaned on the side of the boat, a bony calf stuck out in front mottled with bruises. She swayed first one way and then another, chewing on her lip.

Of course Mr Dodgson had only given her the job of coxswain to patronize her. The inner flesh of her arms was as pale as the underbelly of a fish; the vein at her wrist was a thin river burrowing underground. Perhaps there was a boat on it, with children in, and a governess, pulsing inwards.

Bile rose to Mary's throat. She had had seasickness as a child: her father had once rowed her out to a lighthouse in Devon to look at the birds, in his shirt tails. She had never forgotten the flurry and flap of them as they shrieked down into the water.

She swallowed. Took out her fan.

'Have you still got my lock of hair I sent you?' Alice said.

Mr Dodgson pulled at his collar. 'I dare say. That was a long time ago.' He leaned down on his oar and brought it up without making a stroke. Bright beads spilt from his paddle.

'I should think you need to keep rowing, Mr Dodgson,' said Alice. 'Otherwise poor Reverend Duckworth will have to make do on his own and I should think the boat is far too heavy for him to manage.'

'You are quite right, Alice, I was being very selfish, and besides, I must take advantage of your steering, for I have noticed up to now that we have managed not to crash into anything at all, and that is a great triumph on your part. You must be particularly pa-pa-pa-pa . . . Oh dear, that was rather ambitious! *Partic. Ularly.* There, I have got that one right . . . Per. Spic. Cacious. Perspicacious. Good. If I could only exert my will over the various bits of my body on every occasion I need to, well, things might turn out all right.'

'What is per. Spic. Cacious?' said Edith. Her voice seemed to blend with the water so she could hardly be heard.

'Usually, my dear Edith, it means to see clearly, but I cannot be sure about today.'

'What on earth do you mean?' said Mr Duckworth.

'I mean that in this heat it may decide to take on another meaning if it feels like it.'

'You are being absurd.' Beads of sweat stood out just below the brim of Mr Duckworth's hat.

'Not at all, my dear Duckworth. If, say, you were from a tribe of Aboriginals, "perspicacious" might mean something else altogether.'

'That is true, I suppose,' said Mr Duckworth. 'But then language would be following another set of rules.'

'But there are no rules as to why one sound should mean one thing and another sound another. It is all quite random. Unless perhaps language developed at first in an onomatopoeic way. Soft sounds and sharp ones. Soft, *douce*, *dolce*. They are all soft sounds. Sharp is another word that expresses itself. But most words do not follow in the same way.'

'You are far beyond me, Dodgson, in this heat.'

When Mr Dodgson was in front of her, Mary stood behind every word she said, weighing up its suitability. But Mr Dodgson's own words spiralled out of her control. She tried to follow them but she was always running after them somehow, out of breath. And they wound themselves nonsensically into her mind, to replay themselves in sounds that seemed to mean something but didn't. She remembered Mr Wilton's church, how words had poured out of her. They had meant something to her then. But now, when she recalled how she had been taken by the Holy Spirit, it was a different woman standing there and letting the words out.

'And prick!' said Alice.

'And prick,' said Mr Dodgson. Alice smirked over at him; Mr Dodgson put a hand in front of his face.

'Alice, what is funny? We might all like to know,' said Mary.

'Oh no, nothing! I just had a funny thought, that was all.'

'About what?'

'About . . .' Alice scanned the river. 'About a story Mr Dodgson told us once. You weren't there.'

'No need to go into it, Alice. I dare say it is not remotely funny now,' said Mr Dodgson.

The boat continued on slowly. The river twisted over rocks and slithered down slopes in one unbroken coil. It hardly made a sound, even where the water lapped at the side of their boat. Lapped and smoothed and stroked.

Alice leant right over the side and brought her head down to the surface, opening and closing her mouth like a fish.

'Alice. Alice, you had better sit up and take notice,' said Ina from the front of the boat. 'We may crash. It was you who made such a fuss about being coxswain in the first place.'

Alice stayed leaning out over the water. 'We are going perfectly well, Ina, in the middle of the river, and are not about to crash into anything.'

'Well, how would you know? You aren't even looking.'

'I AM looking.' Her hair shone, the ruffles of her dress

dazzled against the spangled water; it was hard to see where she ended and the water began.

She shook her fringe out of her eyes and looked back at Mr Dodgson.

His coat was a solid shape against the water, his face unusually red.

'Oh, Mr Do-Do-Dodgson!' Alice sang.

He smiled at her.

'Tell me a story!'

'Not when I have my hat on.'

'Weh-aall,' she drew the word out in two notes, 'take your hat off!'

'It is far too hot for stories. I must have told you at least twenty this summer alone.'

'Take off your jacket, and then it will not be so hot, and your gloves and your hat!'

'We are on a boat, in the middle of the river; I don't suppose it matters much, Dodgson, if you were to take off your jacket,' said Mr Duckworth.

'I already have my summer attire on, Mr Duckworth. Just because it happens to be hot does not mean I should undress myself out of doors.'

Sweat trickled from Mary's armpits. She clamped her arms to her sides in case it was blooming through her dress, but that made her sweatier. She took off one glove and inserted her fingers in the water. They looked green and bulbous, as if they belonged to someone else.

'Tell me a story,' said Alice again.

The sky was a white haze. Humidity coated every leaf and blade with stillness. Beyond the banks, cows pressed heavily on the grass, motionless except for the swish of their tails. The pulse of the river was counterpoised by the men's weak pull on the oars.

The boat was suspended, not moving forwards or backwards. Time going nowhere, hanging motionless over them all.

Alice leaned forward and put both hands on Mr Dodgson's knees. She looked up at him. 'Tell me a story. *Please*. Otherwise we shall be bored.'

Mr Dodgson turned his head away to the bank.

'Alice,' he said. His voice was unsure. 'Alice . . . Alice was beginning to get very tired of sitting by her sister on the river-bank, and of having nothing to do.'

'You cannot stop already!'

'I am thinking which way to go, only I can't. Think, that is.'

'Carry on!'

Mr Dodgson began to row again. 'Once or twice she had peeped into the book her sister was reading, but it had no pictures or conversations in it, and what is the use of a book, thought Alice, without pictures or conversations?'

'Carry on!' said Alice loudly.

'Alice was considering in her own mind, as well she could, for the hot day made her feel very sleepy and stupid, whether the pleasure of making a daisy chain was worth the effort of getting up and picking the daisies, when a white rabbit with pink eyes ran past her. Please sit straight, Alice, you are upsetting the balance of the boat. Now there was nothing very remarkable in that, nor did Alice think it so *very* much out of the way to hear the rabbit say to itself, "Oh dear, oh dear, I shall be too late!"'

'But it *is* out of the way to hear a rabbit speak,' said Ina.

'Normally I suppose it would be, but not today. But when the rabbit took a watch from its waistcoat pocket and looked at it, Alice started to her feet, for she realized she had never before seen a rabbit with either a waistcoat pocket, or a watch to take out of it—'

'Just like Father!' said Ina.

'Yes, just like your father. Alice ran across the field after it, and was just in time to see it pop down a large rabbit hole under the hedge.'

'Oh, what happened then?' asked Edith.

'Why, she went down after it, of course,' said Mr Dodgson.

'But how would she get out?' asked Ina.

'Well, she didn't consider that.'

Mary had heard Mr Dodgson tell the children stories before. This one wasn't so very different, only it was longer. Mr Dodgson talked on, his voice dizzy against the water. Occasionally he said, 'That's enough till next time!'

'It *is* next time,' said Alice.

It was unfair to the other girls to reward Alice's obnoxious behaviour by making her the heroine, thought Mary.

She stared at Mr Dodgson's elbow, rising and falling as he manned the oars.

He had hardly looked at her today. It might be because he was shy – God knows, sometimes she could not bear to look at him.

She heard Nanny Fletcher again, her embarrassed voice, and grasped on to it. Other people thought it was true. It *must* be true then.

'That's enough till next time!' said Mr Dodgson for the third time. His chin fell down on his chest and he pretended to snore. But Alice got to her feet, unnerving the boat, and prodded him. She must have the story, she was determined; she would never make it home without it. Otherwise she would be bored to death. Otherwise Alice would become quite savage.

Mr Dodgson pretended to wake up and began telling the story again, speaking very fast, still looking out over the river, until they told him to slow down.

Down the rabbit hole, the tale spooling out like a river weed, winding round them all.

A secret door, like the one in the Deanery garden.

DRINK ME.

EAT ME.

Mary watched Mr Dodgson's mouth, no hint of primness now.

Alice changing size, changing shape; there was no centre to it, no solid ground.

No moral, no happy ending.

'Dodgson, is this an extempore romance of yours?' asked Mr Duckworth, after a while.

'Yes, I'm inventing it as I go along,' said Mr Dodgson.

'But will I grow small again?' said Alice. 'I cannot stay that big for ever.'

'You can stay big and you will, though happily for me not

yet,' said Mr Dodgson. He pointed at Mr Duckworth with his oar. 'There was a Duck, a Dodo, a Dodo, a Dodo . . .'

'Dodgson!' said the children.

'A Lorina,' Mr Dodgson pointed at Ina, 'or Lory for short, and an Eaglet.'

'Am I Eaglet?' asked Edith.

'You are, and you are all in the pool with several other curious creatures who happened to be there. At length everyone got out on to the bank, but the first question was how to get dry. Indeed, Alice had quite a long argument with Lory, who at last turned sulky and would only say "I am older than you and must know best," and this Alice would not admit without knowing how old the Lory was, and as the Lory positively refused to tell its age, there was nothing more to be said.'

'I do not mind my age being known,' said Ina.

'No, but in a year or two you may – at least I know a lot of ladies who prefer not to be asked.'

'Why ever not?'

'Because it is rude.'

'But why is it rude to know someone's age?'

'Because ladies are never meant to grow old, unfortunately for you. They are meant always to stick at one-and-twenty, though I think they ought better to leave off at seven and a half. Which means that you, I am afraid, dear Alice, have already gone too far. And so have you, Edith.'

'But what happened next?' said Edith.

'Well then, at last the Mouse called out, "Sit down, all of you, and attend to me! I'll soon make you dry enough!" They all sat down at once, shivering, in a large ring.'

Mr Dodgson's voice rose into a squeak: '"Ahem! Are you all ready? This is the driest thing I know. Silence all round, please! William the Conqueror, whose cause was favoured by the Pope, was soon submitted to by the English, who wanted leaders, and had been of late much accustomed to usurpation and conquest. Edwin and Morcar, the Earls of Northumbria . . . "'

Although Mary kept her eyes fixed on the water, she could tell the children were looking at her. Grinning, she knew it, by the change in the shape of their faces, though she would *not* give them the satisfaction of having noticed.

Her cheeks were hot, her neck was hot. Perhaps they would think it was the heat of the day. She shifted her weight on to her outer thigh, pressing hard down on the wooden seat, to the bone.

He was mocking her because he felt comfortable enough. He was mocking her because he felt close enough to her to be able to do it. He mocked everyone.

'"Edwin and Morcar, the Earls of Northumbria, declared for him, and even Stigand, the patriotic Archbishop of Canterbury, found it advisable to go with Edgar Atheling to meet William and offer him the crown." But since all were as wet as ever, the Dodo moved that the meeting adjourn, for the immediate adoption of more energetic remedies.

'"Speak English!" said the Duck. "I don't know the meaning of half those long words and I don't believe you do either!"'

Mr Duckworth laughed. 'I may take offence, Dodgson, if you are not careful.'

Well then, everything was still all right. She must show how she could take a joke too.

She used the muscles of her mouth to pull her lips up into a smile. But everyone was looking at Mr Dodgson, and Mr Dodgson stared at the river, moving past in its bright pieces.

❖

Mary had not known that all this time inside of her was a gaping hole, that she could have lived for twenty-eight years thinking that she was a person, but she was not. She wanted Mr Dodgson to look at her with half-lidded eyes, as he had on the bench in the darkness. She wanted him to speak to her.

She wanted him not to speak to Alice.

'Carry on with my story!'

No more story. Mr Dodgson had told them enough for one day.

Mary took a breath. She pulled herself up, as sharply as she could – her ribs tore with the effort of it – into the afternoon. 'Stop!' she said. 'Please!'

She stared at the bank, at the couple walking by. He had hold of her gloved hand and was kissing her fingers.

'That is what I thought you would say.' Did Mr Dodgson mean her or Alice?

'*Please!*'

'It is not *your* story,' said Ina.

Mary was about to say, no, she knew that it was not her story, but she had had enough. Hadn't they all had enough?

But Alice said: 'It is! I am the heroine.'

Mr Dodgson sighed. 'Very well, Alice, I will finish it. But it is only for you that I make such an effort.'

Mary let her shoulders slump and her spine bend. She stared down at her boot. Water swilled around in the bottom of the boat and over the tip of it, making its own watermark.

The boat drifted on, the only sound the drop of the oars and the voice of Mr Dodgson rippling out again over the river.

The children and Duckworth laughed, the sound of it skimming over the water.

Alice's neck stretched out as long as a serpent.

Alice, who played croquet with ostriches, who expanded and contracted.

Two Alices, impertinent and cocksure; one had powers of the grotesque.

'"Hold your tongue!"

'"I won't!" said Alice. "You're nothing but a pack of cards! Who cares for you?"'

The boat was drawing near at last to Folly Bridge as Mr Dodgson finished his story; the sun had stained the fields a dark purple. The river was a deep black pulse and pushed the boat like a heartbeat towards the bank.

'It was all a dream?' said Alice.

'Yes, the best stories are.'

'It feels like a dream,' said Alice. 'The same way that a dream sometimes feels more real than real life. I should like you to write it down so that I might remember it always.'

'Write it down? If you'd like. But we must get home; your mother will be wondering what has happened to us all.'

Mr Dodgson helped Mary to the bank, his hand firm on her arm. Usually this would have given her consolation.

Alice kept going on at him, would not leave him alone.

'Promise me you will write my story down, so that I may have it by my bed.'

'If you'd like, I will promise. Though I hope you don't start asking me to write down every story I tell you.'

'Just this one,' said Alice.

CHAPTER 26

$\mathcal{M}$ARY HAD INTENDED TO READ HER BOOK FOR THE whole evening, in her room. But she had been staring out of the window, the book unopened on her lap, and she saw him just at the exact moment that she felt her head might burst with the thinking of him. And she was sure he looked up at her window. Perhaps he always looked up as he passed, to see if her light was glowing, just as she always stared hungrily at his as she went by with the children.

Mr Dodgson must be thinking of her – the look proved it. If she could secure a meeting, make it seem by chance, then he would be bound to reveal himself to her, just as he had on the bench, or at the play.

She quickly put on her cape, pulled the hood over her head instead of a hat, and ran downstairs. It was still bright daylight, even though it was past seven o'clock.

As she turned into the High Street, she saw Mr Dodgson on the opposite pavement, at a fair distance and heading away from her, his back straight and immobile, his knees lifted an inch higher than other people's knees, about to disappear into the crowd. She stepped into the road to follow him. A carriage passed close by, spraying a ribbon of mud up her cape.

She fixed her eyes on his top hat. The High Street was full of people, even at this hour, all of whom seemed to be going the other way. Mr Dodgson always walked fast, even if it was a stroll by the river. All his movements were precise – unless he was telling them all a story or a riddle. Then his words were the ribbons that weaved in and out, and his very face seemed to lose substance.

Mary looked up the street. She could still make out Mr Dodgson's top hat, merging with all the rest. She wanted to run but she did not dare. She could not fly up behind him and tap him on the shoulder, gasping for breath. But she had to move quickly.

The silk of her skirts swashed against her legs as she walked; the hem of her dress was splattered with damp. He was at the corner of Turl Street now. What would she say to him? He would wonder why she was out on her own at that hour. She would say something about the children. One of them was sick and she was sent to get medicine. But that would not work – he would worry and he would ask them to their faces about it tomorrow.

His head turned in her direction. He saw her. He would wave. She could go to him, he would wait, they could walk on together. She would say she was just going for a stroll.

But he had turned away again. He must not have seen her. Another carriage sparked past, hitting her ears like an assault.

Alice had been going on and on about her story. How she wanted it written down. Perhaps she could mention that.

They had turned into Broad Street, where there were more people. She must get to him – make it seem natural, as he had done in the meadows. But it was so much harder for a woman. Near the Sheldonian Theatre a crowd aggregated on the pavement, ready to be assimilated within. They all had an excitable sense of belonging: the men in their top hats, the women with their bare shoulders and jewels around their neck.

Mr Dodgson had stopped on the edges. Mary had almost caught up with him: if she spoke loudly he would hear her, but she shrank from doing so. She pulled her hood tighter around her neck.

When she had stepped out of her room, she had not meant to find herself at the theatre, standing alone in the middle of a crowd, and she thought about turning back. But she had come too far; he was too close. She could not face the exile of her room when here he was near enough to touch. Perhaps she would not need to say anything to explain herself. He would look at her and understand.

Mr Dodgson took out his pocket watch and scanned the crowd. Now was the moment. Mary stepped forward.

'Hullo!'

He looked at her. His face was blank. 'Good evening,' he said.

'Are you here for . . .' She looked in through the doors to see what was on. 'Are you here for *The Tempest*?' Her words came out stretched and tight.

'Yes. You?' Still he spoke to her politely. She realized he did not recognize her.

'No. I was . . . I was just passing, when I saw you.'

Mr Dodgson stopped looking at the crowd; he stared at her then. His eyes widened. 'Miss Prickett!'

'Mr Dodgson.' The heat of the crowd transmitted itself to her, made her cheeks burn.

'What are you doing here?' He took a step away, pressing himself on to the back of a broad man in a topcoat. The man looked round in surprise; his eyebrows were great caterpillars.

'I was just passing, when I saw you,' Mary repeated. She saw the impossibility of it now, surrounded by people ready for their evening out. No intimacy would pass between them tonight; she had been a fool.

Mr Dodgson looked from side to side again. He resembled the white rabbit he had told them about on the river, his eyes darting this way and that.

He had heard the gossip.

'I am meeting Mr Southey,' he said. 'He is late.' He tried to take another step back from her, but the crowd was too tight. 'I ought to find him, before the performance begins.'

'Yes, it is late.' Mary had the feeling that she was pretending to talk, that she didn't exist, that her words could not be heard.

Inside, a bell rang. Immediately there was a move inwards by those surrounding them. Mr Dodgson used it to turn away from her towards the theatre.

Mary stayed where she was, rubbing at the material of her cloak between her thumb and forefinger.

'Good night,' he said, but without turning back to her, pushing with the sharp edge of his shoulder through the crowd to get inside more quickly.

If he had heard the gossip, he would not want to be seen in public with her, for fear of adding heat to the flames. He hated gossip, whether it was true or not. She knew that about him.

But he might want to speak with her privately, still. He was a man of different faces, each one unrelated to the other. He could pass between several in the course of a day. Tomorrow might be different. Still, Mary wondered why she felt as if she might cry and why her legs were heavy, would not carry her away. She leant against the wall, listening to the hubbub from the pavement being sucked ever deeper into the theatre, until it was silenced.

She closed her eyes.

She didn't know how long she had been standing there, but when she opened them again there was another man, a stranger, standing quite close. She wondered if he had to do with Mr Dodgson, if he had been sent for her.

'Good evening, miss.' There was wine on his breath.

'Good evening.'

He put his hand on the wall just above her shoulder and leant in. 'Are you having a pleasant evening?'

Mary didn't know how to reply.

He squinted at her. 'Do you work around here?'

'Nearby,' Mary said. He was not from Mr Dodgson, then. 'And I had best be going home.'

'Can I come with you, to your rooms? If you name me a price.'

Mary stared at him. His nose was engorged; three black hairs sprouted from the tip. The surprise of what he had said surged through her breast.

Could he see her, did he know why she was here, that she had followed a man?

She could name him a price, an extortionate one. She could change her life, for good. It was as easy as stepping off a cliff.

'I'm afraid.' She leant over, away from his arm. 'I'm afraid you have mistaken me.'

She ducked down and around and walked away, feeling his eyes boring holes into her back, her shoes loud on the pavement.

CHAPTER 27

'*W*HERE WERE YOU LAST NIGHT?' MRS LIDDELL asked. 'You came in late. Past curfew.'

Mary's hand went to her necklace, a small gold cross hanging on a chain. She pulled the ring from side to side. 'I was . . . out. I was taking a walk. Sometimes I find it hard to sleep.'

'You look pale. You might try a sleep remedy. Better than going for a walk at that hour.'

Mary looked at the carpet: the design of flowers in a bouquet circled round with ribbon expressed certainty of function and purpose. 'Yes, Mrs Liddell.'

'Are you well now?'

'Quite well.'

Actually Mary had slept very little. A band gripped her round the head, just above the eyes. She could feel, from the heat along one side of her face, that Mrs Liddell's eyes were still fixed on her.

'Mr Dodgson is coming today. To photograph Alice. I have said he may use the garden. Ina and Edith will come with me to Lady Astbury's. *You* may have the afternoon off.'

'Thank you, Mrs Liddell.'

'Perhaps you might visit your family. I am sure your mother would like to see you.'

Never had Mrs Liddell looked more hawk-like, with her curved nose, her penetrating eyes and the thick hair that swooped away from her head like wings.

Oxford was a small place and Mrs Liddell knew everything that went on in it. Although she could not know *everything*. Not Mary's visit to the theatre, unless she had spies all round town. But she might have heard that Mr Dodgson came to the Deanery to pay court to her. And if she had heard – what did it mean? Did it give the gossip more weight or less?

But in spite of Mrs Liddell's command that she visit her mother, Mary decided to stay in. She had seen her mother only last week and had no news. As well as that, she was tired. It would be much better to sit in the garden, where Mr Dodgson would be, with a book.

That way she might have a chance to write over the awk-wardness of last night. She would ask him about the play – she had read on billboards around town that it had a real sea into which a ship was wrecked. She would ask him about Caliban. It would be a topic for them; she would tell him that she was thinking of going herself.

Mary positioned herself with a book on a bench, near enough to see him and hear him, but far enough away, she told herself, not to be intrusive. If he *did* want to speak to her, she could be incorporated into the conversation quite naturally.

'I thought you might like to pretend to be somebody else for a change,' he said to Alice, there on the lawn. 'It can get very dull being oneself all the time, if there is such a thing as oneself.'

'Have you written down my story?' said Alice.

'Which one?'

'You know which one!'

'Not yet, Alice, I have been busy.'

'*Please* start, otherwise you will forget it.'

Mary risked a glance up. Alice was on her knees, dismembering the contents of the dressing-up box, pulling out its bright innards: a Red Riding Hood cape, an orange parasol, a pile of rags.

'This looks like something that might be worn at a circus,' she said, holding up a slippery black jacket whose yellow leaves and birds were embroidered at a frantic pitch.

'It is from the Orient.'

'I'll try it.'

She took off her jacket. Underneath she wore a thin blouse. Mary could see, through the material of the blouse as Alice bent over to unlace her shoes, her breasts. Buds of breasts.

She looked away, but the shape of them would not let her go. They reminded her of the springtime protrusions on a sapling: high and tight.

Another night and another morning to follow. Rolling on and on like a celestial carriage wheel, crushing her beneath its constant motion.

Alice put on the Chinese jacket and stuck her hands on her hips. She rolled her eyes up to the sky, as her mother did. She pointed her toe on the ground in front.

'Look at me!'

Mary looked. Mr Dodgson smiled. He held up a pair of culottes. Alice stepped out of her skirt and her petticoats – left them there on the grass like the cast of a worm. Her legs were pale and smooth and she ran to him and grabbed the trousers.

She was always full of self-regard, poisonously so, but now – Mary stared at the back of Alice's legs: she was making a display. A girl ought never to revel in herself.

Mary looked at Mr Dodgson for help. Surely they would be in agreement on this. They had always agreed before! About manners, about the need for rules.

If she could only get his attention.

Make him see her.

But he was looking at Alice.

Frustration built in Mary's ribcage, overflowed into the joints of her, her elbows and wrists, making it impossible for her not to move. She flexed her fingers in and out. She must cut Alice down to size, it was her job, as Mrs Liddell would want her to. She must hack at her.

Pushing the book off her lap, she got up and went to where Alice was. She gripped her hard on her bare arm, below her shoulder. Pain pulled at the girl's features.

She let her fingers press into Alice's flesh. Just a little scrimp of muscle, then bone. She dug for the bone with her fingernails. 'I will not have you running around like that! You are noisy and insubordinate and . . .' As she gave way to her rage, Mary felt soothed. Alice's face was the reward: twisted away from her, her mouth in the downward turn of a much younger child, as if she was about to cry. In one smooth motion Mary brought her other hand, as hard as she could, up and across to meet Alice's cheek.

The slap rang out across the lawn, bouncing off the walls of the Deanery and back to the three of them, frozen in a tableau, in the middle of the lawn.

Mr Dodgson took hold of Mary by the shoulder and pushed her backwards. Two red spots burned high up on his cheeks, as if he had been slapped himself.

'Miss Prickett! Please leave us. We are here to take a photograph. Leave us, please!'

Mary looked at him, for a sign, but his face, apart from its colour, was quite blank.

She found she was shaking. 'Over here? Yes. I merely . . . Alice ought not to . . .' What could she say to appeal to Mr Dodgson? Mrs Liddell would not want her daughters . . . Alice was nearly a young woman . . . She ought not to . . . It was for her own good!

Alice met her gaze stubbornly, her chin thrust forward. As Mary walked away, she heard Mr Dodgson ask her, in a low voice, if she was all right.

Yes, said Alice. She did not mind. Where should she stand?

Swifts screeched and doves sang out to one another. The chestnut tree next to the house fluffed up a top portion of its branches and was quiet again.

The sickness in Mary's stomach pitched her forward as she

walked. Her nose itched, her eyes were red with rubbing, her nostrils were full. She had forgotten her book on the bench, she realized. She could not go back for it now.

◆

When Mrs Liddell came back later that evening, Alice was still in the garden with Mr Dodgson.

'It is getting quite gloomy out there. I can't think they can *still* be making a photograph.' Mrs Liddell pulled the strings underneath her bonnet and threw it off. 'Could you fetch her for me, Miss Prickett? I cannot face going out again.'

'Perhaps Ina might like to go,' said Mary.

'Ina is tired, and as you know, Miss Prickett, the photographing of Alice is not her favourite topic. You go, bring her to me.'

There was no sign of them outside. Dew was forming on the lawn, staining the toes of Mary's slippers as she walked. Perhaps the plate had not come out well. By now it would be too dark to prepare another one.

They must be still inside the darkroom. She could hear Alice's voice, wheedling, whining. In the tone of her words she could divine the shape of Alice's mouth: bottom lip pushing forward, tight at the corners. Mary had her hand on the heavy black curtain that served as the darkroom door.

Then Mr Dodgson, his voice rising and falling:

'If you only spoke when you were spoken to, and the other person always waited for *you* to begin, nobody would ever say anything.'

He was talking of manners again, but upside down. That was strange.

'That is not what Pricks says,' said Alice.

'Well, Pricks is full of thorns.' Both of them laughed, as if at an old joke.

Mary hesitated, not yet understanding, but not going in.

'Pricks will not get married, at least I cannot imagine it.' Alice's voice, careless.

'No. The man that would marry Pricks must have a very thick skin, to keep from getting stuck.'

Alice laughed. 'I should not like to see the man Pricks would marry. He would be too ugly. But there was that man, that common man, who used to visit her with us.'

In a rush, Mary understood. In the turn of a phrase she found herself standing on the other side of the bank, alone, watching Alice and Mr Dodgson, together.

'Yes, I know, Alice. Step away from the tray, please.'

'I don't know what happened to him!'

'Your governess's love life is nothing to do with me. I would rather you did not mention it.'

The kernel of the thing that had always been there, that Mary had always known, sprang out and grew up and covered her over. Of course it was impossible – it had always been impossible, she saw now – that Mr Dodgson had loved her.

She crammed her fist into her mouth.

'If I were engaged to be married, I could tell her what to do, couldn't I? I mean, even if I were very young and she very old? If you are married, you are higher up than if you are not.'

'I suppose so. But you must submit to Pricks for another year or so, until you have finished with her. Governesses are something regrettable to be endured, I am afraid.'

Mary closed her eyes. Every word she heard now would live within her always, written on her brain like it was on her phrenology chart. *Regrettable*, *endured*. Just above her temple.

'She ought to be nicer to me.'

'Thorns are spiky. But that is what you have *me* for. I shall be as nice to you as I can for as long as I can until you are grown quite sick of it.'

'I know! And I am glad for it. But can you come up to the nursery for tea? I saw some strawberry jam, I think.'

'Bread and jam, how tempting. But it is late, I still have some work to do.'

Mary started to cry, silently.

'Strawberry jam is my favourite kind of jam. And you always have work,' said Alice.

'Have a thought for all the poor strawberry pickers next time you put it in your mouth. Bent over all day in the fields just to get enough strawberries for your tea.'

Mary needed to be in her bedroom, alone. She needed to not let anyone see the tears that fell down her face. She turned at last and went unseeingly into the garden. Nobody was there. Once inside, she ran upstairs, one hand over her nose and mouth, the other pulling the rest of her up the banisters.

CHAPTER 28

*M*ARY SLEPT VERY LITTLE THAT NIGHT. THE following morning she rose as if in a dream. The air was still damp with night.

She opened her mouth, as the pastor had told her to in Mr Wilton's church. But nothing came. She was a dry river. All stones and pebbles. When she was a child, her mother used to tell her that God always answered a prayer, however trivial. It was just that he usually said no.

Her gaze fell on the picture of the Deanery given her by Mr Dodgson. In another moment she had ripped it off the wall – it was not framed – and torn it off its mount. The photographic paper was flimsy and it was nothing to tear it into pieces and crush it in her hand so that nothing but shreds of blackness remained.

She looked around for a waste-paper basket, but there was none; the maid must have taken it downstairs. She had an urge to be outside; she thought she might like to let the pieces go in the river, see them drift away from her.

She threw off her nightgown, fumbled on her chemise and drawers and stepped into her first petticoat, and her hoops. Her second petticoat she tried to force down over her head, for now that she had conceived the desire for the river, she was desperate to be outside, but it would not smooth out. She took it off again and stepped into it the normal way, breathing heavily. Her dress she snatched from the wardrobe and hurried down over her face, its dense silk scratching at her cheek.

She opened the front door slowly; there was a hinge that strained and she did not want any of the household to see her leave. But as she looked outside, she thought she must still be dreaming. Mr Wilton was sitting on his own, on a bench, waiting for her. He must have been there all night: the bench and he seemed both to be carved of stone.

Mary's lungs registered it before she did; they lurched up into her throat. Perhaps she could make it up with him.

She stepped out into the quadrangle, a smile on her face. She stuffed the torn photograph into her pocket and began quickly to tie the ribbons of her bonnet. It was still early and only one other set of footsteps could be heard approaching. Mary's lips were pressed together in a hum, ready to say *Mr*, Mr Wilton, but his head was turned towards the footsteps, and he rose from his bench and stepped forward.

Mary looked in the direction of Mr Wilton's gaze, and saw Mr Dodgson coming towards them both, making his way slowly, probably on account of the glass funnels he was carrying, in a bag, gripping them by their snouts. She had seen the same in the darkroom.

Mr Dodgson had not seen Mary or Mr Wilton yet, though he must be coming to the Deanery.

As Mary pressed herself back into the doorway, Mr Wilton went forward. Mr Dodgson was fiddling with his funnels, but he looked up to see Mr Wilton, quite close now. *I beg your pardon*, he said. Mary thought: they don't know each other, and she thought: they will pass each other by.

But Mr Wilton did not step out of the way. He looked into Mr Dodgson's face. His eyebrows tightened and a deep furrow appeared between them.

Mary bit her bottom lip, the taste of metal leaking into her mouth.

Mr Dodgson tried to walk on towards the Deanery, but Mr Wilton was blocking his path. Mr Dodgson brought both hands up to his chest, his package dangling in front of him like an awkward pendant. He started to step round Mr Wilton. But Mr Wilton would not let him go.

The hard crying of a child broke out behind her. Mary heard it as if it were connected to the scene unfolding in front.

Mr Dodgson stared at Mr Wilton with surprise.

'Excuse me, may I pass?'

'Mr Dodgson.'

'Yes,' said Mr Dodgson. He stopped and stood with his chin pressed towards his neck, very stiff. His face was perplexed.

The child wailed. Mr Wilton's cheeks were dark red. Mary could see the flesh on them shaking. He grabbed for Mr Dodgson. Mr Dodgson reared back, but not quickly enough, for the other had surprise on his side. Mr Wilton snatched at his chest and seized the package of glass funnels.

Mr Dodgson was too shocked to speak. He seemed to want to, but his jaw moved up and down wordlessly, like a pump with no water in it.

Mr Wilton swung his free hand back. He is going to hit him, Mary thought. Right there in the middle of Christ Church. Mr Dodgson would fall straight down on to the ground and never get up. It was impossible that he should be bloody and dishevelled and involved in a brawl and be able to get back up again into the world.

Mr Dodgson smiled in astonishment, as if he thought the same.

The tendons on Mr Wilton's neck stood out. Without stepping back, he swung his other hand, the one holding the package, and hurled it at the ground next to their feet. It exploded out of the paper bag into fragments, which lay glistening around them: on their shoes, on the hems of their trousers.

Mr Dodgson looked down in amazement at what remained of his funnels. He bent down and tried to brush off the hem of his trousers, with the side of his hand.

And then, as he straightened up, he looked across to the Deanery, in the way that people do when they sense they are being watched, and straight into Mary's face.

He nodded at her; embarrassment was the first thing on his face. She tried to smile in return, and nod, as if all this still remained in the realms of the ordinary. But something in her own face, in the way she had frozen herself in the doorway with her hand twisted behind her, caused Mr Dodgson to look at her again.

Mary felt herself pinned to the door; she felt his gaze strike her. They stared at each other, locked together, Mary aware of her face hanging down below her eyes and the blood draining from it.

Only now did Mr Wilton skirt round him, his feet crunching on glass, and walk away.

Mr Dodgson came towards her. In one hand he still held a fragment of the brown paper that had contained the glass funnels. 'What are you, what are you doing?'

'I just . . . I just came outside.'

'Did you . . . did you *know* that man?'

'No! Well, I may have seen him, at the store. At Elliston and Cavell.'

'Elliston and Cavell?'

'Yes. He is employed there.'

'Employed? What is he doing *here*?'

'I don't know!'

Mr Dodgson squinted into her face. 'You *did* know him. And he knew me!' He shuddered, visibly. A kind of horror overtook his face. 'I think it better, Miss Prickett,' he said, the glass still glittering on his shoulders, 'that we take no further notice of each other in public.'

'No further notice,' said Mary. 'No.'

Mr Dodgson's head was reared back on his neck as far as it could be, but Mary thought she saw something like shame pass over his features too.

And then the same blank look fell over his face, the one that she had seen after the incident with Alice.

'As I said. No more notice.'

He turned from her, back to the shattered glass. And then he swerved away again, as if he did not know where he was going.

CHAPTER 29

THE WHOLE OF OXFORD HAD BEEN IN PREPARATION for the royal wedding for weeks: flags, banners and bunting stretched across every street in celebration of the marriage of the Prince of Wales to Princess Alexandra.

Mary had stayed indoors, in her room. That her pain was insignificant to the universe was brought home to her in every ironmonger's cry, in every tap of every hammer that put up every gas lamp on every wall.

Marriage! the whole world seemed to cry. But not for you.

God had said no – once again.

There was no sense in anything. No one watching or guiding her. No need to be good.

Mr Dodgson and his brother Edwin had come to the Deanery to pick up Alice on the night of the Illuminations. Alice had been sitting by the door in her red cape and beret for half an hour, waiting, kicking her foot against the chair.

'Let us go,' said Alice.

The taste of desolation was in Mary's mouth. She swallowed. If she could leave here, go to a different country . . .

'Well,' she said, putting on her bonnet.

'Oh, are you coming with us?' said Mr Dodgson.

Mary flushed. She had tried to refuse, but the Dean had insisted that she accompany them. 'The Dean has said so, yes.'

Outside, instead of the usual darkness, they found heat and light and bursts of noise. The ancient walls of the college had lost their substance, while the air seemed more substantial, pregnant with smoke and smell.

Three enormous stars and a giant replica of Cardinal Wolsey's mitre, fired by twelve hundred jets, hung along the walls of Christ Church. A glass transparency of the Prince of Wales's emblem shone out.

Alice walked in between Mr Dodgson and his brother, holding on to their hands. Mary walked behind. People loomed up and vanished just as quickly.

All of Oxford was a darkroom: night turned into day, shadows into light, faces into dark.

'That emblem is just like the one I have in my crest book,' said Alice. 'Only bigger, and brighter too. When I get married I should like to have my initials blazing on the top of Tom Quadrangle.'

'I am sure the Dean could see to it,' said Mr Dodgson.

Mr Dodgson's brother frowned. 'The path to God is not by upholding vanity.'

'Wouldn't it be grand to be a princess? Mama says Prince Leopold is near my age; she says that I am bound to meet him.

Mama says that Her Majesty the Queen will come to stay again with us and she will bring him. Though I don't know when, now that the Prince of Wales has returned to London.'

Mary stared at her shoes. The ground was littered with the remains of food from the street vendors: the crusts of meat pies, curls of glistening eels, pickled whelks. Crowds of people passed them on all sides.

'Aren't you rather young to be thinking of marriage?' said Edwin.

'I am eleven,' said Alice.

'I have heard of some engagements as young as eleven,' said Mr Dodgson. 'It is not unusual.'

Edwin grimaced. 'I shall never get married. I intend to dedicate my life to God.'

The smoke from the Illuminations got in Mary's nostrils and in her mouth and choked her.

She had known all along that it would turn out this way.

She had been mistaken; she had revealed herself, the gaping thing at the centre of her, and now she was paying for her mistake.

She had lost Mr Wilton, and for nothing.

Sometimes at night she took out the Belgian lace from its drawer by her bed. She let its bumps and nubs graze her cheek, inhaled its damp smell.

He had proposed, and she had laughed. And still he had loved her enough to be stirred into a fever, into a rage! She saw him dark and brooding now, she saw him striding across somewhere wild.

Mr Dodgson couldn't love as much in eighty years as Mr Wilton could in a day.

Now she would be a spinster; she would live in the Deanery for the rest of her days. Watching Mr Dodgson and the Liddells living out their lives while she . . . while she – Mary closed her eyes, a lump in her throat – grew older day by day and new lines crept their way across her face. Every night the same and every morning too, until she was an object of pity, even to her own mother.

Mr Dodgson was talking on. 'It's a pity that I wasn't able to get the Prince to sit for me! Prince Edward would have looked fine in my photograph book. A charming man, if a little ordinary. But he had the most delicate of hands, each finger tapered to a point.'

How, after the other day, could he continue in such a pleasant voice? He seemed unchanged by the affair, while she was ruined. There was something unfathomable about him. He was like a series of locked cabinets, with only one door open at a time.

They turned into St Aldate's. All along the street gas jets fired the shapes of stars and crowns, and down the side of one tall building in three-foot-high letters of flame ran the words *May They Be Happy*.

'Oh, I do like that very much! May They Be Happy,' said Alice.

'May They Be Happy? Is that a question?' said Mr Dodgson.

'I should think the Prince and Princess ought to be happy,' said Alice.

'Happiness is not an assumption that ought to be made,' said Mary. She looked away, up into a house with a pyramid of candles in its window, their flames slanted in the breeze.

They turned up on to St Giles'. Even though they were a hundred paces away from the bonfire, Mary already felt the smoke in her nostrils. A cloud of angry sparks juddered above the rooftops. As they drew nearer, the fire itself was barely contained, blasting out boiling air, belching smoke. Only the men who fed it stayed close, outlined in black, gripped with a feverish motion as they worked to condemn faggot after faggot to the flames.

They went through the outer part of the crowd to get a better view. When the bodies got more closely packed they stopped, but Alice wanted to go on.

'A shower of sparks may come down on your dress,' said Mr Dodgson. 'Or they may land on your hat and then your hair would catch on fire, like in "Harriet and the Matches".'

'I want to go nearer,' said Alice.

Mary's cheeks were hot and her eyes stung. But Alice slipped out of the men's hands and led them all towards the fire, weaving in and out of the crowd, until they were out in front of the semicircle of people. Mary could feel the heat all down the front of her. The fire flung its arms towards them and instantly retreated, then again pushed out some unspeakable part of itself with a manic crackle until she could hardly hear or speak.

'Let us go,' said Mr Dodgson.

'Please, Mr Dodgson.' Alice shouted at him above the snapping flames. 'One more minute.'

The fire bullied and belched, a monster of tongues served by the outlines of the poor blackened people. The protruberances of Mary's face were rubbed by heat; her nose, her lips, her chin.

Alice twisted round, her own cheeks glowing orange. She was saying something to Mr Dodgson but Mary could not make it out. She had snatched her beret off in the heat and her hair was an awkward shape. She looked coarse, ugly even, the light exaggerating some parts of her, hollowing out others.

Mr Dodgson put a hand up to his neck, another on Alice's shoulder as he bent down to listen.

Mary couldn't tolerate it. Every word they spoke to each other might be a jibe against her. She stared at the fire, letting the flames burn themselves on to her retina. When she looked back at Alice, she was burned out, a glaring yellow gap.

◆

St Aldate's was now so crowded they could hardly walk. Throngs of people were jostling and shouting and shuffling past one another, so many that after five minutes they turned into Bear Lane, hoping to escape. But the narrow street was even fuller than the broader one, although quieter. There was only the sound of scuffling and a murmured apology as someone stepped on another's toe or a lady's hat was knocked off.

Mary was behind Mr Dodgson, who was behind Alice.

'Are you all right?' he asked Alice.

The lane smelt of cabbages. Unwashed necks and feet.

'Am I hurting you?' he said.

'No,' said Alice. 'Though it is cramped in here. And I can feel the whole of you pressing on my back.'

'Yes. We are nearly out.' Mr Dodgson's voice was high and tight.

'I can feel your breath on my ear,' Alice said. 'It is making my skin into goosebumps. Could you please breathe somewhere else?'

'I could try, if you would prefer me to expire,' said Mr Dodgson.

They all moved forward in tiny steps, almost in unison but not quite. Mary's breasts were crushed against the back of Mr Dodgson's coat. The breath squeezed out of her. If she pushed herself harder on him, she might hurt him.

She pushed harder. Mr Dodgson did not say anything. She pushed harder still, her eyes closed and a lump in her throat. The bones of her chest ground into his shoulder blades.

He did not turn round. But his body was very still.

'Why, I think I could lift my feet up and still be carried along, you are pushing on me so tightly,' said Alice.

'Alice, for pity's sake try to move forward!' said Mr Dodgson.

'I cannot help it.'

'Put your feet down and do not press on me so!' Mr Dodgson's voice came out as a thin line, urgent.

Mary found herself falling down, very slowly, in the darkness. *Down down down. Would the fall never come to an end?*

Alice's voice, annoyed. 'I can hardly help pushing on you, in this squash.'

Down down down, there was nothing else to do.

CHAPTER 30

*N*O MORE NOTICE OF EACH OTHER, MR DODGSON had said. But that was impossible when he came so often. When he came nearly every day. To Mrs Liddell, with infuriating good humour, he suggested more boat trips, more picnics. With Alice, in the afternoons, he played games of croquet, puzzles, doublets. It was only Mary he would not look at, or say anything to. The change was so marked she felt as if she alone were in Siberia while the rest basked in the sun.

But there was still something that caught at her, that did not rhyme. At night she saw his face again and was certain that she had not invented his intimacies, his stares, his touch. Some mystery lay at the bottom of it.

✦

One day the family went on a boating trip with Mr Dodgson and Lord Newry, all the way to Newnham. Mary could not stand the idea of their chatter and laughter; she pleaded a headache, which she did not have, though oppression hung over her like a cloak, blocking out the sunlight.

As soon as the house was quiet, she got up and went to Alice's bedroom. She opened Alice's wardrobe, with its ranks of shiny shoes and jutting dresses, its smell of lavender. She was searching for something but she did not know what. She went through Alice's pockets, turned over all of her shoes.

Nothing.

Her eyes fell upon a wooden box that sat on the dressing table. Mr Dodgson had given it to Alice. She tried to prise open the lid.

It was locked!

Something must be in there.

Where did a child keep a key? At the bottom of her drawers. Mary hurried over. Alice's clothes were crisp, like so many leaves of paper. Mary's hands were red-knobbed, grappling. She found the key at the bottom, as she had thought, made to look like an ornate twig, threaded on to a red ribbon.

She turned it in the lock. It fitted perfectly: the lid sprang open.

But there was nothing inside but childish treasures: a pressed maple leaf, a shell. The drawing that Mr Dodgson had given her that he had made of the Illuminations. He had copied 'May They Be Happy' and adorned it with garlands. Underneath he had drawn two hands holding formidable birches with the words 'Certainly not.'

She replaced it all, carelessly tearing the leaf in half as she did it, back in the box and the key back in the drawer.

She closed her eyes. *May They Be Happy* blazed behind her eyelids. The Prince had taken his Princess Alexandra on honeymoon, the paper had told her.

The house was very still. She could hear only the wind in the trees and the shout of an undergraduate in the quadrangle.

She found she was crying again. She dragged her hand across her nose. She ought not to have left her handkerchief behind in her room.

She looked at her pocket watch and then out of the window. No sign of the Liddells returning.

She could not face the exile of her floorboards and the cold little picture of Jesus. She sat down on the floor, the wool of the rug warm under her fingertips.

The upper floor of Alice's doll's house was at the level of her eyes. The beds were unmade, the piano on its side and the chairs upturned. She pulled away the house's facade, and saw, in the bedroom, a pile of letters tied together with pink ribbon, so tall it reached up to the ceiling.

She reached in, scattering the tiny inhabitants on to their backs.

The letters were written in purple ink; she knew immediately they were from Mr Dodgson. She pulled on the ribbon. Mr Dodgson had sent Alice so many letters in the preceding months; perhaps there would be something more in them about Mary. She wanted to see herself talked about, even if it was in the worst way.

My darling Alice,

This really will not do, you know, sending one more kiss every time by post: the parcel gets so heavy that it is quite expensive. When the postman brought in the last letter, he looked quite grave. 'Two pounds to pay, sir!' he said. 'Extra weight, sir!' (I think he cheats a little by the way. He often makes me pay two pounds when I think it should be pence.) 'Oh, if you please, Mr Postman!' I said, going down gracefully on one knee (I wish you could see me go down on one knee to a postman – it's a very pretty sight). 'Do excuse me just this once! It's only from a little girl!'

The childish sentiment grated on her, rubbed at her skin until it was raw.

'Only from a little girl?' he growled. 'What are little girls made of?' 'Sugar and spice,' I began to say, 'and all that's ni—' but he interrupted me. 'No! I don't mean that! I mean what's the good of little girls when they send such heavy letters?' 'Well, they're not <u>much</u> good, certainly,' I said, rather sadly.

Mary crumpled the letter in her hand. Mr Dodgson loved Alice, she knew that. But reading the letters was like listening to the man talk privately. Like eavesdropping.

My own darling,

It is all very well for you and Edith to unite in millions of hugs and kisses, but please consider the <u>time</u> it would occupy your poor old very busy friend, even during the holidays! Try hugging and kissing Edith for a minute by the watch, and I don't think you'll manage it more than 20 times a minute. 'Millions' must mean 2 millions at least.

20)2,000,000 hugs and kisses
60)100,000 minutes
12)1,666 hours
6)138 days (at twelve hours a day)
23 weeks

I couldn't go on hugging and kissing more than 12 hours a day and I wouldn't like to spend <u>Sundays</u> that way. So you see it would take <u>23 weeks</u> of hard work. Really, my dear child, <u>I cannot spare the time</u>.

Mr Dodgson kissed her, she had seen it often. She was a child, it was quite safe to go about kissing children.

But a girl who was almost grown!

And now Alice was almost grown.

When a little girl is hoping to take a plum off a dish, and finds that she can't have that one, because it's bad or unripe, what does she do? Is she sorry or disappointed? Not a bit! She just takes another instead and grins from one ear to the other as she puts it to her lips! This is a little

fable to do you good; the little girl means you – the bad
plum means me – the other plum means some other friend
– and all that about the little girl putting plums to her lips
means – well, it means – but you know you can't expect
every bit of a fable to mean something!

Outside, a carriage pulled up. She must go, she had said she
was not feeling well, she must get back to her room. She rose to
her knees and gathered the pages together, smoothed out the
crumpled one.

Downstairs the front door opened. A man's voice, more than
one. She must fold the letters exactly as they had been, else Alice
would notice.

You lazy thing! What? I'm to divide the kisses myself,
am I? Indeed I won't take the trouble to do anything
of the sort!

Mr Dodgson was coming up the stairs with Alice and Ina.
Mary could not get the ribbon on right. One loop was far bigger
than the other – it would have to do. She had no time to put the
dolls upright; Alice would not notice.

She was out and into the corridor before she saw them all.
'Did you have a nice day?'

'Very nice!' said Ina. 'We rowed up and Bultitude brought
us back in the carriage. Lord Newry was exceedingly droll,
though he didn't like the humidity, he said, and Papa ate too
many slices of cake. Lord Newry is still downstairs. I think I

will go back down after I have changed my shoes.'

Alice and Mr Dodgson followed behind.

'Of course one day you may abandon me altogether,' Mr Dodgson was saying.

'Abandon you? Why should I abandon you, Mr Dodgson?'

'When you are eighteen, perhaps, another prince may come along. It happens all the time.'

'I shall *never* abandon you. I hope we shall be friends always. But can we pretend to be the Prince and Princesss again? Only you must promise *not* to make fun.'

They went past Mary and on into the nursery.

Downstairs she could hear Lord Newry's monotone, modulated occasionally through his nose.

As the door shut on her, Mary stared straight ahead at the wall: creeping tendrils of ivy.

❖

The next morning Mary woke early, before the sun was up. No birds were singing.

In the night, something had come to her.

She had not been mistaken, or stupid, or naïve. Or any of the things she had been calling herself.

Mr Dodgson had used her to get to Alice.

Mary got up in her white nightgown and stared at her face in the looking glass. She did not recognize the person who stared back, with the new creases between her eyes.

Now that Mrs Liddell had changed her mind again, and he was back in the centre of the family, he did not need her.

Mr Dodgson had often told her that his love for children was innocent: by loving children, he said, he was made purer.

But the man was not innocent. He had hurt her, ruined her. And she must have her revenge.

CHAPTER 31

*Y*ESTERDAY MR DODGSON HAD COME TO TEACH them chess and had stayed an hour, Mary with them all, watching, listening. To see him now was to look at him from the other end of a telescope; to hear the rhythm of his voice, in the same light tone as ever, while she sat there in utter blackness.

Most of the following night she had lain in her room, in the darkness, awake, sharpening her plan.

Between the stage of her mind and her eyelids she put up one character and then another, made them speak, get up, sit down.

She smiled as she went up the High Street. *May They Be Happy? Certainly not.*

Mr Osmond, the watch- and clockmaker, had his shop in Magdalen Street. His window was crowded with faces: long-faced grandfather clocks with hanging pendulums, chubby-faced mantel clocks, watches whose insides were visible, even a cuckoo clock in the shape of a wooden house.

Mr Dodgson had often talked about the problem of where the day began. Suppose you started from London at midday on

Tuesday and travelled with the sun, reaching London again at midday on Wednesday, he had said. At the end of every hour if you asked the residents of the place you had reached the name of the day, you must at one point be told Wednesday, even though it was still 1 p.m. on Tuesday at the place you had left an hour before. The children had not understood this and neither could she. But Mr Dodgson had told them it didn't matter, because neither did he, and that was the point.

Mary shook her head and looked down at the pavement. She walked on past Theophilus Carter, the antique dealer, who stood at the door of his shop with his top hat on the back of his head, his hooked nose, and receding chin that vanished into his collar. Past the bookshop, towards the pharmacy, with its mahogany pillars standing on either side of the door, its polished tiles and its glass jars stacked to the ceiling in antiseptic ranks. The smell of lavender and liquorice soothed her. Sanitized her intent. The horrid mess of human bodies and illness and excrement could all find its antidote here, in one of those jars.

On the first afternoon she bought a bottle of Loring's Fat-Ten-U, imported from America. A spoonful every day, the pharmacist told her with a nod, implying that she would be plump in no time. Even so, the next afternoon she was back, having told Mrs Liddell that she needed something for her cough. She did not have a cough, but spent some time staring at cough drops and bowel exciters, finally being forced to buy a bottle of Vin Mariani, a French tonic wine intent on restoring her health. It cost her dear, but she still went back on the third day, this time pleading a headache to Mrs Liddell, until she was sure the shopkeeper was staring at her, his eyes sunken in his angular face. He must think she had a disease of such noxiousness and embarrassment that she could not tell him what really ailed her.

After that, she crept out of the Deanery as soon as she had a break in her duties, and sat on the bench opposite the pharmacy reading *Vanity Fair*, or pretending to. Men and women, children and dogs came from nowhere and disappeared into nothing, and nobody took any notice of Mary, sitting and staring at her instalment.

At last, on the fourth afternoon, when her excuses to Mrs Liddell were wearing thin, she saw the woman she had been waiting for: Mrs Chitterworth. Her face was glassily implacable; she was entering the pharmacy, as Mary had known she must.

'Good afternoon,' said the pharmacist, his eyes widening as Mary came in. 'Are you having a recurrence of your old problems?'

Mary flushed. 'Old problems, yes. That is to say, similar problems.' She moved purposefully towards a shelf near to Mrs Chitterworth and arranged her features into a mask of surprise.

'Oh, Mary. I thought I recognized your voice. Your mother said you had not been well. And you look quite feverish. I am not well either. My head aches when I wake up and again in the evening. And I have a terrible itch on the arm that will not go away, day or night. I came to see if I could get a cream for it.'

Now that Mrs Chitterworth was in front of her, Mary could not think how to steer the conversation in the direction that she needed, that she had rehearsed so many times in her head. 'I have a headache too.'

'Have you tried this Skin Soother Herbal Relief? That one is good, I believe, for all sorts of maladies.'

She knew, Mary thought. Mrs Chitterworth could see into the pathways of her mind and find Mr Dodgson there, and then her plan for revenge would come to nothing. She was about to turn out of the store when Mrs Chitterworth said:

'I saw Mr Wilton yesterday. He looked better than he has been recently.'

Mary nodded, trying to appear blank.

Mrs Chitterworth lowered her voice. 'They say he has turned his sights to the milliner, Miss Preston. Which must be a reprieve to you.'

Mary did not feel reprieved. She turned away to the racks of opium pain relief. Of course Mrs Chitterworth would know about Mr Wilton. She knew everything; that was why Mary had chosen her.

'Mary, do you need some air? I can pay for these later.'

Mary nodded and breathed out sharply. She turned to Mrs Chitterworth. 'Some air would be very good, just what I need. Shall we go to the meadows?'

✦

It was strange to sit in the meadows with Mrs Chitterworth, not too far from where she had once sat with Mr Dodgson, in geography at least. It was quiet; a wind scuttled the leaves from the trees and whipped a strand of Mary's hair into her eyes.

Mrs Chitterworth looked eagerly at Mary. She wanted Mary to give her something, it was clear, a piece of confession, in the guise of Mrs Chitterworth's helping. And so it was easy to do.

'I am glad Mr Wilton has moved on. I would not want to be the cause of any unhappiness. He is a good man and will find a good wife. On that topic, I have learned something that may surprise you,' Mary continued smoothly.

This was not what Mrs Chitterworth had been expecting, but she leaned in.

'Of another engagement. A secret engagement.'

Mrs Chitterworth leaned in further, her mouth falling open in a O of pleasure. Mary could see a moist glistening inside her cheeks.

'Between Mr Dodgson and Alice,' said Mary.

The O broadened to a capital. 'Mr Dodgson and *Alice*? But I thought Mr Dodgson was visiting the Deanery so much because he is paying court to you! And that is why you refused Mr Wilton.'

Mary shook her head, as if it was unimportant. 'No, no, nothing like that. I never suspected the same. No, no.' She stared at the metal bench; she could feel the nubs of it sticking into the backs of her legs.

'*Alice?*' said Mrs Chitterworth again. 'But she is only, what is she, twelve years old?'

'Eleven.'

'Do they intend to wait until she is eighteen? I suppose they must. And what does Mrs Liddell say?'

'It is a secret engagement. Only I know, and I came upon it by chance.'

'What chance?' Mrs Chitterworth was flushed, her hands in their gloves agitated on her lap; her whole body, with its rounded shoulders, formed a question mark.

'I heard it by chance, I should say.'

'Heard it?'

'I was outside the door; they did not know I was there.'

The scene that Mary was about to describe to Mrs Chitterworth had replayed itself as she lay in her room that night.

Alice and Mr Dodgson were playing chess, she said.

Alice was making remarks about the Queen's face and the grumpy King and the dear little Knight, about to take off at a gallop. And Mr Dodgson was showing Alice how the Knight moved.

'Do you think the Queen will pay us another visit? The real one, I mean, now that Prince Edward is married,' Alice said.

'I shouldn't think it is unlikely.'

'Oh, I wish it could be a royal wedding every day!'

'But I almost forgot. I have brought you a drawing.' Mary saw Mr Dodgson pull out the drawing again, and Alice's pout. She did not approve of marital unhappiness, especially in a prince and princess.

'Mr Dodgson is being unkind. Aren't you, Mr Dodgson?'

'If they ask, they must expect a reply.'

'But they didn't ask. And I dare say they would not expect that reply.'

Mrs Chitterworth sat very still on the bench, her gloved hands gripping the bars.

Mary paused.

'And then? And then?' said Mrs Chitterworth.

'Mr Dodgson, as far as I remember, said that he wasn't serious, that their marriage was a fine thing, and the fact that he spent the celebration of it with her even finer. Then Alice said that she should like to wear a dress, all in white, with pearls at the collar, just like Princess Alexandra, and suggested that they play a game where she pretended to be the Princess.'

'Let us begin at the marriage,' said Alice.

'I don't think we ought to play a game that is set in a church, Alice dearest, even in jest. We can begin at getting engaged, if you like.'

'Oh yes, Mr Dodgson. I should so like to be engaged to be married.'

Mary went downstairs, the voices of Alice and Mr Dodgson still very clear in the corridor.

All this, as she remembered it, was true, and all of it she told to Mrs Chitterworth, as the wind chilled her cheeks and blew against her ears.

And then, instead of going to her room, as the real Mary had done, Mary told Mrs Chitterworth that she had returned to the nursery to fetch her gloves. She told her this easily; she almost believed it herself, because in the night this fictional Mary had grown her own life, just as Alice did in her story.

As she had been approaching the door (she told Mrs Chitterworth), Mary had heard Mr Dodgson say:

'My dearest Alice, will you marry me?'

Mary, as she told it, had stopped then and peered in through the crack in the door, only to see Mr Dodgson down on one knee. She thought they were still playing the game, but there was something about Mr Dodgson, she said, that arrested her.

Alice said: '*Yes!* There is no one in the world whom I would like to marry more.'

'I am the happiest man in the world.'

Mr Dodgson got up, Mary said, his eyes flashing. Alice got up too and put her hands on his shoulders.

'I love you, Mr Dodgson!'

'I love you too, Alice.'

And then, said Mary, Mr Dodgson had wrapped both his arms round Alice and buried his face in her hair. They had stood like this for an age. Mary stood with a beating heart, hoping not to be heard.

And then Alice had turned her face up to his, her arms still round Mr Dodgson's neck. Very slowly (Mary had thought she might explode with holding her breath), Mr Dodgson bent his head down and kissed her.

'Kissed?' Mrs Chitterworth's eyes were wide. 'Where?'

Mary had often seen Mr Dodgson kiss Alice, on her eyes, her hair, her cheeks.

'Her lips,' she said.

'They are engaged then,' breathed Mrs Chitterworth. 'And Mrs Liddell's hopes are dashed!'

'There are letters that show his intent. Not outright, but they show his feelings,' Mary said casually. 'I have seen them.'

'Letters! How careless. I will tell no one, of course,' said Mrs Chitterworth.

'Of course,' said Mary. She put her hands by her sides and pushed herself up. 'It has been good to see you. I feel quite revived! It is a secret. I only told you, well, because you are a friend.' She smiled.

'Oh, no one!' said Mrs Chitterworth. 'I am the servant of discretion.' She yanked on her bonnet and pursed her lips, as if to emphasize that nothing would pass through them.

If it was a secret, Mrs Chitterworth could not reveal her sources, Mary thought. There would be no way to trace the rumour back to her.

CHAPTER 32

$\mathcal{I}$T TOOK THREE DAYS. THREE DAYS FOR THE INFOR-
mation that Mary had poured into Mrs Chitterworth's ears
to flow all the way round Oxford, and back in through the
Deanery's front door.

Mary was sitting in the schoolroom, staring through the
window at the grey sky pressing down, when she heard footsteps
hurrying up the stairs. Mr and Mrs Liddell were arguing: she in
a fury and he, lower, restraining.

As they came closer she could hear Mrs Liddell say: 'It is an
outrage! Does he think he is good enough for her? And why
would he not come to me first?'

'Lorina, caution. It is just another rumour.'

'And when I think of all the kindness I have shown Dodgson,
to be repaid like this! I cannot believe it.'

'Then don't believe it until you know it to be true. We must
all live together here.' Mr Liddell had a hand on his wife's arm,
trying to pull her back. His hair was unbrushed; he looked as if
he had been surprised at his desk. He was not slowing her down.

Mary went out into the corridor.

'Mama?' said Ina.

Mrs Liddell went towards Alice's room. Mary stood at her door.

'Is Mr Dodgson here?' Mrs Liddell asked Alice.

'No, Mama, he has just left. He said he would take me out riding tomorrow; may I go with him?'

'No, Alice, I am afraid you may not.'

'Oh, please may I go? You know I love to ride and he has promised to take me the prettiest way.'

'Your mother means that it is the Long Vacation in a couple of days and there is plenty to do before we leave for Penmorfa.'

Mrs Liddell turned to stare at her husband. Her hair had come loose where she had passed her hand unseeingly through it; strands of it fell down over the collar of her blouse with its high neck and amber clasp.

'What shall I tell Mr Dodgson?' said Alice.

'You shall not tell him anything, Alice. I shall tell him you are too busy.'

'But I am not too busy. You ought not to lie.'

'And you ought not to keep things from your mother.'

'Keep things, what things?' Alice looked at her mother and sat back down on the bed.

Mary stepped in closer. You moved the first piece along the chessboard and then the second, and the third followed suit.

'You cannot go about with Mr Dodgson whilst the rest of the house is in turmoil. You know very well how much there is to be done. Really, Alice, you are too demanding! I ought to have kept a stricter eye on you.'

'What have I done? What is wrong?' Alice saw something in her mother's face that made her lower lip start to shake.

Mary put her hand to her own face, to cover her mouth, going in a different direction.

'You have done nothing wrong,' said the Dean. 'Come, Lorina, let us go back downstairs.'

'Where are the letters?'

'What letters?'

'The letters that Mr Dodgson sent you.'

'I don't know.'

'She does know! She looks at them all the time.' Ina stepped forward.

Alice looked very small, sitting on the bed.

'Where are they?'

'They are in her doll's house,' said Ina. 'The one you gave her for her birthday.'

Mrs Liddell crossed the room. She was too big for it, and the feeling increased when she knelt down next to the doll's house and wrenched off the front.

She untied the letters and began to read, her lips forming the words. With each one finished she let it fall on the floor or passed it silently to her husband. Her face was a deep red.

Alice was crying now, silently too. 'What have I done?' she said. 'I don't understand. Why are you reading my letters?'

'I did not know he sent you so many,' said Mrs Liddell.

'Lorina, you ought not to read the child's letters,' said

Mr Liddell. 'Come downstairs and we shall talk about it.'

'Henry, I shall come in a minute. Listen to this one: "Oh, this pride, this pride!" Mrs Liddell's voice was surprised and resentful. "How it spoils a child who would otherwise be quite endurable! And pride of birth is the worst of all. Besides, I don't believe the Liddell family is as old as you say: it's all nonsense that idea of yours, that you can trace your ancestors back to the ark, I do not believe it for one moment – unless perhaps you are descended from a monkey. Besides, I am descended from Noah, so you needn't turn your nose up (and chin and eyes and hair) so *very* high!"'

'Well, you know how the man is, Lorina. It is a joke,' said Mr Liddell. He stood angled towards the door as if he meant to step out of it at any second, his mouth miserable with embarrassment and awkwardness.

Mrs Liddell held on to the last letter, the one about the plums, with both hands. She shook her head violently.

Now Mary would see; she had been waiting for it.

But instead Mrs Liddell grew very still. She folded the last letter up into squares.

'Ina, could you get the rest please? I am taking them downstairs.'

'Why, Mama, what is wrong?' Alice's eyes seemed to take up all of her face.

'I should not like anyone to find these; they may fall into the wrong hands.'

'Wrong hands?'

'They are too affectionate.'

'But why should they not be affectionate?'

'You will understand, Alice, when you are a grown-up.'

Mrs Liddell took up all the notes and letters, the product of seven years of friendship, and turned to the door. Then she turned back to her middle daughter. 'Did Mr Dodgson *say* anything to you?'

'What do you mean?'

Mrs Liddell stared at her. 'I mean: do you have an *arrangement*?'

'What kind of arrangement?'

Mrs Liddell said nothing.

'We are supposed to be meeting tomorrow, for riding,' said Alice at last.

'Does he take you on his knee?' said Mrs Liddell.

'Yes, you have seen him do it!'

'Mr Dodgson's manner is *too affectionate*. He has made this family the subject of gossip, not for the first time.' She turned to Mary. 'I thought he was supposed to be courting you!'

Mary smiled painfully. 'Me?'

'Of course, I knew there was no truth in *that* rumour.'

Mary felt the blush start at her breast and burn upwards past her neck, her cheeks, and into her hairline.

'This rumour is much worse.' Mrs Liddell shut her eyes, her mouth a thin line. When she spoke, she barely moved her lips. 'Alice, was there any talk of marriage?'

'Marriage? Yes. We always talk of marriage. He says he will be my prince.'

Mrs Liddell opened her eyes wide again, turned and pushed past Mary through the door.

Alice was confused. 'The Prince and Princess's marriage, Mama. The Illuminations! What did you mean?'

Alice followed after her mother but could not get up to her; she was moving so fast and her dress took up all the width of the corridor. The Dean, Mary and Ina followed behind.

'You are a child. You cannot be expected to know.'

Mrs Liddell got downstairs and pushed through the doors into the servants' quarters and the kitchen. Mrs Cook was preparing dinner, rasping away at a large cow's tongue that arched over the sideboard. The windows were opaque with steam.

'Mrs Liddell. Has there been a change to the menu?'

'No change, Mrs Cook. I need a box of matches?'

Mrs Cook stopped and took in the mother, the children, the governess, the bell jar of weight that surrounded them all. She did not ask what the matches were for, but fetched the greasy box and placed it in Mrs Liddell's outstretched palm.

In the drawing room, Mrs Liddell crouched down over the waste-paper basket, her bustled skirts pooling out behind her on the floor, and lit a match to the first of the letters. It flared up immediately, the flame burning her hand so that she was forced to drop it flaming into the basket.

'You will set the whole house alight,' said Mr Liddell.

Tears fell from Alice's eyes and pooled at the velvet round her collar.

'They are my letters,' she said.

'Not any more.'

'Why not? I don't understand! Tell me why?'

Mrs Liddell lit the next letter, and the next, until the basket, which was made of wicker, began to smoke. 'At least the Long Vacation is soon,' she said grimly. 'We shall be away from here for three months.'

The Dean hurried from the room and returned with a pail of water, which he slopped into the basket, a stain spreading unevenly beneath. He grabbed his wife's wrist and pulled her away. Then Mrs Liddell contented herself with ripping every letter into tiny pieces, and throwing them into the fireplace, watched by the silent members of her family.

CHAPTER 33

THE NEXT DAY, MARY, MRS LIDDELL AND THE CHIL-
dren were walking across the quadrangle when they saw Mr
Dodgson at the corner. He was standing, as if waiting for them.
He half put his arm up in a salute but then his face changed and
he began to hurry towards them.

Mary instinctively stepped behind Mrs Liddell. He could not
know that the rumours originated from her – she had gone over
and over it – as long as Mrs Chitterworth had not mentioned her
name. But it would be against her own interests to do so. And
even if Mr Dodgson knew, Mrs Liddell so thoroughly believed the
rumours now that it would make no difference. But still Mary
felt she might give herself away somehow. She was no actress.

Mrs Liddell saw Mr Dodgson at the same time as Mary did.
She stopped. She seemed to be about to lead them all back
indoors. But she changed her mind and carried on walking in the
same direction, giving him no sign. She pulled Alice by the hand.
Mary saw from the corner of her eye Mr Dodgson breaking into
a limping canter.

Mrs Liddell was walking quickly at a perpendicular angle to him. Alice craned round on her mother's arm. Mr Dodgson drew nearer until it was impossible not to acknowledge him, although Mrs Liddell did not slow her pace.

'I know you are busy preparing for the Long Vacation, too busy of course for tea, as your note said. But I thought perhaps, perhaps, I thought perhaps . . . It may be . . . I came to bid you goodbye before you and your family left.'

'Mr Dodgson. Yes, well, goodbye.'

Alice looked up at him but did not speak. Mrs Liddell started to move forward, leaving Mr Dodgson standing alone. Mary glanced back at him. He hadn't noticed her. He was staring at Mrs Liddell's face with a look of confusion and alarm.

Mrs Liddell took a few more paces and then came to a halt again and turned back to him.

'It will be best if you cease communication with this family, Mr Dodgson.'

'Cease communication? Why?'

'Why? Do you ask why? The whole of Oxford is talking about it and you ask why!'

'You know Oxford is a dreadful place for gossip. But forgive me, surely you do worse to give in by stopping our meetings than to show Oxford they have no foundation.'

'Give in? No foundation?' said Mrs Liddell, speaking quietly but pushing her words out between her teeth so violently that each of them was a kind of stab. 'No, there you are wrong. It is best that we don't speak today, I think.'

'Do you think? Perhaps next week then.'

'Not next week. Not ever. You must know what I am talking about.'

Mary felt as if she were looking down at them all from the roof of the quadrangle. The disc of Mrs Liddell's skirts, the rest of them insects, ants, thin-limbed.

'I have heard, huh-huh-huh, one thing. That my visits to the Deanery have been misconstrued as attentions to the governess. But Miss Prickett will be the first to assure you that I have no plans that way. None at all!'

He looked at Mary, as if expecting her to say something. Mary stared back at him until he dropped his gaze.

'Not the governess.' Mrs Liddell paused. 'I must ask you, Mr Dodgson, just out of curiosity. Did you really think I would allow it?'

'Allow what? What, allow what?'

'Marriage.'

'To Miss Prickett?'

'No, Mr Dodgson, not to Miss Prickett. For there are other rumours, more ugly.'

Mr Dodgson looked from Mrs Liddell to Alice, who stood silently with her head hanging down. 'Can you mean to Alice?'

They were still standing in the middle of the quadrangle, windows looking in on them and doors like mouths.

Imperceptibly Mrs Liddell nodded.

A red stain burst out over his cheeks and his forehead, the colour of blood. 'I deny it absolutely! Alice. You cannot say it?'

Alice started to cry again. She shook her head. 'I'm sorry.'

'After all my kindness to you. God knows there are others

who would have been more congenial to have in the house, but I let you come, for the sake of the children. Alice . . .' Mrs Liddell let the word trail off in a long hiss. She shut her eyes and continued in a quieter tone. 'Did you really think I would ever allow marriage between the two of you? The idea is ludicrous. Ludicrous! To a mathematics tutor? To *you*, Mr Dodgson? You, who have taken advantage of my home and my hospitality. As I said, it would be better for all if your visits to my family cease.'

Mr Dodgson's face was shocked and confused but Mrs Liddell was already starting to turn away, pulling them all after her.

'Can you deny it?' said Mrs Liddell, stopping again.

'I do!'

'But everybody says differently. And I have your letters. Alice kept them hidden in her doll's house.'

Mr Dodgson looked to be in physical pain. 'They do not mention marriage!'

'The friendship is over,' said Mrs Liddell, adding, 'Good day,' out of habit before she could stop herself.

◆

'When will I see Mr Dodgson again?' said Alice as they walked away. Her nose was red and her cheeks blotchy.

'I have told you, Alice, his visits to you will cease. It is not appropriate, especially as you grow older. You must develop friends of your own age. The Acland children.'

'But Mr Dodgson is my friend,' said Alice, tears and mucus shining on her face. 'My one true friend.'

'Alice!' Mrs Liddell stopped again and towered over her middle daughter. 'Do not be so childish. I have said that you cannot see Mr Dodgson and I expect to be obeyed. Stop crying before somebody sees you.'

Alice stopped crying. Her wrist hurt where her mother had been grasping it and she cradled it to her chest.

'Alice, there is a great deal to get done, stop hanging back. We must get to the draper's before they close, otherwise we shall have no curtains in Penmorfa.'

But Alice would not speak and she would not hurry until her mother took up her arm again and forced her to walk more quickly.

CHAPTER 34

THE LIDDELLS ALWAYS MADE THE TRIP TO WALES BY railway: Mary and the family took up one carriage, the servants and the luggage occupied another. There was no conversation in the Liddells' carriage. The Dean worked his way through several books in Ancient Greek, piled up in front of him on the table. Mrs Liddell's face was obscured by Wilkie Collins. Harry and Ina each had an instalment of Dickens. Alice had *The History of Sandford and Merton* open on her lap but was not reading it; it was boring she said, she already knew how it would end: the good happily and the bad unhappily. After a while she snapped it shut and turned to stare out of the window.

Mary was already staring out of the opposite window. Her book, *The Christian Observer and Advocate*, was still open, but similarly unread. When she turned her eyes to a paragraph she found that her mind mechanically recited the words but would not take them in. They were just useless sounds that rattled around in her mind, much as the train rattled on along its track.

Things passed outside the window. The various hedges that demarked the fields from the railway track blurred into a thick jagged line that seemed to lead somewhere. She could move through the landscape like this lightly and forever.

Nobody knew that it had all been set into motion by her.

She was not nothing. She was not something to be toyed with as if she had no consequence.

Behind them in Oxford the gossip still raged – Mary imagined all the small rooms of the college chattering with it. Mr Dodgson would always now be the man who was in love with Alice, who wanted to marry Alice and was turned down.

She saw again his face as she had last seen it in the quadrangle. But it had looked – how? Clouded this time. Like an animal's, in pain.

She pressed her forehead to the glass of the carriage. It was warm in the train; the smell of breakfast still lingered: kippers, milk.

He had picked her up when it suited him and then let her fall. Wafted her away without even explaining what he had done. Such carelessness in a man who seemed so precise.

Mr Wilton, with all his size and stubble, had turned out to be the better man after all.

One day they would find that love was a chemical such as could be made in a laboratory and drained away just as quickly. It was simply a matter of waiting for Mr Dodgson to drain away. In the meantime, she had her pride.

As the hours ground past, the rolling pastures roused up into steeper hills. Cows were replaced by sheep, hedges by stone walls. A bleaker place, but more honest. Bare crags rose now on top of the hills, as if Nature had failed with its usual cover.

The roundness of Alice's cheek was still turned away from her. Mary could see the length of her neck as it twisted, the tiny pulse that beat at the base of it. Every so often Alice rubbed at her nose with the palm of her hand.

After many hours the family climbed into a horse-drawn carriage that jolted and heaved over the road that led to the coast. Round the first sharp bend Alice's knee was shoved into Mary's, and Mary's into Mrs Liddell's. Alice looked for a second at Mary and their eyes met.

Alice had lost a friend. But she would make another. In another year she would have needed an escort to go out with Mr Dodgson anyway, and the friendship would have faded off. Mary had done no more than push things forward.

Mary tried to smile, but Alice looked quickly ahead, towards the horses.

In any case it was a lesson to the child. Alice had too much as it was; she must learn that some things would be taken away.

Mary's life would be more comfortable now. Small distractions, small comforts. A normal life, with normal things to look forward to. Mrs Liddell would have more children. Might even be with child already – Mary had heard retching the other morning coming from her bathroom, and all day she looked pale and ill. The Dean was taking more care with her too, settling her into the carriage with a fussiness that was not usual to him.

As Penmorfa came into view round the final bend, Mary saw a bird, bigger than a sparrow, smaller than a hawk. Swooping and diving, plunging down and managing to rise again without any seeming effort, on wings that curved perfectly into the mountainside. Alice saw it too, and for a moment she and Mary were united, in the dance of it.

Then the bird caught something, or lost interest, it was hard to see which, and flew higher and higher till it was obscured by the sides of the carriage.

EPILOGUE

CHARLES DODGSON SAT AT HIS DESK IN HIS father's house in Yorkshire, the light fading around him. The summer was already over and soon the Long Vacation would be over too. He was always surprised, and a little gratified, at how quickly summer faded after August was gone. The sheets of paper that spread out over his desk were filled with handwriting he had tried so hard to make neat: Alice's story, finished but for one last drawing. He would give it to her for a Christmas gift; she would have to forgive him the two and a half years that had passed since the telling of it.

Alice would be quite changed by now.

Charles saw her of course, at Christ Church, in glimpses. The cherry red of her hat heading across Tom Quadrangle. Her awkward smile as she and her governess passed by him under Tom Tower. Last summer – *mirabile dictu!* – he had been asked to the Deanery for the day (by the Dean no doubt) to enjoy croquet and all the other pleasures he had once been so used to. The children had been friendly, and for a few moments of blissful amnesia – if he was showing them a magic trick, or telling them a story perhaps – he had even forgotten that everything had changed between them.

Mrs Liddell had kept her distance all afternoon. The governess, when his eyes had mistakenly met hers, had looked at him with contempt possibly. But governesses were full of contempt, not least for their charges. He had liked her once, it seemed a long time ago. But she was limited in intellect, pedantic to the tenth degree.

This last spring he had hoped for a resurgence in his relationship with the Liddells. The new growth on the trees had given him hope that such a thing could be achieved. In May he had applied for leave to take the children on the river (except Ina, of course, who was now too old to go without a chaperone), but Mrs Liddell wrote that she would not let any of them come in future.

A boat beneath a sunny sky,
Lingering onward dreamily
In an evening of July.

Charles turned back to *Alice's Adventures Under Ground*. The difficulty of making his handwriting neat enough for a child to read had turned out to be nothing compared to the difficulty of illustrating the thing. Over many laborious months he had scratched out his pen-and-ink drawings in the spaces he had left in the manuscript. The process had made him painfully aware that he was not a draughtsman. The animals were easier; he was not too displeased with them – their faces could be quite without expression. Even Father William and his son, absurd as they were, were pleasing enough. In deference to Mrs Liddell, who, he was sure, would not like to see her child represented in a book, he had not attempted to draw Alice as she actually was, instead giving her long pale hair. But even this unreal Alice had come out flat. He had managed to capture no essence of little girls as they were, at all.

He had left a space at the end of *Alice's Adventures* in which he intended to put a drawing of *his* Alice, and it was this he wanted to do now. Surely Mrs Liddell could not object to *that*.

He took up his pen and worked in silence, looking for reference at the photograph of Alice he had taken several years ago.

But inspecting the photograph so closely gave him pain. Her features were so even, her gaze so clear, but beneath it he could still sense *her*, the riotous, inquisitive child, his dream child.

He could see very quickly that his own picture was nothing like her. His pen and its awkward scratchings could never do her justice. He started again on her dress, white cotton with a frill round the neck – that was easily done. But her hair, of which he had always been so fond, its short fringe cut halfway up her forehead and its sides so soft in her photograph, quickly became a bulbous spiky mass under his own pen.

He stood up and went to the window. The grass of the lawn was blackening to the colour of ink. He tried to imagine Alice walking across it, but he found he could not picture her face, only the horrible spikiness of his pen's re-creation.

Still she haunts me, phantomwise,
Alice moving under skies
Never seen by waking eyes.

Every minute night seeped into day and made it darker.

Alice would be twelve and a half years old. He would hardly know her now. She would be going through that awkward phase of transition.

Charles sat down again in front of his papers. *So the boat wound slowly along, beneath the bright summer-day, with its merry crew and its music of voices and laughter, till it passed round one of the many turnings of the stream and she saw it no more.*

He would start with her nose; not too much expression in a nose.

Now then, her mouth. A smile, or the idea of one.

But he put too much ink there and it looked pinched. He gripped on to the pen until he could see the creases that ran over his knuckles, dead-end pathways.

He was not an artist. Was he always doomed to fall so far short of what he wanted to achieve?

He straightened his back without releasing his grip on his pen. He permitted himself a long sigh. He must continue, imperfect as he was.

Her eyes. What was the expression that he was trying to capture? He stared at her photograph. Wistfulness; her eyes seemed to contain within them the knowledge that childhood could not last.

He bent very low over the page, his breathing shallow. He looked at the photograph, then back at the page. The eyebrows slanted upwards; the eyes were dark, almond-shaped.

Then she thought (in a dream within a dream as it were) how this same little Alice would, in the after-time, be herself a grown woman: and how she would keep, through all her riper years, the simple and loving heart of her childhood.

When Charles sat back up and looked at his drawing, he saw he had got nothing of her eyes. Nothing, in fact, of Alice at all. No coolness, no beauty, no softness, no arrogance. None of the things he had loved her for. She looked more like a beetle than a girl.

His own eyes stung and he rubbed them with the palms of his hands.

Oh God, I pray thee, for Jesus Christ's sake, to help me live a more recollected, earnest and self-denying life. Oh, help me break the trammels of evil habits, and to live better year by year. For Jesus Christ's sake, Amen.

He opened his eyes and left the table to fetch a pair of scissors. He cut into the photograph he had been working from, going round Alice's head. Then he fetched some glue and stuck the photograph on top of the hated drawing.

There now, there she was, his dream child. It was no wonder he could not approach her with his pen.

Charles gathered up his papers. It was dark now. He had finished Alice's story at last. He was glad, but his gladness was tinged with melancholy.

Although, of course, he had not finished.

He took off his shoes, loosened his tie. Last year he had given the manuscript to his friends the MacDonalds to read. He had lent the story only to amuse the children, but Mrs MacDonald had written back to him exhorting him to publish. Publish! That had not been his intention at all, but the idea had taken hold. The vanity of such a project could perhaps be excused if the story could give pleasure to other children.

He had gone to meet Mr Macmillan, who to his surprise had liked it. He needed an illustrator, of course, and Duckworth had suggested Mr Tenniel. Mr Tenniel was already well known from his cartoons in *Punch*, but when Charles had called on him at the beginning of the year he found him very friendly and favourably disposed to do the pictures.

The original story needed to be expanded on if it were to be published. And the name needed to be changed. *Alice's Adventures in Wonderland*, perhaps.

It might be well received, there was no telling. Children's pleasure, that was the main thing.

Well then, time for bed. Pray God his sleep would not be haunted by some worrying thought that no effort of the will could banish.

◆

POSTSCRIPT

M̲y STORY IS BASED ON REAL CHARACTERS AND real events, but I have moved the scenes around and, of course, fictionalized them. I have also compressed the seven years of Alice's friendship with Mr Dodgson into the space of one year.

But because I have based most of my characters on real people, it may be of interest to recount what did actually happen to them, in the Victorian tradition.

Charles Dodgson was forced to watch from the sidelines as he was replaced by a far more important suitor, Prince Leopold, Victoria's youngest son. Oxford gossip had it that Lorina was angling for a royal match; she was satirized by Dodgson as a 'kingfisher' in one of his pamphlets. Nothing came of the affair, however. Queen Victoria would never have allowed her son to marry a commoner and she put an end to it. But Alice and Leopold's feelings endured: each named one of their children after the other, and Leopold was godfather to his namesake, Alice's second son.

In 1880, Alice married Reginald Hargreaves, a well-off

country gentleman whose favoured pursuits were dispatching animals in the name of sport. She settled into life as the wife of a county gentleman: village committee meetings, running her household, bringing up her three sons. She does not mention it in her letters but I cannot help thinking she must have been bored: Reggie was not an intellectual match for her, and they were often apart as Reggie embarked on one shooting party after another. It was a far cry from her glamorous childhood.

Alice saw Dodgson very rarely after her marriage. She asked him to be godfather to one of her sons, but he refused when he found out it was a boy.

Dodgson did not forget her, however. The memory of Alice as a seven-year-old girl endured, grew more perfect even, fed by Dodgson's fondness for melancholy and nostalgia. 'My mental picture is as vivid as ever,' he wrote in 1885, 'of one who was, through so many years, my ideal child-friend. I have had scores of child-friends since your time, but they have been quite a different thing.'

Mary Prickett continued to work for the Liddells for many years. In 1871, at the age of thirty-eight, she married Charles Foster, a prosperous local wine merchant and owner of the Mitre Hotel, one of the best hotels in Oxford. Mary, at last, had a place of her own, and as proprietor, social standing too.

❖

The story of the Alice books, of course, continues to run and run. Alice treasured the handwritten manuscript until she was an old lady, selling it only just before she died to pay her husband's death duties, for the then astronomical fee of £15,400. It came into the possession of Eldrige R. Johnson, the American phonograph millionaire; and when he died it was bought by a group of Americans, who presented it to the British people 'in recognition of Britain's courage in facing Hitler before America came into the war'. The manuscript now lives in the British Library. *Alice in Wonderland* and *Through the Looking Glass* have entered the public psyche and are said to be the third most quoted works of literature after Shakespeare and the Bible.

◆

A short untangling of fact and fiction. The letters at the end of the book that Mrs Liddell reads are actual letters Dodgson wrote, but to other children. 'My mother tore up all the letters that Mr Dodgson wrote to me when I was a little girl,' Alice told her son, my grandfather, Caryl, in 'Alice's Recollections of Carrollian Days' published in the *Cornhill Magazine*. And yes – his name really was Caryl, and although Alice denied that it had anything to do with Lewis Carroll, it seems a pretty big coincidence.

Dodgson's diaries do not reveal much about his inner life, except for his exhortations to be a better man. My suggestion that he suffered sexual abuse at school is based on a quote, written later: 'I cannot say . . . that any earthly considerations would induce me to go through my three years again . . . I can honestly say that if I could have been . . . secure from annoyance at night, the hardships of the daily life would have been comparative trifles to bear.' Added to which, sexual abuse was common at public schools in those days.

There is no evidence that Dodgson was a paedophile, except for in the classical sense, as a lover of children. After Alice's time he had many other child friends. He met new children on the beach, where he advanced towards them with pins to save their dresses from the sea; he fell into conversation with them on trains; he approached mothers he knew to have daughters of a suitable age – that age being in Dodgson's case around seven years old – even, once their mothers' permission had been gained, photographing them nude. One must not forget that in those days this was more normal than it is now – it was the pursuit of women of one's own age that was absolutely not allowed.

And yet I find something odd in this quest, even trying to look at it through Victorian eyes. Whilst I believe that he did not actually touch any of these little girls, I think his lens was focused on them to an unusual degree, especially in his later years.

Alice remained silent on the matter, in private and in public, except for a rather anodyne piece written by her son, my grandfather, in the *Cornhill Magazine* in 1932. Dodgson used to tell her stories, she said, and then take her picture. 'Being photographed was therefore a joy to us and not a penance, as it is to most children. We looked forward to the happy hours in the mathematical tutor's rooms.'

The gossip at the time in Oxford, and the tradition in my family too, was that Dodgson was too fond of Alice. Some said he wanted to marry her. For my part I cannot imagine him actually proposing, to Alice or anyone else. But that does not mean that he was not in love with her in his own way.

My mother owned a letter written to Alice by Ina when they were both old ladies. Ina had been questioned about the split that occurred between Dodgson and the Liddell family by Florence Becker Lennon who was writing a biography of Dodgson. 'I don't suppose you remember when Mr Dodgson ceased coming to the Deanery? I said his manner became too affectionate to you as you grew older and that Mother spoke to him about it and that had offended him so he ceased coming to visit us again as one had to give some reason for all intercourse ceasing. I don't think you could have been more than 9 or 10 on account of my age! I must put it a bit differently for Mrs B's book. . . . Mr Dodgson used to take you on his knee . . . I did *not* say that!'

This letter can be read in two ways. Either Ina is lying, and the truth is elsewhere, for example, that Mr Dodgson was courting Ina. The other explanation is that Ina felt under pressure to come up with a reason for the split to Florence Becker Lennon, and is explaining to Alice why she let the truth slip. The comment about Alice sitting on Mr Dodgson's knee seems to bear this out.

As far as character goes, I have coloured in interior lives from known facts. Some examples: Mary was called Pricks by the children, 'the thorny kind', as Dodgson put it. As Alice later wrote, she was not 'the highly educated governess of today'. She came from a relatively lowly family and was ashamed of it: her father was a steward at Trinity College, but she called him a 'gentleman', which he was not, according to the standards of the day. There were rumours around Oxford that Charles Dodgson was courting Mary, and no doubt she would have heard those rumours, although there is no textural evidence that Mary had feelings for him.

For the character of Mrs Liddell I read the letters that she wrote to her husband and children, which were owned by my family, and of course Charles Dodgson's diaries, which document the split from the family as well as her various ups and downs. She was a well-known figure around Oxford; the ditty, 'I am the Dean, this Mrs Liddell,' was current at the time.

Mr Wilton, Mary's mother and Mrs Chitterworth are all entirely fictional.

Wherever possible I have relied on existing source materials, which include Lewis Carroll's diaries; *The Rectory Magazine* and *Mischmash* (ed. Dodgson Dodgson); *Curiosa Mathematica, Part II: Pillow Problems*; *The 'Wonderland' Postage-Stamp-Case, Invented by Lewis Carroll (Eight or Nine Wise Words about Letter-writing)*; *The Collected Verse of Lewis Carroll*; *Collected Letters of Lewis Carroll* (ed. Morton Cohen); *Lewis Carroll Interviews and Recollections* (ed. Morton Cohen); *Memoirs of H. G. Liddell* by Henry Thompson; Alice's recollection of Carrollian days as told to Caryl Hargreaves in the *Cornhill Magazine*; the *Historical Journal*, Vol. 22, Alden's *Illustrated Family Miscellany* and *Oxford Monthly Record*. Also a number of family letters once owned by my mother; Henry Liddell's handwritten diary which, although it does not cover the events of *The Looking Glass House*, were good for atmosphere and character. And of course, family recollection.